It was lil

mercury. I b

and felt a tho pressure

on all sides. T was only six feet high and the whole place was blank, gray lead. This thing was a tomb, a psychic tomb. Dawson was lying in the corner, on her back, eyes staring at mine, struggling to breathe. The maddening thing was, I couldn't probe, couldn't make contact. This was no simple interference, it was a steady oscillating pressure. Any normal mind would have been crushed in minutes. There was no chance to relax my defense long enough to send anything. It was no surprise I hadn't been able to sense her earlier. I inched along the wall, knelt and took her wrist. *CONTACT*.

Her mind was screaming, every synapse wide open and firing. The link took too much energy; I collapsed. I pulled the two flares from my pocket and wriggled around, slapped one on each of my boots. I let my right arm go numb and took a deep breath. I dropped the concentration against the room entirely, and sent with all my energy, *CUSHION THE IMPACT!*

The world caved in.

AGENTS OF INSIGHT

STEVEN KLAPER

AGENTS OF INSIGHT

TOR

A TOM DOHERTY ASSOCIATES BOOK

For J.J. and R.W.

This is a work of fiction. All the characters and events portrayed in this book are fictional, and any resemblance to real people or incidents is purely coincidental.

AGENTS OF INSIGHT

First printing: October 1986

A TOR Book

Published by Tom Doherty Associates, Inc.
49 West 24 Street
New York, N.Y. 10010

Cover art by Barclay Shaw

ISBN: 0-812-54308-4
CAN. ED.: 0-812-54309-2

Printed in the United States

0 9 8 7 6 5 4 3 2 1

Prologue

No one noticed the little man slip into the apartment. The police downstairs didn't pay any attention; they thought he was from the Inspector's office. The fingerprinting team just leaving figured he was with the medics, and the ambulance crew didn't care one way or another. He was a dark little man wearing a long coat with the collar turned up. Sometimes the coat looked gray, sometimes brown. Depended on the surroundings, depended on the projection. He had a sad, flat face that had spent too many years monitoring its own mannerisms, and anyone asked to describe him later would state that he'd seemed "unremarkable." This wasn't due entirely to indifference on their part. Finney possessed prodigious psychic ability. It was child's play to keep shifting the optic vibrations of anyone glancing at him, to keep a muddy flicker on his face. It gave him the aspect of a shadow, a tired nonentity from some government office on official and routine business. He didn't bother moving the lock of mouse-brown hair from his forehead, didn't take his hands from his pockets. He just leaned against the wall next to the door and watched them carry the mountainous woman out on a stretcher.

They've got a heavy-duty job, thought Finney, lots of muscle to get her down four flights. But then, it had always taken a lot of muscle to handle Mary.

He psi-scanned the body as it passed. Dead six hours.

Loaded with drugs. Not a vibration left, all the wavelengths stripped bare. Any message she'd left, any clue, was gone. He memorized the imprint: strong, just like the others. He probed the attendants, then the two policemen. Nothing. Routine suicide, as far as they were concerned. Counting the hours till the end of their shift. He scanned for residue imprints. Tanner had already been here; he could feel it. Tanner loved leaving his cold, professional imprint everywhere. With Mary dead, he was in charge of the Paris network now. Big shot punk.

He scanned the bed. Nothing. It figured. The local network would jealously guard any information they got from this. Correlate it, process it, send the official conclusions to HQ in Chicago and, if he wanted it, he could damn well sign the report out like anyone else. A month from now. Wonderful teamwork.

The hell with them. Finney concentrated on one last deepscan. No point looking for papers or messages or physical clues at all. Mary was sharp. Anything she'd leave would be psi-impress. The problem was, it would fade a couple hours after she died. He'd gotten here too late. Damn it.

He'd been in Paris a week. When he'd arrived, there'd been two suicides to contend with; now there were three. Poli with his head blown off, LaRue a pile of bloody meat from ten stories up, now Mary. It was no good. He was turning up nothing and every other network in town was probably on to him by now. He couldn't send a message without risking a leak, couldn't leave one without leaving it for everyone.

He walked over to the window. Latched. Well, of course. She couldn't have jumped. No one could even have fit Mary through that window. In a way, it was fortunate. Until now, it had been too easy to accept the official explanations. Not this time. Not a drug overdose. Anyone who'd known Mary would find it ridiculous. Energy fields all over the place; the patterns were beginning to make sense. It was time for an intuitive leap. If he was wrong, then fifty years in the espionage business would have gone for nothing. Either way, it was time to stop following other people's trails.

The little man closed his eyes and slipped a signal into the Eurotrans computer across the city. One reservation booked to Munich, backdated three days. Next he triggered the vidbox in the 15th district, and the autorelay coded a request to another box in Johannesburg, setting up a Mafia meet two days from now. One step at a time. Place enough steps around and you create the impression of a man running in circles. He keyed the vidphone on the desk, called in a reservation to San Francisco, then switched off and relayed a psi message via satellite to the Frisco Pool saying he'd be tied up in Chicago before he arrived. Those would go out in the morning. Timing was important here. He stared hard at the phone, impressing the false vibration of a shuttle reservation to Luna. Good. All that remained now was to leave a sloppy trail toward Zurich that ended at the French border.

Was that it? He went over everything slowly, the contacts, the meets. He ticked them off: Tanner, Andre, South Africa, Germany, U.S., Luna, Zurich. Yeah, they overlapped properly. It really *was* all timing.

"Hope you find me, pal," he said quietly, looking out the window. "I just hope it's not too soon." He didn't bother considering the corollary.

He blanked himself off the Pool wavelength, cut the autotrips. The hell with the Old Man too. No triggers, no flares. You're on your own, baby, like old times.

Finney glanced at the huge bed, shook his head in disgust. What a waste. He opened the door with a wave of his finger, and slipped back into the warm, drizzling night.

One: Paris, 2089

I

Finney had made a serious mistake. I didn't know what the mistake was yet, but he'd vanished. In this business, that's serious. Dawson had gone in a couple days ahead of me, and she must've followed his trail perfectly, because she'd vanished as well. We were out of contact, at any rate. I had to figure she was on to something, but who the hell knew? With the communications block that'd been covering Europe for the past four months, you couldn't transmit more than a couple blocks. It was maddening. People you're in telepathic contact with don't just disappear.

I was glad to finally be in Paris. Traveling isn't one of my favorite pastimes anyway, and this had been one scorcher of a day. Taking a shuttle to the moon or the stations is one thing—it's always exciting to be off-planet—but this zipping about in hovercars frays the hell out of every nerve it doesn't bore. I must be getting old.

The glass doors to the Hotel St. Claude were thirty feet high. They looked too heavy to move. The street was as wide as a broomstick and if that glass slab *did* swing it would probably crush the *boulangerie* across the street. The whole building seemed designed as an illusion. Everything was elongated, drawn way up into spires and towers joined by walkways and circular ramps. Completely decorative. With all the glass and silver, the place looked like a cathedral to a god with very bad taste. I touched the handle and the huge door swung silently out, then slid into the wall. I was both right and wrong. It *was* too heavy to move by hand, but the little shop was safe.

Once inside, it was all familiar. Hotel lobbies in 2089 may have a lot of fancy gadgets, but behind the flash the basic activities have changed very little in the last hundred years. Two guys stood near the front desk, smoking cigars, big clouds rising as they boomed in German: sports, local gossip, undoubtedly the dirty morsels. They spoke much too loudly, purposefully attracting attention, as if the action in and around the St. Claude were *the* news of the planet. A kid sat in front of the lifter, shining jetboots, his eyes darting around, eager for news, while his mouth practiced the proper subservient grin. Another guy molded into the corner, chewing on his cigaret while the lines in his forehead argued with his eyes. He kept his hands deep in the pockets of his zipcoat, tried his damnedest to look sinister but still available to the highest bidder. Any information he had was on page seventy of yesterday's news flash. Punks.

I scanned up through the hotel, a light pass, trying to pick up a trace of Dawson. This was supposed to be our meet, but nothing registered. I crossed to the desk, slung the bag off my shoulder to the floor. Something broke. I no longer gave a damn. I'd sweated clear through my suit and had a dozen inaccessible itches. I just hoped to God I wasn't going to have to deal with an incompetent desk clerk.

He was a young guy, twenty-five maybe, but starting to go bald in front. Big bug-eyes and tiny round glasses. The edges of his cheek looked normal through the lenses; I wondered if he wore the glasses for show. He had a straight sliver of a mouth that you weren't supposed to notice, and he could've left his nose home for all the good it did him. He knew his job, though. Pegged me for an American right away.

"What can I do for you, sir?"

"Reservation for Mollitor," I said, looking around.

A lot of agents don't like to use their real names. Some of the older ones hold onto their code names from the War, others like the sense of camouflage an alias gives them. The problem is, once the alias is blown, you need a new one. I'd go crazy trying to remember who I was this week: Bill, or Rebus, or Bobo. I'd just as soon advertise my presence; no one's going to take me by surprise anyway. This kind of lax attitude isn't encouraged by Insight HQ, of course, but then, I pretty much make my own rules.

The guy got the keys, watched me closely while I signed the register. I scanned the book by fingertip. Nothing interesting. I glanced at the clerk. I wasn't in the best of shape to try a probe, but some things become automatic after enough years. I figured I'd pick up something. I put down the pen.

"You the regular desk clerk?"

"Why, yes, sir."

"You seen a woman in here the last couple days, blond hair, mid-30s? She's pretty."

I scanned as I spoke. His mind was a file system, very orderly, lots of blondes going by; he was leafing through people he'd seen, nothing triggering . . .

"Got a limp on the left side," I said.

Nothing . . . no, wait, heartbeat up, respiration changing, ah hah! He hadn't seen Dawson, that was certain, but someone had warned him about *me*.

"No sir, I haven't seen anyone like that." He was smiling, twisting that sliver up into a curve.

"Yeah, well, thanks anyway," I said, grabbing the keys and my bag.

"Enjoy your stay here, sir."

"Yeah," I said, moving toward the lifter. "It's nice to know I'm expected."

It registered. Let him take that back to them.

I thought about it as I glided up the twenty-two floors. If Dawson had never been here, then either she'd spotted something wrong with the place, or she'd gotten sidetracked. A tip? Could've come from anywhere. Finney, maybe a setup by whoever had him. Bah. I always suspected the worst. Well, if she hadn't been here, then how did they know to tip the desk clerk at this particular hotel? I'd made the reservation today, from the other side of the Atlantic. Unless they'd covered every hotel in Paris. Ridiculous. It depended on who *they* were. Johanson might have figured it out. The trouble was, the Pool had acquired so many independent enemies over the years that you rarely knew who you were fighting until it was almost over. Oh well. A few hours' sleep and I'd be ready for a deeper probe.

I walked down the hall to my room and shifted the bag to open the door. I looked at the key, then at the lock. Well, someone had known I was coming. The vibrations from inside were normal, but the lock was blank. Odd. I deepscanned it, found a light mindscreen shielding some sort of nastiness. Jesus, the banality of all this. I stepped back across the hall, leaving the key suspended. I slowly *pushed* it into the lock. Sparks flew, a low buzz sputtered. Couple thousand volts, I figured. Maybe I was wrong about Johanson; this had Intertel written all over it. Cloak-and-dagger crap. I turned the key, then, aggravated, mentally kicked the door open with a bang. The electricity cut off. I let the key drop to the carpet, walked in and threw my bag on the bed. I slammed the door with a wave and lay down. I was exhausted. I'd take care of all this when I woke up.

I've got a mental clock that never needs winding; years of use have just made it more accurate. I woke up three hours later, three hours of deep, blank sleep. I scanned the room for sensors, got out of my clothes and stepped into the bathroom. I pulled the curtain aside, scanned the showerhead. Once you accept the fact that any number of people are being paid to kill you, precautions become second nature; you don't think about it, you just scan. This nozzle was a nozzle, though; the water, water. So far, so good. I gave the mirror a tentative push. Mirrors can be tricky. You get glass when you scan, but they make viewers awfully thin these days, and some of the rumors you hear about dimensional-portal experiments are pretty bizarre. I couldn't believe I was important enough to use such an expensive piece of equipment on, but who can tell? Any network capable of blowing away our agents wasn't to be taken lightly. I put an alarm shield over the glass and got under the hot water.

Five agents dead in under three months. One in Frisco, one in Germany and the other three right here in Paris. No particular connection between them, no warnings to HQ, which meant they'd suspected nothing until it was too late. Hell, none of them had even been on sensitive assignment. Poli had been investigating the communications foul-up, LaRue had been doing routine talent scouting, and with Basil and Avery it had been business as usual. God knows what Mary Z. had been up to. She hadn't had an active field assignment for three years. Slowing down, the Old Man had said, letting her run the Paris Pool from a desk. Now they were all dead. The method differed from case to case, but the official line throughout was suicide. That was the outlandish part, that was what had us stumped. Five high-level T-paths just *don't* commit suicide. If they'd tried hard, and long enough, they might have convinced me of one or two, but not Avery, not that cocky young kid. And to consider Mary Z. committing suicide?—it was absurd. The crusty grande dame of Insight, that long wolf of a smile sitting above more chins than you could count, and those ridiculous, huge, button earrings. What a mind. She could run a security meeting, assess data coming in from all over Europe, *and* map research projections all at once—that mind, trapped within an arthritic mountain of flesh. Mary Z. was awesome; three generations of agents knew it. There was nothing that could induce her to—but that was the point. Something, someone had toppled her, had pushed them all over the edge. They'd either been murdered and the crimes framed to look like suicide—although having five separate cases stretched the plausibility—or they'd been mentally assaulted by something stronger than any of us could imagine. It didn't make sense. Finney would've warned us if he'd been on to anything; there was a hypnoplant in his mind set to trigger, had he died. I shivered in the hot water, rubbed my shoulder. Dawson. No, I was too closely linked to her mind. Block or no, I'd feel it if she were in trouble. I hoped.

I dripped my way back into the bedroom and unpacked the bag while drying myself. I laid everything out on the bed: the one-piece insulsuit that went under the coat, boots, transmitter, flares, wallet with local currency and ID, transliterator, a big spool of vibrawire, the shimmergun that HQ had insisted I take along. I could dump that now.

I don't like weapons of any kind. You carry a gun and you depend on it, your reactions become dulled.

It was the transmitter that had broken when I dropped the bag downstairs. Ordinarily, this wouldn't have mattered; I could have just bounced a message off one of our relay satellites. But that damn block had been fouling the satellite transfers from Europe. The transmitter had been insurance. I wasn't even going to attempt four thousand miles on my own, not in this atmosphere. I was out of contact with Chicago; those were the breaks. It wasn't my problem, anyway.

My problem. Yeah. I put on the insulsuit, brushed the curtains aside and scanned the window. Nothing but a thin paste of soot and bugs. No, my problem wasn't the relay foul-up, although the Old Man wouldn't mind my solving it.

"Play it by ear, Mollitor. Ask some questions, dig around. Finney was on to something. Just don't vanish."

Yeah, sure. Technically, I wasn't even trying to solve the suicides just yet. I had no illusions as to where my loyalties lay. Step one was to hook up with Dawson. This was a joint mission; I had no intention of pursuing it without her. After seventy years in the Pool, I guess I owe them something, but she and I go back a lot further. These telepathic comrades of ours really *are* children, the Old Man included. He's no old man to me. Dawson and I learned to regenerate our cells twenty years before Insight was ever conceived of, before there were enough active T-paths alive to bother forming such an agency. We worked plenty hard on our own for a long time. It wasn't until the Wars that we were even approached. Christ. I was still practicing medicine in those days, and Dawson was keeping the pieces of the corporation together. They offered the easiest way of working with other T-paths; at least we didn't have to train them all ourselves. And, of course, there *was* a war going on. I'm not knocking it; the agency is nice to have around, but this secret-agent game does become a little silly.

I stared out the window. Paris was beautiful from twenty-two stories up, even through the grimy drizzle, all lit up and glittering. Thousands of little stovepot chimneys, clotheslines stretched at every angle imaginable, the huge, pulsing City of Lights wearing its entrails like scarves. It was good to be back. It was very familiar, so little ever changed. I'd preferred the Eiffel Tower to that neon plasteel monstrosity in its place, but what the hell. Anyone who would've agreed with me was fifty years dead anyway.

I let my focus expand until the lights were a single line, then cleared my mind, drifted into the color spectrum. I fixed on the blue, Dawson's color, and probed on the widest band possible. You never realize how alive a city is until you actually hear it breathing, sense all the individual lives dovetailing to form a single, great life. There's a mental hum, a blend of tones, and once you've felt it, you never have any trouble distinguishing it from the others. There was something wrong, though; I felt a net hanging over the city. Nothing directed by a mind, nothing alive, just a tight, static net interfering with vibrations moving anywhere in Paris. It was subtle, set very deep in the blue, but something tipped me off. Dawson must've put a crimp in the wavelength to draw my attention. I pulled it closer. I could feel two or three points of emanation, but I couldn't focus on them; they would shift as I got close. I had to peek at it from the corner of my mind. I tried pinpointing it with quick jabs, and got the same shadows dancing out of the way. I had more success with the other bands. Whatever they were hiding was being kept well out of the main stream, and it was that stream they wanted me to see. There was lot of activity going on. No direct transmission from Dawson anywhere. I drew back to the dotted lights of Paris, the window, the room. This was obviously going to take some legwork. They were up to something, but there were still too many *theys* to even begin speculating *what*.

I finished dressing and started for the door. Then I remembered. Childish games. I closed my eyes, concentrating, and short-circuited all the electrical current in the four walls, floor and ceiling. It was the simplest way. The lights went out.

The kid was sitting behind the desk, holding a vidphone, looking at a little book in the other hand. Numbers. He was looking for a date. He glanced at me as I crossed the lobby, then his head jerked up, unable to hide the surprise.

"Uh, shall I call a cab, sir?"

I looked him in the eye. A happy prison guard, just doing his job.

"No, I'm sure I can manage."

I thought of kicking the chair out from under him, the bastard, but people like him never learn. I picked the numbers out of his book with one scan. He was going to get a lot of busy signals tonight.

II

Once on the street, I flipped the transliterator to French, pinned it to my collar and looked around for a cab. My French isn't bad, if a little rusty, but trying to understand the accents can be a full-time job. You miss one key word, and by the time you've fished the translation out of your memory the guy's eight sentences down the road, waiting for your response with the patience of a cigaret ash.

The cabbie was an Arab with a face like a flat pincushion. He had a terrible twitch in his eyes, and his hands shook, but he couldn't seem to synchronize the two. His cigar had a faintly sweet odor to it. I hoped he wasn't spiking it with krillweed, not in Parisian traffic. I gave him the address of the Wooden Cafe and he began jerking in and out of the crawling lanes, making a point of ignoring the latest fashions in horns.

Andre's place was our fallback. There was nothing official about it, no Pool surveillance or relay transmits, but Dawson and I had spent years in Paris before the War. We had our own system of meet and fallback here, which we'd never bothered clearing with HQ and had never stopped using. The Wooden Cafe wasn't the most inconspicuous place in town, but Andre was my buddy from the '60s. He was loyal as hell to his friends, and he had his own gang of urchins running information on the streets.

My driver slouched back while we stopped for a light, and let me know how he felt about the weather and the traffic and the Syndicate's plans to screw Europe. It was the type of tired, practiced monologue that didn't require a response. This fellow didn't have a thing in the world but his cab, and what they charged him for monthly power units ate up most of what he made in fares. And he was doing well, compared to some. I kept my mouth shut and tipped him too much.

The familiar tinkle greeted me as I opened the door and went down the three steps. Long varnished beams ran diagonally across the ceiling, curved down into pillars, railings, all wood, all designed for comfort. Little blue lights flickered from somewhere along the ceiling. No bulbs, no wires. Nice touch, Andre, keeping up with the times. The place was fairly empty, the curtains drawn. Two blondes were leaning over a table, waving long cigaret holders at each other and chattering in Italian. A meaty guy in a blue apron took up two spaces at the far end of the bar, alternating between gulps of beer and whiskey. He had a face you would never argue with. One little toothpick of a man blended into a corner chair, dark shades over his eyes, leaning against the wall. I could barely hear him snoring over the Italian laughter. Business as usual. Andre came out of the kitchen wiping his hands, and the seams in his face smoothed out as he smiled.

"Mollitor," he said loudly, using both tattooed arms for emphasis. He leaned over the counter and grabbed me. A soggy one on each cheek. "Ah, *mon ami*, how long has it been?" He cocked his head. "What's the matter, you don't get old like the rest of us? A little gray, maybe, but it's the same face. So?"

"You know. Professional secret and all. How've you been?"

He poured two glasses of wine, set one in front of me. I took a sip.

"How should I be?" he said. "Making a living. What ever changes in this city? The people who rob us have different names sometimes, but the hands sneaking into my pockets always feel the same."

"Meaning, you still cut them off."

He laughed.

"Like the old days, eh? We string everyone along and sell them back their own information at a profit. Ah, Mollitor, it's good to see you. I wish we could sit and talk about the old days."

"That's the truth, Andre. It would be nice. I don't know. Why don't the times ever seem old enough?"

"Why? Because the people live so long. Because the grudges last so long. What old times? You try to tell me you're here on new business, unconnected? Never happen. There are no social visits." He sighed. "Is not hard to guess why you're in Paris."

"You've heard?"

"What do I need to hear? They kill Mary, and Finney makes a meeting here, doesn't keep it . . . Am I stupid?"

"The police say it was suicide," I said quietly, fingering the rim of the wineglass.

Andre snapped off a backhand wave. "Not even a fool believes that."

"You saw Finney?"

He shook his head. "No. He sets up meet, flashes an all-clear, then he doesn't show."

"Hmm. You know who he was meeting?"

"No idea. Your codes are beyond me."

"When was this?"

"Day after they found her. I've got my people looking around as soon as I hear. Drug overdose. This points East, as far as I see."

"Intertel?"

"Sure, Moscow. Who else controls drug flow on this continent? So I check. Is quiet everywhere. No one wants to push any operations; maybe they know your people are investigating. So. I lose three kids. Gone, vanished. No messages, no communication possible in this city. Something is wrong with the transmitters. Maybe with your signals too?'' He raised an eyebrow at me. I didn't say anything. ''Okay, none of my business. I try to contact your people, but they don't want nothing to do with me. Tanner tells me to keep my nose out. Doesn't come by, just bops me in the head with it, long distance. I don't like that business, Mollitor. I give your people the best for years. I don't like guys like him crawling into my head.''

''Tanner?''

I pictured him, the tough guy who liked to throw his weight around. He was the type of limited T-path administrator who felt his meager abilities entitled him to some kind of automatic respect from *normals* like Andre.

''The *canard*. So I don't tell him about Finney.''

''What about Finney?''

His eyes sparkled. Andre was proud of how he could dig up information.

''The call box. The one to Jo-burg. Finney activated it the night Mary died. Maybe he sees a Maf' connection, who knows? All Tanner sees is Finney supposedly going to Zurich, but no Finney on the flitter. So? Am I going to give him updates? *Merde!* I call off my people, take precautions to keep what I know to myself. I figure . . .''

''What precautions, Andre?'' I said with a laugh.

''You think I'm a punk? I feel the tickle, I know when someone's trying to break in. Go ahead, Mollitor, read my mind. What am I thinking?''

He closed his eyes. Andre's face always seemed to want to congeal into a ball, but his nose stood guard and kept its neighbors from clashing. Right now, the bushy eyebrows pointed down while the moustache leaned up, and the nose had no chance. Andre had a short neck and a small powerful body. Muscles on muscles, with a few tattooes thrown in. Twenty years ago, he had been the perfect bodyguard. I probed lightly, got the edge of a defiant attitude, and then I thought I'd hit a radio by accident. A dumb, popular song danced around, the jingling chorus repeating over and over. I pushed deeper; the tune got louder. Full orchestration. I tested the edge of it and smiled. I could get past it if I really wanted to, but it would take a concentrated effort. It was a brilliant impromptu shield for a man with no telepathic powers.

"Okay, Andre," I said. "You win. That's an awful song."

"But catchy, no?" He had a smile wide as the Seine. "Look, I tell you what I told Finney. Is house at *Sevres-Babylone*; Moscow safe-house, I think. Mary knew of it. Finney says he goes there to suss it out, then to meet someone back here. Last I hear from him."

"And Dawson?"

His eyes widened, pushed the seams in his forehead up. "Your girl? No. Is she in Paris?" He shrugged. "I haven't seen her."

"All right. What about Mary? Anything I should know?"

Suddenly, I was hearing another message. Someone was on the Pool wavelength, asking for a crash meeting at Beauborg. They hadn't realized I was in Paris, and Tanner felt I should be briefed by the local Pool. Interesting. There was no reason they should've known I was around. This trip was completely unofficial.

Specifics? I flashed.

Johanson angle. There's a lot that hasn't been declassified for Chicago yet. Must meet tonight.

I got a sub-intimation that this wavelength wasn't safe. Christ. How full of holes had the French Pool become? Maybe Dawson had had good reason for dropping out of sight. I keyed the codes for *20 minutes*, and turned my attention back to Andre's description of Mary's death and the quick, official burial the case had received. It was clear he suspected Intertel. Like everyone in Europe, he had Moscow on the brain.

"The same methods could point to Central, you know," I suggested.

"Washington?" he said, surprised. "I suppose so. But—I mean—you guys don't control them?"

"It's never that neat, Andre. We owe a certain amount of allegiance to the same country, but trading useless information is the closest we've been to a partnership in many, many years. Forget about controlling."

"You should keep that quiet," he said, nodding. "No one really believes it."

"Then there's no reason to keep quiet about it, is there?" I said. It was amazing how people sought to complicate this business. I stood up. "So what do I owe you?"

He held up a hand. "Not a franc. I won't take—"

"The Pool pays for it, Andre. Come on."

"I'll send them a bill. I won't take money from you, Mollitor."

"Okay, look—you be careful. Silly songs or not, you play on the edge of dangerous games, with people a lot more powerful than you."

"*Bien sur*. I made my decision thirty years ago when you run into my cafe, in trouble. I'm careful enough, for a tiny fish. *You* walk carefully, *mon ami*. You've outlived all the other big shots. You're the only prize left."

I looked at the counter. There was nothing more I could warn him against, nothing more I could request. He would do exactly as he pleased, in his own good time.

"*Salut*, Andre," I said.

"*Salut*."

He grabbed me and assaulted my cheeks again. A nod, a short laugh and I left.

Rue de Rivoli was one huge sparkle show. Lights are very in these days. Holos, hovering flashers with no supports, suspended advertisements—the big thing is to grab the attention and dazzle it quick.

An incredibly tall woman in kaleidoscopic furs breezed by, both she and her escort wearing knee-high jetflo cushion boots. Most of the sidewalk cafes were really above-the-sidewalk cafes; anyone who could afford the exorbitant price of drinks hovered at tables fifteen feet above the pedestrians. The noise was light and jingly; every language imaginable was represented. Everyone seemed utterly determined to have a pull-out-the-stops good time, simply because Paris expected it of them. What the hell, they had the money.

Two blocks down, I crossed a square and passed into the winding, alley-wide side streets, and the glitter and bustle could've been a dream. I stepped back two hundred years; I was waiting for the twentieth century to begin. The little shops were closed, boards up, awnings pulled tight, and water bubbled out of the gutter to wash the cigaret butts along the cracked red brick to the river. I passed a gang of kids in a wide doorway, jostling each other on and off the curb. They had eyes like bright, plastic tile that won't scuff no matter how many people walk on it. Their clothes were just this side of rags. They laughed at me, pointing, ducked away, muttering in-jokes until I passed, then went back to playing got-you-last, kicking stones around. Not a penny to spend, nowhere to go. Life had been like this for most people since the War. The bastards lucky enough to be rich played with all the technotoys of the twenty-first century, and the kids, as usual, got screwed.

The little guy from the corner at Andre's was tailing me. He was pretty good—hung back a couple blocks and blended in—but you can't shadow a man who's telepathic and expect him not to notice. So he had to know that I was aware of him. Did that mean he was prepared to handle me if I took offense to the tail? I kept walking, hands in my pockets, and scanned him. His mind was shielded, so I concentrated on the physical. He was all loose flesh, like he used to weigh a lot but forgot to trade in the skin when he lost the fat. Baggy cheeks and sunken eyes, sunglasses in the middle of the night. Sparse, khaki hair. Trenchcoat. No weapons I could pick up. I led him through Place du Chatalet. A big, deserted square with tree-lined paths was just what I wanted if he was interested in a confrontation. I slowed down, getting set; he hung back. The hell with him.

I glanced up at the worn gargoyles on Tour St. Jacques. My old buddies, always leering, always waiting for nothing. They were losing their horns and teeth as the years went by, features blurring with the windy drizzle. They were no longer the forbidding warrior sentinels of old, only stubborn stones playing out their roles with whatever strength history had left them. Just like Mollitor. They were born to a different world and, through fortune or misfortune, had outlived that world. You could reconstrue their purpose to fit the present, but it would never be more than a close approximation. Yep, just like Dawson and Mollitor. We had no claim on this era. There was nothing left to own that wasn't already locked up. Nothing but illusion and power over the illusion. The networks grabbed what they could, and every agent grabbed a piece of his network. Empty power. Christ. Why've we stuck around this long, Dawson?

I saw her face, one side tilted up, with that half-smile and tough-guy squint, hand on her hip, telling me, "It's the only game in town, Mollitor, that's why. Don't take it so hard; things are always looking up."

I looked up. The gargoyles were gone, back there watching my baggy friend slink past. Beauborg was a couple blocks ahead. The sky was a black wave. I felt like hell. I closed my eyes, clenched my fists and filled the widest band possible with a blast:

DAWSON!!

Nothing answered but the damp wind. Great, Mollitor, brilliant move. You just blew through every transmission in Paris. Nothing like sending up a flare when you want to stay undercover.

I got to Beauborg and stood at the railing overlooking the plaza. It was quiet. The museum was closed and the only people out were the *clochards*, passing bottles and cigarets. A couple dogs sniffed along the museum wall, looking for scraps, side-stepping the moonlit puddles. So where was my contact? I scanned lightly, followed a dirt path between a cafe and a newsstand. The impress felt fresh, though a little odd. There was residue from a lot of energy fields here. The gravel was scored with long furrows, no clear footprints. I glanced up. Trash cans hung from hooks imbedded in the spotched stone. High walls pocked with blackened windows, a sliver of moonlight splashing into the narrow space between the walls. Not enough moon to matter, not enough sky to matter. Nothing of interest in a tiny curved alley tucked behind an empty plaza but two legs and the lower torso of a man twisted into the gray corner. The top of him, from the chest up, was burned off, fused into the wall at the end of the alley. I scanned, and it was hot. Nuclear. Whoever'd burned him wanted to make sure. It didn't look like Johanson's work; too messy. Christ. I touched what was left of my contact, and the top half crackled as it crumbled away from the blackened blood. Move fast, Mollitor, your stomach's out of practice, you haven't played doctor in thirty years. I went through his trouser pockets, came out with some change. Well, that wasn't surprising. You don't carry clues in your pocket when you can store them in your mind. The nuke burner pretty effectively blew that, though. I probed, picked up an intimation of tunnels. Johanson. Hmm, anything was possible. Messy operation or not, this agent had been on to *something*.

I dropped the coins on the gravel and scanned back out the alley. High intensity. I was nervous now. Anyone waiting for me had better have more than just a shield. I came out onto the square, moving fast from a crouch, felt around. My toothpick shadow had vanished. No mistakes, Mollitor.

A dog barked. I scanned again, and hit a wave, a blankout shield above. I dived into the empty magazine rack as the air went *FOOM!* and a big chunk of sidewalk vaporized. I rolled to my feet, locked the guy's shield and tore it away, flashed a nervethrust. I heard a muffled groan from the roof of the cafe. There he was, the huge pistol still leveled. His muscles were locked, but the final spasms would be all he needed. I leaped again, sliding on my stomach across the gravel, and the newsstand exploded into millions of splinters. I rolled onto my back, ignited the oxygen in front of him. The concussion folded him in two and blew him off the roof. He crashed into the metal railing, bounced, dazed but still awake. Now I had time to solidify the lock on his nervous system, keep that trigger finger from moving.

I brushed myself off and scanned him. Nothing. He had a hypnoblank primed across his mind. No ID, fingertips plasteened, a custom nuke burner with the serial-impress blanked. Yep, one well-prepared torpedo. Not any more though. I knocked him out and fused the neural receptors in his right arm. He'd pulled his last trigger. Too late for that guy in the alley, but just in time for the next one.

I probed the area again. All quiet. I transmitted the location of both bodies to Tanner's office and started off down the empty street.

III

I checked a few of our impress drops around the city and got nothing. Something strange was going on here. Finney had been too careful. We use buildings and walls all the time for impress; you key to a staggered series of bricks, and it's perfectly safe. I didn't like this. Why would he contact Andre and Tanner, why such easily traceable paths? Because it was smoke. Anything blatant had to be a false lead, and he knew I'd realize it.

So where was he really pointing? Intertel just didn't make sense. Central would've spotted it months ago and we would've picked up something from them. You couldn't suspect Moscow of anything anymore without suspecting Washington of arranging an elaborate frame, and vice versa. They'd been monitoring each other, matching move for move, for so long, that they really were inseparable. Central and Intertel's agents were little more than B-movie spies, good at shadowing or taking mini-holosnaps, but they were unable to handle any of the subtleties of psychic espionage. The sharp ones didn't stay with them long enough. Dawson and I specialized in recruiting agents with previous network training. No, Johanson seemed the more likely angle. The trouble was, tracing his network led down more blind paths than you could count. I should know; I'd spent decades trying.

Johanson. Insight's most illustrious traitor. You'd think telepaths could see through a double agent without any trouble. You'd think we would've known what he'd been up to before he wrecked the Pool. It should've been obvious. Even when he was chief of communications at Insight, he'd been aloof, his thoughts always shielded behind that thin, oily face. There's no law against reticence, and he'd certainly done his job well, but we should've read more into his neurotic attitudes. He'd had no patience with people who couldn't keep up with him, and had suspected the ones who could. Dawson, especially, had worried him because she was able to focus such immense power with so little effort.

It was obvious later that the double-cross had been well planned. Over the years he'd built up a cadre of agents within the Pool loyal to him—it was easy to arrange since he was in charge of all comm nets worldwide; nothing entered the computer without passing his office—but Dawson had forced him into the open before he was ready. For all his intensity, all his ego-buoyed power, Johanson still couldn't beat her. They fought an hour-long probedown, and Dawson came running into the gym afterward. I was supervising a training session and she was transmitting like wild.

Hold it, kiddo.

I've got to—

Verbal. You've got to get off the wave. These guys are working.

We were in a room full of cadets straining to keep objects afloat, concentrating on P-K flow. If I let Dawson give me an overview, at the intensity level she was registering, the whole vibration balance in the room would collapse. Of course, I didn't realize the importance of her message at the time.

She stopped and blinked, put two fingers to her forehead, like she was remembering how to talk. This actually wasn't so far from the truth. After a session like the one she'd just had with Johanson, shifting back to a linear mode took a lot of discipline. You suddenly had to squeeze intention, nuance and image into one narrow band of single-word-at-a-time, and you had to take turns talking and listening. She took a deep breath and pushed the blond hair away from her left eye. She didn't touch it.

"Okay," she said. "Let's see if I can give it to you in baby talk. Johanson's a double. We've got to stop him now."

"How do you know?"

She clenched a fist, then jabbed a finger out of it, at me. "Don't ask questions you won't let me explain. I just spent an hour dueling with him. I beat him, for the time being. We've got to hurry."

The left eye glittered. Dawson's left eye was spooky. Both were a clear sky-blue, but the left one had a sliver of brown running from the upper inside corner, diagonally, across the blue. They would've burned her as a witch in the old days. She had very light skin, high forehead, a button-and-a-half nose and a wide line of a mouth that gave her a deadpan look, until she smiled. A smile animated the whole face, accentuated the cheekbones. These were her proudest accomplishment. She'd spent her first thirty-five years the unhappy owner of a round face. She'd always thought cheekbones were exotic.

"What's he after?" I said.

She shook her head and snapped open the door with her fingers.

"Mollitor, get out of this dummy mode. There isn't time. I need you. I can knock him down, but I can't hold him without help."

We took off at a jog down the corridor. She hadn't been able to contact me from Johanson's office because of the lead-lined walls we used in HQ. Now it was clear.

Flash it.

She did, and it was a boggle of intrigue. Subnets all across Europe, a whole group linked on unused frequencies, gathering information from rival networks into his own system . . .

What end?

Domination. The man's a maniac.

Computer didn't catch it?

Foxed. He's been feeding it false leads.

Duration?

Three years, anyway. Maybe more. He slipped. Rerouted my report on South Africa before I finished it.

Stupid move. Why?

Payoff to the Maf'. They're squeezing satellite time for him.

The Old Man know?

He's scared of J. He'll know soon enough, though.

Can we put a lid on it, Dawson? Or is it too late?

He knocked the trips out of the program before I could move.

Damn. Anyone overseas blown?

Plenty. Frisco and Jo-burg too.

You broke him?

Near enough. He went to impulse-block.

Should keep him for a while.

You don't know how strong he is.

Plan?

Get his nerve centers. I'll deflect.

I was almost flying as we came around the corner, and I was so intent on the transmission that I reached for Johanson's door without scanning. I felt Dawson shout in my mind, but there really wasn't any time, my hand was already touching the frame. By the time I reacted, I would've already pushed it open, and by then . . . Well, as it turned out, Dawson blew the door inward with a mental blast and physically tackled me out of the way as the room exploded. She caught most of the impact along her left side. She countered automatically as best she could, but the blast broke her ribs on that side and tore her leg open to the bone. The concussion almost killed her. There was no time for ambulances, certainly no time to stop Johanson. So I became Dr. Mollitor again, and worked like hell to keep her going, right up until they wheeled her into surgery and finished the job I'd started. We saved her life and her leg, but the big man was gone, safe with his partners in South Africa. Later, he surfaced in Europe with an international network and began fighting us on our own psychic ground. I never forgot it. He was my responsibility from that day on, my mistake having let him escape. Thirty-two years now, and that mistake still stared at me every time I had to watch Dawson walk with that little limp. The bastard owed me and, one of these days, I was going to collect.

There was little doubt in my mind that Johanson was

behind the communications block. After all, he was the expert. He'd designed our microwave satellite system, and helped create the teletransmission seminars at the Academy in Chicago. Whether he was involved in the suicides, though, was anybody's guess.

My toothpick shadow was on me again, two blocks back, same coat, same sunglasses. He'd added a soft, round hat, pulled low over his baggy forehead—protection from the drizzle. I turned my collar up, checked my watch. 10:25. I'd spent enough time wandering empty streets; I had better things to do than confuse my tail. I found a taxi at St. Georges. The driver was safe; there was nothing left in his old mind but a grid of Parisian streets.

"St. Michel," I said, slamming the door with a blink. I was out of bright ideas. If everyone else was tracking Johanson, I saw no reason to do otherwise.

IV

Place St. Michel is an old triangular plaza lying where boulevards St. Michel and St. Germain meet the Seine. You look across the river and to your right, and there's Notre Dame, sprouting spires and gargoyles through the mist. You turn around, and there's St. Michael above the fountain, one foot on Satan's neck, a long rippled sword in one hand. The payoff is coming; the griffons on either side of him can tell. They're enjoying every minute, and it's been going on for centuries.

The plaza was full of people. Tourists constantly readjusted their scarves, convinced that, once they achieve the proper angle, they'd be indistinguishable from Your Native Parisian, and wouldn't have to keep paying double for everything. A young French couple went by, wrapped around each other step for step, pointing out every little thing and getting an uproarious kick out of it. Kids kept running by, street kids with black strobe eyes, darting in and out, too fast to follow, waiting for an opening, a careless move, an available pocket. Lots of general riffraff, making noise.

I walked around, picking up snatches of thought. I was probing lightly, didn't want to arouse the attention of any other T-paths in the area. There was a lot of the usual business of the street going on: people looking to buy an ounce of krillweed or some zephyrs, buying and selling custom weapons, tired eyes looking for action, cheap whores. I was partially scanning for Dawson—though I didn't really expect her to have left any obvious vibration here on the street—and partially just waiting for a meet I could stick my nose into. It didn't much matter whose contact I was disrupting. When you're completely in the dark, any glimmer you move toward is the right direction.

I put myself in Finney's place. He'd gotten here right after Poli had shot himself. Since Poli had been talent-scouting, the obvious approach would've been to find out who he'd been recruiting. Lots of questions, lots of contacts. It would have let everyone know that Finney was in town. Knowing that, they—assuming it's the same they—still went ahead and knocked LaRue out a window. Nobody would have had that kind of nerve but Johanson. So, at that point, Finney should've started digging at the comm block, checking Johanson's recent contacts with the Maf', etc. Instead, he books a flight to Munich, where Basil died a month earlier. It's only two days later, when he finds Mary dead, that he sets up a meet in South Africa and fakes an impress of a shuttle to Luna. It didn't make sense; it was all out of order. The following morning, he relays contradictory messages—to San Francisco, of all places—and leaves for Zurich without notifying Tanner. Then he drops right off the wavelength, no hypno, no autos, just gone. The Zurich business was an obvious screen, and the rest was just crazy. Did he go anywhere? Did he get caught? I had to find Dawson. I had to turn up *something* here.

I got my break on the third pass through the square. He was standing under the lefthand griffon; a young guy in a heavy leather zipcoat, strange for this time of year. Maybe it was a signal. He had a long, delicate face, shiny sand-colored hair, nice straight nose. You could've mistaken him for a choirboy, but for those eyes. They were cold, gray pools, completely gray, with two black ovals dead center, and they had nothing of humanity left in them. I don't know what they were doing on that face; they should've been ammonia pools on Jupiter.

I scanned him. It was no problem; he had an untrained mind. He was waiting for someone named Rizi to pass information to. Or was he picking it up? I don't think he knew, himself. I scanned deeper for passwords or signs. Apparently, he didn't know this Rizi. Then what was—ah, got it. I walked up to him from the side, scratched my head and asked him for a cigar. He turned, his left hand diving into the coat pocket.

"How many you need?" he asked, looking me up and down. His eyes narrowed; something was wrong, his pulse was jumping. Damn it. They'd told him this Rizi was young. There was nothing I could do now about the gray in my hair. I played with his vision a little; the lighting in the square wasn't very good anyway. I added a few moving shadows. I had to go easy, keep the monitor going—heartbeat, respiration, nerve-to-muscle impulse.

"One will do it," I said, not taking any chances. "Things are moving from the East."

I transmitted a big dose of *meaning* in that. If he was supposed to pick up as well as deliver, I had to give him something. If not, it didn't matter.

He reached into his top pocket for the cigar case, not sure he liked what was going on, but figuring he was just the messenger boy; this was all out of his league anyway. He shook his head to clear his eyes, handing me the case. He was getting restless; he didn't like his eyes twitching. I gently pushed alpha waves at him. Calm, boy, calm. Oceans. Quiet oceans, campfires.

"Hey, you can't be Rizi, you're too—"

"Sure I am," I said soothingly. "Who the hell else is going to ask you for a cigar in the middle of the street?" *Calm, boy.*

"Oh, well, I guess . . ." He stopped. The hand in the pocket held a slipknife. I didn't care how fast he was with it; his fingers weren't going anywhere. I keyed on the bicep as I turned away.

"You tell 'em to be good now," I said, and poured the alpha waves on.

That damn knife. I was so worried about a knife in the hand of a kid I'd fooled that I didn't sense the other guy until he swung. I caught a beard, big meaty face, electro-stud shockshirt and something heavy about his hand. I managed to move enough so I only took a glancing blow to the head, but I felt it cut me. I staggered to the street with the next swing, jumped between two cars and, suddenly, vehicles were blaring and swerving into one another. I slapped the hood of a Flamer and vaulted over it, spun out of the way of a skidding slicebike and stumbled between two Photons a second before they collided. The parts of me that weren't spinning were falling. I got up from the curb and ran to the wall above the river, looked back. The big, bearded one was running *over* the mass of stalled cars, bellowing as he jumped from roof to roof, caving each one in. The kid was right behind him. Weapons were coming out of pockets. This was getting serious; no time for subtleties. I put one hand on top of the wall and swung myself over, fifty feet of rushing air, hit the pavement and staggered involuntarily a step and a half to the river's edge, then fell back against the wall. My ankles were killing me. Thank God for the boots.

I was still holding the cigar case. I slipped it into my pocket and zipped it shut. King Kong was at the top now, leaning over and yelling at me. I saw him throw something, and I *pushed* it into the wall and took off, running along the river. Whatever it was blew up against the wall, splattering concrete into the river. Chips hit me in the back. Christ, this was some cigar. I focused on my muscles, my legs, *speed*. I ran like hell. The important thing was to stay on this side of the river. If I crossed, I'd be on

Île de la Cité and they could easily surround me. I kept scanning. This walkway wasn't going to last long. The iron rungs stopped growing out of the wall at the next bridge. No more mooring, no more lover's lane, just a dark, swirling river with an indiscriminate appetite. Like it or not, I had to go back up.

There was a guy standing at the bottom of the stairway ahead, facing me. He was heavyset, fleshy jowls, dumb-looking. I had no way of knowing if he was one of them or just some fellow who happened to be in the way. No time to probe. His jaw dropped, and I kicked his legs out from under him before I got there. He fell down and I went over him with a leap.

I got to the top and felt around. There were a lot of them and they were coming from all directions. I could hear the Old Man, back in Chicago, telling me, "That's why you're such a damn good agent, Mollitor. You get right to the root of things, you stir up the nest."

Yeah, lucky me. I probed the layout of the streets, got my bearings. I wasn't far from Elena's. Sanctuary. No, I couldn't do it, they'd have no trouble picking me up. I couldn't lead these bastards to an old lady's house. Oh well. The Metro looked like the obvious choice. I ran down the steps, slammed open the electronic doors and shorted them out after me. I got down to the platform and heard a train rumbling away; the station was just about empty. My boots clicked against the concrete, and the echo answered on a slight time delay from the long, arching tile ceiling. The tile used to be white, the lighting down here used to be yellow, but the dusty uniform green admitted this only in isolated spots.

A dozen *clochards* hung out at one end of the platform, spilling down the steps into the tunnel itself. They were happy to be here, dry, warm, the cheapest hotel in town. Bottles passed with dull clinks through the bags. Cigarets.

I felt the back of my head and winced. I didn't detect anything broken, but there was blood running down my neck. He'd hit me with something sharp. My jacket was ripped. Christ, my knuckles were skinned raw; I was smearing blood on everything. I wiped my hands on my pants, turned up my collar and shuffled toward the group, mumbling and coughing. The leader gave me the once-over with his one good eye, and I let my own eyes go as dumb and empty as possible. I concentrated on radiating a harmless misery. He thought about it for a minute, then scratched his stubbled cheeks and grunted his approval. As simple as that. Someone handed me a bottle, and I drank while scanning them. I was perfectly safe here. What brain cells they had left wouldn't hurt a fly.

I leaned against the wall and shut my eyes, worked on closing the wound in my scalp. My legs ached, and a muscle in my back felt wrenched. I was getting too old for this business. I found the cigar case, opened it and slid a roll of plastic sheeting out. Yellow, translucent, very thin. It was covered with hundreds of dots and lines, cut into the surface. I had no idea what it meant, but someone in Chicago would. I stared at it awhile, memorizing it. Contrary to popular belief, a photographic memory *can* be developed. I'm proof. Most people just don't have the hundred or so years it takes to work at it.

I put the case back in my pocket and got up. There was no time to relax here. The bleeding had stopped, and my thick skull had avoided any concussion. All I had was a headache, and I could work on that while I moved.

I started mumbling good-byes to my newfound buddies, instinctively throwing a light scan over each as I clapped him on the back. The oldest guy lifted his paper bag in salute. A toothless smile.

"*Salut, Granpère,*" I said with a wave. I was past him before it struck me. I whirled around.

Dawson!

What was she doing in his mind?

I probed, gently but thoroughly. The old bum, François, lived in these tunnels. He'd seen a blond-haired woman carried through here two days ago. He'd remained hidden from her captors, but Dawson had managed to lock a vibration, picture and all, into the old guy's mind. This was beautiful. A vibe on our private subwave was as good as a homing signal. I restrained myself from kissing François, and bounded into the tunnel.

It was late. Soon the Metro would stop running for the night but, for now, I could still feel the tracks vibrating. I looked at the broken patches of wall, the peeling arches of stone and concrete and masonry and steel supports all jumbled together. These tunnels were old, always crumbling a little and always being repaired, the new slapped onto the old until you had a hodgepodge only an archaeologist could appreciate.

I kept close to the wall. Every twenty minutes or so, a train sped by, and I wasn't interested in trying to knock it off the track. Telekinesis is not my strong suit. I could push that bomb into the wall, move keys, knock people over, but the really intense stuff—crumbling walls, blowing holes in metal—I leave all that to Dawson. I just haven't got the razor concentration. I'm the deep scanner. I can peel away layers like turning the pages of a book. I was a doctor for years; I know, literally, what makes people tick. Probes come as naturally to me as a bedside manner. Dawson's parents died when she was twenty-five, and she was left to run the details of a multinational finance corporation. She had a mind honed to precision from years of dealing with cutthroat executives, and she'd learned how to get nasty when the situation called for it. At this point, after almost ninety years of perfecting her psi powers, Dawson was not someone to mess with. You could fool her sometimes, but that's what I'm around for. I like to think we're an unbeatable team, but what do I know? I have no perspective.

I'd been walking for about an hour, tracking the exact same vibration, when it struck me that there should've been some variance, some fluctuation due to my proximity or as a reaction to my steady scan. There had been no change. Something was leading me in circles. I concentrated. It had started when I was sitting against the wall with the *clochards*. I tried a pinpoint scan; it danced out of the way. What the hell? This was just like the comm block, except it wasn't coming from anywhere. It was local; more than local, it was *personal*. Very strange. How could *I* be shifting my own signal unconsciously?

Then I got an idea. I unzipped my top pocket and pulled out the cigar case, slid the plastic sheet into my hand. Absolutely. It was radiating a net of subtle interference but, like a ventriloquist, it was "throwing" the point of origin and changing the frequency every few seconds. I concentrated and got the pattern of the frequency shift, but the positioning, the "directioning" of the ventriloquism, was truly random. No wonder it was driving the networks crazy. A couple of these near a transmitter or receiver would disrupt all channels, and you'd never know what it was or where it was coming from. You'd just get an illusion of something much bigger. These codes were probably stashed all over Paris. Hmm. It couldn't be selective, or someone would hit the unblocked channels eventually. That meant the designer had to know how to neutralize it locally. There was only one man on the planet sharp enough to develop such a system.

I looked at the dot pattern again, then memorized the vibration of the actual material. I dropped it to the ground and dissolved it, molecule by molecule.

With the interference gone, I backtracked down the tunnel. There *was* something nearby, but now it felt like it was muffled by lead shielding. My luck was becoming phenomenal. I'd come down here on a spur-of-the-moment decision, merely to escape. Now here I was finding Dawson in the mind of a burnt-out wino and accidentally cracking the comm-block code. I glanced around, peered into the wet shadows, shot out periphery scans. All this good fortune made me nervous. It was a safe bet the Evil Eye was setting me up to get creamed.

Nothing was blocking me anymore. Of course, this meant that nothing was keeping the vibrations from being picked up aboveground either. There were telepathic alarms going off across the city. They got stronger the closer I got to whatever it was I was getting close to. Whoever was transmitting those alarms was a first-class idiot. I started jogging through an old, unused section of tunnel. The tracks at my feet had rust on them. Green things were growing on the damp walls. The arches here were red brick lined against the stone, and there were concrete floors fused into the cracking wall, huge iron handles quietly oxidizing. Broken glass was scattered everywhere. Something was nudging at my mind. No clear message, just a steady throb.

Dawson?

I kept to the wide tunnel, scanning the smaller passages at a glance and then, suddenly, I was there. I stood in front of a strip of peeling concrete wall with three doors in it. All three looked like they'd been sealed a couple centuries ago. Long, wet patches ran to the ground. The brown, spongy lichen was a nice touch. There was even the remnant of an old Dubonnet poster clinging to the mold. I scanned, and felt a heavy mindscreen on the middle door. I stripped the screen away and pushed, but it wouldn't move. No recoil, no resistance. Inert. I touched it. Christ. This was no time for heroics, I decided; no time to burn myself out burning that thing down. It was lead, but it was imbedded in concrete. I pulled the spool of vibrawire out of my pocket and molded it along what would've been the edges of the door if this had really been a door. I doubled the strand; I wasn't going to go through this a second time. I trotted down the passage, got inside an arch and ignited the wire. It's a damn good thing vibrawire is ultrasonic. Anything that could chew up concrete like that would've been hell on the ears. A quarter-mile above, the dogs of Paris were having nightmares.

The lead slab rocked as the surrounding concrete disintegrated into sparks. I pushed and pried the hell out of it. Then it slowly toppled forward, crashing into the tunnel with a hollow boom. I ran past the dust and leaped through the opening.

It was like diving into a swimming pool of mercury. I broke the surface, went all the way in, and felt a thousand pounds of suffocating pressure on all sides. One knee buckled, but I grabbed a wall and stayed on my feet. The ceiling was only six feet high and the whole place was blank, gray lead. This thing was a tomb, a psychic tomb. I felt around. She was lying in the corner, on her back, eyes staring at mine, struggling to breathe. It was Dawson. She was a mess. Not a lot of physical damage except for some cuts and bruises, but she wore the signs of someone who's been fighting a strong current for hours, maybe days. Her eyes were glassy, her chest heaving, with one fist clenched tight and shaking. The maddening thing was, I couldn't probe, couldn't make contact. It took all my concentration just to stay on my feet. This was no simple interference, it was a steady oscillating pressure, each wave building on the one previous. Any normal human mind would crush like *papier mâché* in minutes. Nothing to fight, no mind to engage; there was no chance to relax my defense long enough to send anything. It was no surprise I hadn't been able to sense her earlier. With that door sealed—Christ, how long had she been in here?

The time to move was now, before I weakened. I inched my way along the wall, knelt and took her wrist.

CONTACT.

Her mind was screaming, every synapse wide open and firing. The link took too much energy; I collapsed. I put my feet against the wall and let the lower half of my body go numb. I concentrated on breathing, and on the muscles of my free right arm. The left arm was safe. It would sooner leave its socket than let go of Dawson. I pulled the two flares from my pocket and wriggled around, slapped one on each of my boots. Now came the tricky part. I let my right arm go numb and took a deep breath. I dropped the concentration against the room entirely, and sent, with all my energy,

CUSHION THE IMPACT!

The world caved in. As I started to black out, I ignited the flares. Understand, these things were designed to shoot a half-mile into the sky. With two of them on my boots, I was like a rocket that falls over at liftoff. In the quarter-second it took to blur out of the room, it occurred to me that, if she didn't manage to put up an adequate cushion, we'd be another damp splotch on the tunnel wall. For a quarter-second, I knew how an electron feels. Then the shield, with us inside, hit the wall, blew right through it into the next tunnel and hit another wall. This one, being simply a buttress against solid earth, cracked but didn't break. The shield held. Dawson blacked out.

I'd been through a lot, but I was still feeling pretty strong. Dawson, however, wasn't going to be moving until she recharged a bit. We didn't have a lot of time. I set an alarm in my peripheral consciousness, put a pressure shield fifty feet up the tunnel in both directions. I pulled her to me and held tightly, closed my eyes and slipped my mind into hers. This was a familiar routine. We linked up the equivalent channels, relaxed the neuromuscular circuits, locked wills. We were one energy source.

You all right?

Better. That room is a scrambler—bounces vibrations—no source—it's awful, there's nothing to push against—it's—

I know, I know. Easy. You're out.

Right. Right.

Howdy, partner.

I was beginning to think you'd never find me.

You'll never see that day.

Look, Mollitor, I found the source of the interference. They've got specially treated codes—

I know. I got hold of one.

I showed her the picture. She studied it.

Johanson?

Who else?

No one, I guess. What do they mean?

Don't know. Ballard will figure it out when we get back to Chicago.

We're going back?

It was a thought. Why? You on to something?

Finney.

You're a whiz, doll. You found the trail?

Not that easy. Lots of smoke, lots of trails.

She unwound the thread and I scanned it.

There's a method to it, Mollitor.

More like a braid.

Maybe, but it's all on purpose.

Purposefully out of order?

Absolutely. And I'll bet it's the meaningless ones that are important.

Luna.

Could be. Why fake an impress? And why so strong?

It dawned on me.

So we'd notice it.

Also, why San Francisco at all?

More local focus for us? But it should've been Chicago.

It could've been anywhere. Why San Francisco?

He's on to something.

Real close. But he's being shadowed. Look . . .

She showed me the energy field patterns, the same ones I'd sensed on the dead man at Beauborg.

Who?

It's a puzzle. It looks like Central/Intertel, but it's impossible. They're too dumb.

They could've developed a psi division.

If they were any good, we'd know.

Yeah. They'd have to be real good to force those suicides.

Moot.

Why?

You're not that good, and you're the best psi-stripper operating.

She had a point. I tried the other angle.

Johanson?

The comm block, sure. Not the suicides.

Why not?

Just a feeling. It's the wrong MO.

How do you feel?

Exhausted.

Can you make it to Elena's?

I showed her the map.

I'll try.

The alarm I'd set went off. Someone was coming down the passage.

We've got company.

I'll be all right. Let's go.

I detached the circuits and opened my eyes. We were back in our battered bodies, in a rotting tunnel. She smiled and winked at me, felt a bruise on her neck and followed it up to her ear. I got up and brushed myself off. When I had time to pay attention, I was going to be stiff as hell. Dawson pulled her hair into a ponytail, squeezed once, and it stayed put. She got up and stretched her arms, flexing, while she gauged the dimensions of the tunnel. She dropped back to my left a couple steps, leaned on her right leg. Her breathing sounded labored.

You're sure you're all right?

Just tired.

I'll do the jumping around, okay? You just cover me.

They came around the bend with a lot of noise, but

there weren't as many as I expected. My friend with the beard was in front. He was uglier than I remembered. He had a heavy length of chain in one hand, and a long, slim shimmerknife in the other. His shockshirt had a hood coming up over his hairy skull. Well-protected. Not someone I wanted to trade punches with. I broadcast a move to the left, feinted, then came at him from the right. He shifted in time, but his rhythm was a little off. I probed his face, up the cheek, under the eye and along the optic nerve. A fine, healthy nerve. I squeezed, stopped just short of crushing it, and Dawson hit him in the throat with a thick blast of air. He tripped over his chain and went down, choking. I jumped over him and kicked the next guy in the head, landed to his left and ducked. Whatever almost hit me wasn't coming back; the bicep was ripped. *Now.* I grabbed his good arm, dropped a hip and flipped him high into the face of the guy with the pistol. The beam took out a piece of the wall. I caught a movement to my left and spun around. Four more were jerking and spasming in some eerie, malarial dance. Their joints were twisting in weird directions. I glanced back and saw Dawson, facing them in a crouch, her fists clenched tightly in front of her, glaring over the tops of her knuckles, her whole body shaking. Christ. I was glad she was on my side.

I was getting tired, myself. Enough of this. I turned to the two remaining men and popped a couple capillaries in their heads. This was the simplest way to induce unconsciousness in someone not wearing a shield. You just pinched the vessel and let the pressure go bang!, then you let go. Four eyes rolled backward at once, and they collapsed. Dawson dashed past her twitching victims and we ran together, down the tunnel, scanning ahead for ambushes. It was clear. Dawson seemed better already; the action had perked her up.

That was ridiculous, she flashed. *They weren't even shielded.*

It couldn't've been Johanson.

Don't know. It was Johanson's people who locked me in that scrambler.

Did you see him?

J? No. They just threatened me with calling the boss.

Big deal. How did they catch you in the first place?

The interferers. Enough of them create an oscillating field.

Can you punch holes?

Barely a pin.

Did it make you want to commit suicide?

Bite your mind.

Sorry, just an idea. I wonder why these guys weren't shielded?

It's a sloppy operation, Mollitor, no matter how you look at it.

Okay. What about Finney?

Luna.

You really think so?

Well, there is an energy connection to the suicides. Their brains were overloaded. And those E-Field imprints . . .

Who did the psi-autopsies?

Tanner.

What frame?

.02 vibe, not much to hold onto. Good impress, though.

That's strange. You trust him?

Not really. But they got the same results in Frisco on Avery.

Maybe Finney copped on to it.

Maybe.

There was a station ahead, a train right behind us. We swung up onto the platform, and Dawson *pushed* the people out of the way. The train ripped past, screeching to its stop, and we ran up the stairs to the first landing, jumped the turnstile and ran out to the street. I grabbed her shoulder.

Hold it.

Huh?

Go blank.

She blanked. I scanned the area. They were in the vicinity, but they hadn't picked us up yet. Damn. I needed time, just a little bit of time.

A couple dogs ran past, headed for the river, then three more. Perfect. I focused on the two bigger ones, two raggy Alsatian mongrels. They seemed to be the leaders. I impressed Dawson's vibration on one of them, and mine on the other. They didn't mind. The only effect on the dogs would be a little jolt of energy. All the better. Keep running, guys. The imprint would last ten, maybe twenty, minutes.

I blanked my mind, took Dawson's hand, and we started up the street toward Elena's.

V

It was never large enough to be a real street, yet it didn't have the trash-can-and-clothesline look of an alley. The first time I'd seen it, it had been called rue Boulanger, a deadend path curving up from the tangle of boulevards around St. Germain. There'd been flower boxes lining one side, a German bookstore that served pastries and coffee upstairs; it had always been so strange to see the crossed flags of Germany and France jutting out from the eaves. Students from the nearby schools had loved the obscurity of the street. The shops were their little secret, a personal corner of Paris that no tourist could ever find.

That was a long time ago. The shops are gone now, the sidewalk cracked and deserted, spotted with blown-about debris. The street sign's gone, even the plaque on the corner building is erased by dirt and time—you can see the L-A-N of Boulanger, but you've got to know what you're looking for in the first place. It's not on any recent map.

At the top of the path was a strip of sidewalk that's been

taken care of, a clean building-front, a short green awning covering the top half of window and door alike. Etched into the glass of the door, in a curved semicircle, was the single word, "Cafe." The place looked closed, in business only in a theoretical sense, and the students who happened by peer along the red, cobbly brick above the window for a sign of life, a word of greeting or warning, some means of discovering the hours of this quaint little place, were out of luck. No way. The old-timers had their methods. We keyed the frequency lock and went in.

The place was tiny. One wall held nothing but a doorway that opened onto a flight of stairs. There were four wooden tables in the back, with flower vases on them, yellowing abstract prints framed on the wall above. Two globes hung from the ceiling, turned low, giving the room a soft, fireside sort of radiance. On the other wall was the bar, with three stools in front. I looked into the shadow behind the bar, and Elena took her hand away from her chin and smiled faintly, nodding, as if she'd been expecting us all along.

Dawson walked over and took one of the old lady's hands in both of hers.

"Elena," she said softly. "*Comment ça va*? God, it's been years."

Elena gave a long blink, her eyes lost for a moment, just two more slits among the endless lines of that face. The long nose was the same, the high cheeks just a little more gaunt, but everything else was deeply wrinkled skin, feathery white hair spilling to her shoulders. So many decades, so many changes. It was only when I saw Elena that I understood how many years had gone by, only then that I realized how old I was. She was a mirror that wasn't fooled by psychic games, and there was something terrifying about it. God. What in the world did *she* feel, with her only two remaining contemporaries standing there looking like her grandchildren? She started to respond, her chin quivering, no words, the feelings impossible to encompass with any greeting. The green eyes shut tight again. She leaned forward in the chair, kissed Dawson and held her, cheek to cheek, her fingers laced deep into the blond hair, the veins and tendons along one arm macramed against the bone. Then she pulled back and wiped her eyes.

"Dawson," she said in a deep voice, "look at you. My beautiful Dawson. Where did you get that bruise?" She touched the face. "What happened? You aren't still . . . ?"

"Of course I am, Elena. They put us back in the field. It's a crazy business; you can get hurt."

The old woman winced and shook her head.

"My God. Well, sit down. Please. Let me get you some wine."

She started pulling glasses out from under the bar. She quickly set them down, one, two—she stopped with the third one in her hand, held it by the stem, staring into the glass. Reflection? Transparency? Crystal ball? She sighed and set it down. Then she looked up.

"Mollitor."

"Elena."

The eyes almost floored me. Surrounded by a million creases, spots, all the toll the flesh takes from the spirit, the eyes shone like emerald stars, skyrocketing through the years, the exact same eyes I'd fallen in love with a century ago.

"Don't you know you're supposed to watch out for her? Look at her. What kind of doctor are you?"

I smiled. The only people alive who could ask me that question were in this room.

"No kind," I said. "I gave it up, remember?"

She waved a skinny arm.

"Bah. You don't give up pieces of yourself. You use everything you know, always, and *you*, of all people, have a memory that never lets go. *Voila!*, Dr. Mollitor."

"No, just Mollitor."

"Of course. Come here."

Dawson was laughing. Elena came out from behind the bar and looked me over.

"It's amazing. You never change. You're like a postcard. Ah, Mollitor . . ."

She fell into my arms, her hand on the back of my neck as I reached for hers. I closed my eyes, and the years dropped away. Before Insight, before the Wars, there was a world once, a world where everything was available and anything was possible, where the days never ended and we lived in the cafes, talking about history and destiny and love and hope. We were all young, so tickled by the reality of ESP, so enthused by the cosmic potentialities; application didn't really matter, we were going to change evolution just by being who we were. I saw Arthur, with that sly grin and sharp, Germanic face, the research coordinator at the Institute. Weatherly, the wild-haired cockney, could get computers to sing and dance; Dawson could raise any amount of money through the corporation; Elena ran the home base out of this same cafe; Tanya and Josh were our brilliant writers who could explain it all to everyone. Yes, and Dr. Mollitor was the front man, our distinguished American surgeon from the Sorbonne—people of consequence would take note when the good doctor spoke.

Was it possible? Was it crazy? The Wars blew the group to the wind, long before we ever got past the simple fun of it. Arthur and Josh were killed in the first assaults on England; we heard later that Tanya died in a Soviet prison. Weatherly came out after it was over, bitter and totally fed up; he never left London again. Elena was gone, hiding from the maniacs who ran Europe, maybe dead, maybe—who knew? I couldn't find her. I was thousands of miles away, in Chicago. Safe. Lucky. No one remained but Dawson and me. And Central wanted us; boy, did they want us. Run the section, Mollitor, you'll be a big man, fame, money, top agent in the CIA. Think of your country. It wasn't until several years after the Treaty, but we eventually found a lever and pried a chunk loose from the intelligence community. INSIGHT.

Where were you, Elena? Where were you hiding? You could've coaxed Weatherly out of his den; the four of us could've directed the Pool, clearly and sanely; we could've—no, it was too much. It was 2089, and I held an ancient woman in my arms. There were no possibilities left; there was only the remnant of a connection. No avoiding the work to be done.

Dawson?

Nope. She was lying with her arms folded on the bar, blanked, recharging. All right, she needed that. One step at a time. Elena and I sighed at once, though from different directions.

"So?" she said, stepping back. "What is it this time, Mollitor? What happened to her?"

"We were looking for Finney," I said. "Dawson ran into some trouble, that's all."

"Who was it?"

"That's the problem. No one but Johanson could mount this kind of attack, but he has no reason." I paused, thinking. "Short of simple revenge."

"Revenge is never simple," she said with a tight smile. "That pig would kill Dawson if he could, and by the slowest, most painful method he could devise. He remembers who destroyed his operation."

"This is bigger than a grudge, though. It's turning into a psi war. You've heard about the suicides?"

She shrugged, rubbed a finger along the scarred wood. "I hear a little. No one briefs me on anything. I'm just an old woman; I was never part of your Pool. The majority of my information comes from you. Or from Mary. For the most part, it doesn't concern me."

"You knew Mary?"

"I've known her for years. She made contact with me when she first got to Paris in the '60s. She wanted me to compile a history of ESP applications. For Pool files. She said, since I'd gotten in on the ground floor, I was best qualified to chart a complete report. Dear Mary. Ground floor, indeed. I was there to lay the foundation, but I never saw a piece of the building go up. She was flattering me, trying to make me feel important. You didn't put her up to that, did you, Mollitor? No, don't answer; I don't want to know. Mary was a good one, though. For an American, she showed an amazing intuition for the European mind." She gave me a sharp look. "Suicide? Overdose of drugs? Come on, Mollitor, that's not the real story."

I spread my hands.

"That's what Finney was looking for. The hit looked like Intertel, but only Johanson could've accomplished a psi-assault of that force."

"No," said Elena dreamily, "not even him. Hmm. Mary wanted details—you know—of the offshoots, the experiments that we'd dreamed up. She harped on that for years. The ones at the beginning, Mollitor. Especially the ones that Insight never developed."

"She made you privy to a lot of classified information."

"Of course. Mary ran Paris then, ran every phase of your Pool. Before you semi-retired her and put that silly boy in charge."

"That wasn't my fault, Elena."

"Well, no matter. It happens to all of us. Anyway, Mary knew I was safe. I was one contact who could never be turned by another network, and I can keep what I do know shielded. The added advantage was that I didn't officially exist. No surveillance. I was never an agent, never a formal contact. Why, since the War, I haven't even been listed in the French census. But that's beside the point. Pay attention, Mollitor, I'm not talking twenty years now; I can tell you what Mary was working on three weeks ago. None of this is in your official reports."

I sat down next to her at the bar. I tried to look nonchalant, but I could see the twinkle in her eyes. She knew she had me, and she loved it.

"A month ago, Mary contacts me."

"How?"

She tapped her forehead. I was puzzled.

"There's a communications block," I said.

"For short distances, it comes and goes. Mary and I used special subwaves, anyway." She took a sip of her wine. "So Mary contacts me. She wants to know about energy transfers. You remember Weatherly's idea? That business of tapping psi energy and redistributing it? Oh, you remember, he had those computers of his recording each of us as a vibration pattern, trying to express the flow as a series of equations?"

"Sure," I nodded. "We can do that now. Not to the extent Weatherly was driving at, but we can identify individual vibe patterns." I thought about those two dogs by the river. The time they'd bought us was just about gone. I threw a mindshield around the cafe.

"And transfers?" Elena was saying.

"Not a lot. All higher level T-paths in the Pool spend a transfer session with the computer in Chicago every couple months. We collect enough power to run HQ; we've been doing that since the '60s. To that degree, Weatherly's theory works."

"But that was just the tip of it," Elena said. "He was after something much bigger. He wanted to key into everyone, tap the latent psi force that these people are unaware of, that they'll never have any use for. With just a fraction from every individual alive?—my God, Mollitor, you could power this planet *and* Luna *and* the colonies and who knows what else."

It was obvious, but I said it anyway. "Star drive. Interplanetary travel."

"Right. And you have to remember, Weatherly thought of all this ninety years ago, before the War, before Insight, before there was any hope of applying it. It was just another noble idea; our little group was it. You remember, Mollitor? You remember those pages of computer readouts he used to spread over the table, knock the glasses over, you remember Tanya yelling at him? Ah, the wild man, running in from the drizzle with books and papers falling everywhere."

I laughed. "You're the one with the memory, Elena. I can't come close. Keep going. How did Weatherly think this latent energy was going to be tapped?"

"*That,*" she said, stabbing an enthusiastic index finger, "is exactly what Mary wanted to know. She knew damn well that no one but an agent would sit with a computer and let it suck their energy. Most of these people think we're dangerous freaks as it is. No, Weatherly figured we'd train collectors, actual people who could tap the energy psychically, use themselves as the liaisons between the unwitting donors and the computer. Ultimately, it would have to be coordinated by microcircuit, because it had to operate continuously, but the fieldwork, the gathering, would be done by agents. You want to know the problems involved? I thought so. Stop looking so surprised, Mollitor. Why shouldn't I think clearly? I'm younger than you are. Have some more wine.

"First of all, the actual transfer mechanism had to be perfected. The collector had to know the difference between tapping latent power—a low percentage, mind you—and draining life energy. There's a fine line there. We wanted donors, not victims. He also had to learn to use a section of his mind as a reservoir, separate from his own personal resources, into which power could be channeled and held until the time came to release it, all at once, into the computer/processor. Without control of this reservoir, the collector was, in essence, being trained as a psychic vampire, and all sorts of problems could develop."

"For instance?"

"I'm getting to that," she snapped.

I was enjoying this. This was the Elena I'd known in the early days—carefully organized, needing no prompting or interruption. I could almost see the feather earrings dancing between strands of her jet-black hair as she turned her head from side to side, taking in everything in the cafe while her fingers ticked off the numbers. It was easy to see why she and Mary had gotten along.

"Second, there was no point in sending a collector out unless he could amass an appreciable amount of energy with each mission. So, there had to be a way to keep the transfers effective as the power in storage built up. There had to be some trick for preventing them from burning out their own psi-circuits. We're talking about massive quantities here."

"In both directions."

"Of course. In a lot of ways, the discharge process was even more critical. Blow the computer, blow the agent's mind, in a literal sense. It had to be handled just right, but how do you teach someone that? And then, perhaps most importantly, there were the psychological aspects. Consider Johanson. We saw what kind of imperial delusions he acquired from a position of power. You take an agent and teach him to transfer energy from people without their knowing, just *so much*—the implication being that he *could* drain more—how long before even the most dedicated humanitarian feels qualified to play a benevolent god? I'm not talking about malicious personalities like Johanson—the assumption was we'd screen them out—no, I mean even the Mollitors might not hold up as receptacles of such immense power."

"I don't want the job," I said, swirling the wine around in my glass. "Look, what did Mary want information regarding? This energy program? What, precisely—?"

"No, of course not. She had most of that already; I'd covered it in a report, oh, eight, maybe ten, years ago. And you say you've had your computer sessions for at least that long. No, Mary wanted to know about the collectors. What she really wanted were the figures, the actual equations of power levels that Weatherly had made before the War. Of course, I didn't have anything like that, and Gil's been dead for, oh God, it's been years and years." She stopped and held her chin for a moment. "I suppose she could've tracked all that down in London."

"I'm sure she tried, before she ever came to you."

Elena looked up. "She was very serious, Mollitor. She made it sound like she *needed* that information *badly*."

"Uh huh."

"Do you think she was trying to develop collectors on her own?"

"Could be."

"Could she have been killed because of that?"

"It's possible."

"Mollitor," she said, taking my arm with the tightest grip she could muster, "don't play games with me. Don't worry about leaks. A woman my age makes a poor interrogation subject. Anything strong enough to break my shield is going to kill me anyway. Whether I know anything or not. Mollitor! Look at me. What else do I have? Let me conspire with you once more. For old times sake, eh, Doctor?"

She had me. *Those eyes*.

"All right, Elena. If she needed the information that badly, only a few weeks before her death, then I'd say it would have to have been connected. I honestly don't know what the connection is, though."

"What I wonder," she said, "is why Mary would push a program like that on her own. Why wouldn't you have known about it?"

I suddenly felt tired. Poor Mary. After forty years of action, nothing but a desk in Paris. And what was Paris? A backwater, a cloak-and-dagger circus of little men in zipcoats and fake moustaches. Go run a network, Mary; compile reports, keep tabs on the silly political infighting and drug-running, be sure to let us know how it all goes. Christ. It wasn't hard to imagine why a mind like hers would start looking for experiments to pursue. I flashed as much of this as I could to Elena, and watched her squint as she concentrated with the power she had. Ah, Elena, if only we had trained you to really use that power, if only we could've found you sooner after the War. It was a split-second thought, a quick, shivering wash of emotion.

"They put her out to pasture," I said aloud. "I guess she was looking for a way back onto the main road."

"Well, she found it. They killed her for a reason, Mollitor."

"Who did? The power it would take to—"

"Forget all that," she said sharply. "If Mary was fooling around with energy collecting, then you're already talking about stronger forces than you've ever faced. There are no secret weapons anymore, Mollitor. Once one team has them, so does anyone else who's listening."

"I keep hearing how Moscow runs Europe, and I'm getting sick of it. Is that what you're trying to tell me?"

"No," Elena said. "Neither Intertel nor Central have had any real power over the affairs of this planet in years. They spend a lot of time stabbing each other in the back. Loud and messy. I can't believe they had anything to do with Mary, simply because she had nothing to do with them. She wasn't a threat to them."

Then it hit me. *Who was Mary a threat to?* Elena's implication was clear to me, if not to her.

"I just can't believe Johanson has the organization," she went on. "Not this kind of scope."

Hey?

Dawson was awake.

Yeah?

What's happening? We've got to decide which way—

No need. I agree. Luna.

What've you got?

I flashed Elena's information as quickly as I could.

"Johanson's an old man, Elena," I said. "He's got

nothing better to do than devise communications blocks. He just likes getting in the way."

"So?"

"So, who *does* run this planet? Who calls the shots?"

Lights dawned on her wrinkled face. "The Syndicate," she said in a whisper.

OK, when do we leave? Dawson flashed.

Book a shuttle flight.

Through this interference?

Damn it.

I was getting fed up with this. I gathered my energy and let it drift away from my will, just gave it over to Dawson.

Here. Blow the interference right off the fucking band.

I heard laughing in my head.

"A costless, infinite supply of energy would put the Syndicate right out of the picture," I said to Elena. "Forget the stranglehold they have now. No one would give a damn about their precious solar gatherers."

"People would run the world. Just ordinary people."

"Sure, Elena, right after they string us up for tampering with their minds."

Two reservations, if I didn't strip every circuit in their computer.

Time?

Six o'clock. DeGaulle.

"So," said Elena. "You're back on the trail. Chase down the Syndicate. Well, good luck. I'll be here when you return. You know, Mollitor"—she tapped me on the chest—"you have an unfair advantage over me. You both do." She glanced from one to the other, her eyes finally resting on Dawson. "I don't *feel* a hundred and thirty years old any more than you do, but this body keeps telling me otherwise. Ah, well. You'll tell me all about it later, I'm sure. You'll have to excuse me; I must lie down. This has been very tiring. You both know where everything is."

She pulled herself slowly to the stairway, breathing with a heavy rattle. It was still incredible to me that this was Elena, both in the sense that this was the same person who was once our partner, and in the sense that, now, in this altogether different world, she still existed as a bridge to that past, that she spanned history, on her own, without psychic aids.

She stopped, one hand on the railing, and looked back. She knew. There was damn little she didn't know, and even less she could do about it.

"The hell with you, Mollitor," she said. "I'll outlive you anyway."

She smiled and shook her head, and then she was gone.

Two: ENCOM

VI

The tunnel glowed, floor and arch, from end to end, a flickering metallic blue. The surface actually *was* metal, but the greasy shine gave it a plastic look. You had to gaze along the length of the passage to catch the blue radiating an inch or so off the surface. There was a slight crackle.

Dawson moved slowly, crouched over, her legs drawn up, her arms bent loosely. She was a picture of intense relaxation; perfectly balanced, she moved steadily through the passage without touching the pressure-sensitive metal. This was the hard part, as far as she was concerned. Monitoring the computer as she keyed codes would be easy enough; the human guards weren't worth considering and the surveillance equipment she expected ahead posed little threat. Mollitor could've handled any of it. Half the Pool agents could have. It was this hundred yards of tunnel that presented difficulties only Dawson could deal with. A hundred yards of forward-motion levitation was beyond the capabilities of most T-paths. The years of training came in handy now. She didn't think of the crackling walls around her, didn't consider the lasers that the slightest touch would trigger. She was weightless, almost dreaming this scene. She was the barest part of the lightest breeze possible where no wind blew. The intensity with which she controlled her nerve-to-muscle impulses was no less astonishing than the utter detachment she had achieved from her surroundings.

Training. The year following the accident had seen the most rigorous training any agents had ever devised for themselves. Lying in that damn bed, waiting for her leg to heal . . . Mollitor had been kind, wanted to stay with her through it all, but he was too obviously restless, and if she'd had to sit through his self-recrimination once more—no, there was no blame, just the slow process of bone and tissue knitting together and the apprehension, wondering if it would all work properly again. To begin with, there was nothing cosmic about the levitation experiments. It wasn't even business—levitating objects at Insight HQ was a normal training procedure, but no one ever seriously considered "flying"—Dawson developed it as a means of getting to the bathroom with an immobilized left side. Being off her feet, out of the field for a year, had given her the opportunity to hone her powers to precision, and to invent offshoots that no one else had ever attempted. Dawson came away from the accident the most powerful psi agent on the planet.

As she neared the end of the tunnel, she keyed the prearranged code to open the far valve. This was an automatic reflex she'd set back at the beginning of the passage. From here on, the timing was crucial. If something was waiting for her in the next chamber, she'd have to blow through the opening and take them out in a hurry. At the same time, she had to maintain this exactly balanced mindset until she was just about through the valve. There was a split-second shift in mode coming up that had to work perfectly, or she might not live long enough to know it hadn't.

The valve dilated. As her right shoulder cleared, she went into a midair roll and threw a wide scan into the room. Whatever was moving toward her was either made of or encased in steel. Shielded. Dawson was still in mid-roll, her hands reaching out to spring off the floor. She sensed a heavy leg lashing out, and impressed a magnetic charge into the metal. It was only good for a five-second jolt, but it was enough. The guard stumbled as one leg swung involuntarily into the other with a *clank*. Dawson brought her feet up under his chin and pushed off the floor, snapping her legs straight. The helmeted head jerked back. He bent forward at the knee and backward at the waist and went down without a sound.

Dawson landed and crouched next to him, scanned while reaching for his neck. No alarms, no reinforcements. Good. She looked down. Thready pulse. His neck wasn't broken, but his system hadn't appreciated the impact. He'd come on her too quickly; her instincts had had no time to assess the situation and pull the kick a little. Lucky for him he'd been wearing that suit. The pulse was slipping away, though. She found the rhythm, gently smoothed out the beat until it strengthened. One of Mollitor's tricks. He could've explained it from a medical standpoint; for Dawson, it was enough that it worked. She probed for any impress in his mind, but the suit was still working, transmitting a local jamming frequency. No time to decode the helmet and get it off.

She surveyed the room again, this time comparing it with the layout she had in her head. The ceiling here was thirty feet high, with dull gray metallic containers lining every wall, floor to ceiling. Three to a wall. Some kind of storage banks. She smoothed out the black glove on her right hand as she pictured it. The archway to the left must lead to the processing chambers and monitor station. Beyond that were the patchways to the outside, to the actual collecting system, four hundred square kilometers of solar panels. The bulk of the world's energy came from this system, at whatever price the Syndicate demanded. The spoils of a war more than sixty years past. Through that corridor. So where was— There. Four feet from the floor, a little door was bolted to the wall. Not meant to be opened often, no reason to, unless the main computer needed to be worked on. Or worked over. Dawson probed for a shield, found none, and began loosening the bolts.

She moved quickly, ignoring the sudden beep from the edge of the archway. Red and gold lights blinked along its inner edge. The archway didn't concern her. As long as no one came through it, whatever was happening down there could go on happening. She had no intention of wrecking Earth's energy source, nor of setting foot in that monitor room at all. No, this job only had to *look* like sabotage; any damage she did to the computer could be repaired. It would simply throw a scare into ENCOM. But she needed access to the brain of this monster. Mollitor could pry all the information he could out of Ranagen, but they had to know, conclusively, how far along, if at all, the Syndicate was at Mary's energy transfer.

The last bolt came out and the door dropped softly to the floor. No noise. She wiped her forehead and pulled the beret down snug. It was black, as were her boots, gloves and insulsuit. With an optiflicker around her face, she was nearly invisible if she stayed in shadow. There was nothing on her a detecter could pick up; no metal, no weapon of any sort. Cloth and skin covering one hundred and twenty-five pounds of lithe muscle and bone.

She keyed a signal into Mollitor's subwave and grabbed the edges of the opening. Always let your backup know where you are before going off the wave. No mistakes. She set a heavy shield around her mind, glanced once over her shoulder and jumped up into the black.

VII

Going to Luna is no vacation. It's not a sightseeing tour. Sure, they've got charters you can take—they'll show you the layout, astound you with the technology used to maintain L-City, and maybe you'll even get a side trip out to see the panels—but, if you come up from Earth on your own, you'd better have an appointment. Your bags and passport aren't good enough. Although it does seem a little like a sovereign state, it's not—Luna is the corporate headquarters for ENCOM, the Energy and Communications Syndicate. The Syndicate has its own security force, and they're not going to let you off the shuttle except for legitimate business. It depends, though. Notoriety has its advantages.

"Look," I told the looncop, "just vid Ranagen in Research Tech, and tell him Mollitor wants a meeting. That's M-o-l-l-i-t-o-r. Go on. He'll talk to me."

The guy wrinkled up his nose and tried to muster an extra little glint in his eye. "I'm sorry, pal, I'm not authorized to—hey!"

I pointed, snapped, and his screen switched on.

"There you go, it's on. All you have to do is—"

"Mr. Ranagen is a busy man," he whined, the whole tough-guy look ruined. "I can't disturb him every time someone shows up and—"

"Have it your way, then," I said, folding my arms and leaning on the rail. "I just wouldn't want to be in your shoes when he finds out that Mollitor wanted to talk research swap and you sent him packing."

I stared back out over the landing field and yawned, waiting. The guy was getting upset with me, but that was fine. Now there was *no* chance of him spotting Dawson sneaking in the emergency duct. In a way, it was fortunate we'd found such an easily distractable guard; I certainly hadn't wanted to hurt him. No, this phase was moving ahead as planned. Ultimately, he'd call Ranagen—he wasn't going to get rid of me otherwise—and the old bastard would agree to meet me. His curiosity alone would insist on it. That would get me inside, and from there I could maneuver. I'd try to contact our agent within the Syndicate, or maybe I'd really make a deal with Ranagen. It didn't matter. Chicago hadn't authorized this move anyway; the Old Man didn't even know where we were. At this point, we wanted to know what Finney had done and where he'd gone from Luna, but everything on my end was smoke for my partner. It was up to her to find out where we stood.

The clearance came through. They metal-scanned me before letting me in at all, then a microscan, an ultrasound for surgical implants, another, finer microscan—these, as I descended levels—finally an auto-mindprobe before I was allowed onto the executive level. Actually, the mindprobe was the easiest to deflect—you just gauge the frequency correctly—but you can't fool microscans surreptitiously. My aversion to carrying weapons pays off sometimes.

My guide was a young, wormy guy, soft and skinny, with little round glasses and a long face. His one expression was country-club bored; with a large enough bank account, he'd make a good snob. His duty was to make sure I stayed in the hallway and out of the side rooms, though there was little he could do to stop me other than sound an alarm. That was plenty; no alarms, please. I wondered how far Dawson had gotten.

Ranagen's office was typical of the scientist-turned-executive. There were test tubes on the desk, some graphs and formulae framed to look like art on the walls, his certificates in a neat row behind his chair, a whole bookcase of technical works and journals. These were amusing, because Ranagen had always been the type of researcher who shot from the hip, who used reference materials only to verify and validate the results he got as he went along. A well-ordered, scientific library served him no purpose. Hype. As befitted ENCOM's director of research technology.

He entered from the other end of the room a moment after I did. It was interesting. Same burning eyes, pug nose, the black walrus moustache, same stocky, muscular build, same bald skull. It had been close to fifteen years since I'd seen him, but nothing had changed. He had to be well into his eighties by now. Hmm, it was possible . . .

"Mollitor!" he boomed, putting his hands on his hips. "They weren't lying. Chicago really sent you."

I shrugged. "You know how it is. Business."

"Bull-*Shit*!" with a violent wave. "You don't send your top agent on routine business, without an appointment. Not even your Old Man is that stupid. Sit down, Mollitor. Hey, you," he said to the wormy guy. "Thank you very much. Take a walk."

"Yessir. Uh, sir, according to policy, there should always be at least two—"

"Forget it, sonny. If I can't handle any trouble he makes, there's nothing you can do. He's already neutralized every weapon you're carrying, and he's got your reflex timing memorized. I'll take responsibility. Just log it."

The wormy guy nodded, and ducked out.

"So? I told you to sit down."

"I'm waiting for you."

"Oh, Jesus Christ," he muttered, dropping into the chair. "You think I got poison darts in the seat? I'll tell you, Mollitor, it's a relief to see an old-timer like you. You know what's coming? You know who they're going to replace both of us with?" He jerked a thumb at the door. "Guys like that. They'll recite policy to each other. Would you please sit the hell down!"

"At least they'll be evenly matched," I said, taking a seat.

"Yeah, sure. One wimp against another."

He lit a cigaret and dropped it into the ashtray without

taking a drag. I folded my arms, looked around the room. I was in no hurry at all. Quite the contrary.

"Nice place you got here, Ranagen."

"Yeah," he said, deadpan. "Nice place. So what the hell *are* you doing here? I understood they took you out of the field years ago."

"Ten, to be exact."

"Sure, ten. So what's this, an anniversary appearance?"

I shrugged again. "Just a side trip. The Old Man wants this off the record."

"Sure. So he sends his most famous warrior under his real name. Some clandestine operation. You're full of shit, but I'll let it slide for now." He took a drag off the cigaret.

"Thanks."

"You're being difficult, Mollitor, and we haven't even started yet." He sighed, full of smoke. "Okay, we'll play it your way. How's business?"

I smiled. "Oh, you know how it is. We think you may be on to something that could benefit the Pool. If so, I'm sure we have some recent technology we could trade for it."

"We're on to something, huh? No one tells me a damn thing around here."

"You may not be aware of its significance, but—"

"What's *that* supposed to mean?"

His eyes got dark and narrow. Proud of his department? I filed that for future use.

"Look," I said. "We're in two different rackets. You're interested in collecting and disseminating energy, we're looking for advances in psychic control. There may be some overlapping of aims, but there's no real reason why a psychic use for a developmental energy program should ever occur to the Syndicate."

"To ENCOM."

"Okay, ENCOM. Give me a break, Ranagen, you still think of it as the Syndicate, too. Don't play semantics with me."

"All right, all right. So what? You want a piece of this new energy program you think we've got?"

"I just want to talk."

That was the truth. We stared at each other a while, then he sighed and scratched his shiny skull.

"Look, Mollitor, we've been working different sides of the same fence for years, okay? You remember what it was like after the Wars."

I nodded. I remembered, all right. Half the population of the world destroyed, smoking ruins everywhere, and the mad scramble to gather intelligence to form new power bases once it was clear that no side was going to win. Dawson and I had been instrumental in prying Insight away from what was then the CIA. It had been a crazy time. Anyone with the slightest psi powers had been able to take control of their respective leaderships with little problem.

"I remember you," he said. "I was just a tech, a kid fresh from the Institute. You were up here, right after the Syndicate grabbed Luna, looking for a truce, an open channel on research between the Syndicate and the Pool. Don't look so smug. We gave you what you needed—power to run your operation. All right, I learned a few things. You were no kid back then, and we're talking over sixty years. So?"

"So?" I agreed.

"So, look at *me*. I've learned a few of your secrets. As you pointed out, ENCOM isn't primarily interested in psychics. The next man in this office may be an ignorant punk who they'll retire at sixty when his eyes go bad. But for now, I'm here, Mollitor, and I understand a whole lot of your game. All unofficial, of course, but don't try and bullshit me. What the hell have you got, and what do you want that you think we've got?"

I honestly hadn't been expecting this. Ranagen had come a long way in fifteen years. He was much more than the tough-minded scientist I'd remembered. Somewhere, he'd developed a degree of regenerative control and God knows what else. I tried a light probe. Yep, he had a natural shield up. Very interesting. Under different circumstances, I might've tried recruiting him for Insight. As it was, perhaps I could use his desire to impress me. Surrounded by people of far lower capabilities, it could be that he saw me as a natural comrade. We'd certainly never been any worse than friendly adversaries.

"I haven't missed the signs, Ranagen. I can see what you've done, but you've got a ways to go. Control is something that comes naturally with time. It isn't the key."

"What's the key?"

His eyes were lighting up.

"Energy flow," I said. "Look, I'm not here to discuss the finer points of psychic balance. I understand that ENCOM has come up with new methods of energy collecting and processing. I'm interested in these findings in general, and in the tapping mechanism in particular."

"You haven't done your own research on that?"

I leaned back. "As we agreed, this is your area of expertise. Why should the Pool repeat, by hit-and-miss, experiments you've already done? You're always devising new methods."

"Which the Pool can use."

"In ways far beyond powering generators for Earth."

"All right. What's in it for me?" he said impatiently.

I had him. I settled comfortably into my seat and ignored the implication. "There's been a communications block going on for a while now. You're aware of this, I'm sure."

He nodded.

"Okay," I said, "it's been solved. It originates in Europe. I have the codes you need to neutralize it."

The eyebrows didn't look convinced.

"It's a simple frequency shift, but the field oscillates randomly. You won't crack it on your own."

"Yeah?" he said. "How did you do it?"

"Trade secrets, Ranagen. I took my lumps."

"Interesting."

"I should think it'd be *very* interesting. That block's been in our way for six months. I'm offering you the solution in exchange for some basic research of yours that we'll find out about anyway. I just need it *now*."

He put his elbow on the desk, slowly twirled his moustache. He was getting antsy. He didn't even care what I needed it for.

"All right. I think the Board will go for it. But I still want to know what's in it for *me*."

He leaned forward, dropped the hand. I held his gaze, probed, let him know I was making a nudging contact with his mind. I purposefully didn't push through his shield.

"I'm not here to make personal deals with you," I said softly. "I can guess what you want, but this is neither the time nor the place. You come down to Chicago sometime, and we'll talk. Right now, let's leave Mollitor and Ranagen out of it. Do ENCOM and the Pool have a deal?"

"It's all right with me. Okay, look," he said, relaxing a little, "let me check it with the top. You sit tight." He got up and went to the far door, zipped it, looked back. "We'll have that talk in Chicago, right?"

I smiled, shot him a telepathic *Yes*. It was locked up. He wasn't sure what he was trading for what. He zipped the door shut after him and, at that moment, I felt Dawson's signal key into our subwave. She was through the tunnel and entering the computer. The deal with Ranagen no longer mattered. I had been perfectly willing to make the trade, although the Old Man would've hit the ceiling when he heard, but I doubted whether Ranagen actually knew anything about Mary's program, anyway. All the better. There were only a few minor details to arrange before meeting Dawson back at the landing field. The main one was getting out of here. I scanned the door leading to the hallway, and shorted out the mechanism. I slid it open, and there was the wormy guy.

"You don't want to know, pal," I said, as his mouth dropped and his hand moved. It's incredible how slowly most people react. I pushed his brain lightly against his skull and caught him as he fell.

VIII

There are two ways you can play the intelligence game with your adversaries. One is by putting agents in the field and trying to beat the other guys to the information. The theory is, once your team—the "good" guys—gets what it wants, you eliminate the source so that all the other teams—the "bad" guys—come up empty. In practice, this almost never works, but it's what keeps spies employed. The other way involves getting hold of a piece of what the other guys already have. You do this, either by trading seemingly useless information in the hope that you can get more out of what they give you than vice versa, as Ranagen and I had just tentatively agreed to, or you steal what you want outright. The easiest way to steal information is to sneak in and sneak out, with no one the wiser. A far better method, but slower, involves planting an agent, a mole, in the enemy organization, who works his way as far up the hierarchy as possible and feeds you information, while trying to keep *your* really important projects from being blown. This is tricky, in that you have to wait for the data to trickle in—*you* don't ever want to initiate contact with the mole—you never want to do anything that might compromise him and destroy the well-built cover. The other tricky part of it, to my way of thinking, is that once a man's a double, it's a short step to becoming a triple, to start working for the network he's been sent to undermine. I don't trust someone who plays both sides of the fence.

McIntyre was no genius, in any event. If we had it to do over, I'd much prefer turning someone like Ranagen to planting someone like McIntyre. He was a thin rail of a guy, very precise, very British, always impeccably dressed and poised, searching for just the right word with two fingers resting thoughtfully at his temple. He was perfectly at home in ENCOM, as well suited to the board meetings and politics of corporate infighting as he was to the leisurely life of an upper-level executive in the energy/communication industry. It's not that he was a dandy, or had a shallow mind—I just wasn't impressed with his style. He was a shnook.

Finding McIntyre's office was the next problem. I knew he had to be on this level, but it was still a big place. I couldn't just go down each corridor, scanning rooms. I was conspicuous enough; I didn't need to act overtly suspicious. Anyway, Ranagen would sound some sort of alert as soon as he discovered me missing. This had to be quick; just a fast message and then meet Dawson. I was able to deflect the attention of passers-by without too much difficulty. Most of them were couriers, the same wormy bookkeeper type as my unconscious friend. I could walk past them looking like an important man with important business by impressing a vague sense of authority in their minds. These guys had no shields, anyway. That was my big break. I could scan them for a clue to the mole's location, and didn't have to bother with the offices at all.

The ENCOM installation was mammoth. I was on the lowest of three levels, but I could still picture the entire layout from the plans I'd memorized, Christ, it must've been forty years ago. If anyone could be said to have won the Energy Wars, it was the Syndicate. By consolidating their power here on Luna, they'd managed to escape the horrible aftermath of the War, while remaining in control of all major energy sources left. In the long run, their solar collecting project had been to all Earth's benefit, but their isolation had made any checks on their operation difficult to maintain. By the time Dawson found Weatherly in London, four years after the last battles had been fought, any computer espionage we could devise promised only limited results. You couldn't confront ENCOM with showdowns because they held the trump cards: the huge solar panels. You didn't dare do anything too crippling to them; we all *needed* the energy they provided. This was why Mary's experiments with a psychically powered collection-and-transfer system were so important. If it had been perfected, if it *could* be perfected, it would shift the balance of power, not just from ENCOM to the Pool, but from dependence on outside means of energy to reliance on self-generation. We were on the threshold of something very big, and the Pool would be responsible for developing and coordinating the effort, simply because we were the only ones able to implement the system on a planetary scale. Something about that made me nervous, though. For one thing, Finney hadn't trusted Tanner's Paris Pool enough to let him in on it, and I knew of security leaks in every other network on Earth. For another, I knew damn well that we weren't the only organization that had successfully planted moles in command positions. Hell, Johanson had nearly destroyed Insight with only minimal assistance from the Maf'. I had no illusions. There was nothing so pure and noble about Insight that made corruption unthinkable. In fact, that had been Weatherly's attitude when we found him. He felt that the Wars had dragged on precisely because too many people were playing political games with matters of which they had only the vaguest comprehension. He was as disgusted with Insight—perhaps even more so—as he was with ENCOM, Intertel, Central and the rest. For twenty years, he'd given all his strength, all his brilliant concentration, to systematizing the processes of psychic energy. To Weatherly, this was the Ultimate Science; it would be the next great evolutionary step of human development. . . . Here we were playing secret agent man with it and it galled him.

Suddenly, I felt McIntyre's vibration. No muffling, it was right here in the hallway. No McIntyre, though. I fanned out a receptor band and picked up a young guy just around the corner, hefty, muscular. I scanned for clothes and got a mechanic's shocksuit, antigrav discs, mag boots. He seemed like an ordinary panel worker, walked with the slow swagger of a man used to maneuvering in zero gravity. What was he doing on the executive level? And what was he doing with McIntyre in his mind at that intensity? I had neither the time nor the inclination to play with him. I scanned down his hallway, back down mine. No one coming, for the moment. I swung around the corner, fast, snapped open both my hands, freezing him in mid-step. I simply overwhelmed every nerve-impulse channel he had, halted all muscle movement, suspended his mind in mid-thought. I found no shield, so I gave him back control of his chest muscles, the use of his lungs. I'd hit him with a heavy enough paralysis scan to blow through most shields. It never hurt to be sure. I got the location of McIntyre's office with no trouble, but what was this guy's connection? They had a meeting due for this evening, but where any additional details should've been, I was getting nothing. Not a shield, not a re-route, just a blank spot. McIntyre must've impressed a coded wavelength into this guy's head, an impulse defense against the auto-mindprobe he'd have to face every time he came down to this level. So, he had to be one of McIntyre's recruits in ENCOM. I memorized the blond hair, the wide face and heavy lips. No neck, big bull shoulders. The vibration. I might need to know him later. I set a hypnoblank on him for five minutes, and left him standing there. If there was time, I'd dig him up later and figure out the wavelength code. He'd have no memory of this incident, anyway.

I touched the sensor on McIntyre's door, scanned. If possible, I didn't want to keep shorting out mechanisms; the breakdowns might be keyed to alarms. If McIntyre was in . . . No answer. Oh well, I shorted it and slid through, ready to excuse myself if someone else lived here.

I sensed the energy fields as soon as the door slid. It was a vibration that had become painfully familiar. He was sitting at his desk, sprawled in the chair. I recognized the eyes, the forehead, the short, slicked-back hair. Where the pencil moustache had been was a burnt hole running to the middle of his chest. Not a lot of blood; the blaster had cauterized the wound almost immediately. There it was, on the desk, a couple inches from where his hand had fallen. Christ. I shut the door and locked a shield around it, then I scanned the room. No sign of a struggle. I ran my hand along the wall, the bookshelf, lifted the framed photos on the wall. I made damn sure I remained facing the far door behind his desk. A few dead bodies was all it took to get me good and nervous. Whatever was taking these people out was not to be trifled with.

Damn it to hell. *We* certainly hadn't blown McIntyre's cover, and I couldn't believe he'd done anything to jeopardize himself, but here was another suicide on my hands, all the same. No impress anywhere, just the same dissipating energy fields we'd found with the others. As if he'd fought a battle in here. Sure. Except there was no sign of battle. I walked over and probed him. Dead maybe three hours. *Before* we'd gotten to Luna. It didn't make sense. I dug in hard for an impress, a snatch of some clue. McIntyre was too orderly, too methodical, to just blow his own head off without making *some* move for help. I touched his forehead. Any fear, any scream, gone. I tried the peripheral waves, and caught some sort of swirling clouds maybe, or water. A bridge. I stayed with it. I got a glimpse of children playing, then the bridge again, then a little man in a dark coat, collar up, walking into the smoke. There was something familiar about the scene, but I couldn't hold it. I was tearing what impressions had been left in McIntyre's mind at the moment he died, but this wasn't a living mind; whatever I sensed faded immediately and wasn't available for retrieval.

I looked around. Those damn energy fields. But no source. Like a ghost was watching me. It was time to get out of here. I flashed a signal on the subwave.

Dawson?

No answer. Well, maybe these walls were treated. The ones around the computer were sure to be. I was suddenly claustrophobic. Get me above ground, in this thin atmosphere and artificial gravity, and I could send a lot further, a lot stronger.

I ran through the layout of this place again in my head. The air ducts were dual-purpose down here. They circulated the oxygen and served as a fire escape, should the power fail. I zipped the far door of the office and unhooked the grid in the anteroom. I stared up a long shaft. Dull, green light all the way. I grabbed the lowest rung and started up.

It was beginning to look like we were wrong, that Finney had never come here at all. He certainly hadn't contacted anyone at ENCOM. Maybe he'd been here and avoided them. In Finney's case, that was entirely possible. He was the only agent I'd ever met who could become invisible at will. It was a special trick of his. He not only could blend into crowds of four people, he could meld into walls like a chameleon. It was really uncanny. That was why I was on this case in the first place. Finney and I knew each other's style. His expertise was in covering things up, mine in uncovering.

Still, if he'd never come here, then the only explanation for leading Dawson and me into believing that he did was because he felt someone had to check it out, and he was being followed too closely.

I couldn't shake the feeling that Johanson was mixed up in this, though. The communications block seemed nothing more than a dodge, at this point, just a tricky puzzle he'd been waiting for someone to solve. His operatives in Paris had been too easy. He'd let us escape—why? So we wouldn't follow him further? So we wouldn't read anything more into his plans than a new type of oscillation device? No. We hadn't even thought of that. Dawson and I had no bright ideas as to the suicides—we were following Finney, plain and simple. And Johanson had let us. He'd accepted the loss of his block, the discovery of his secret frequency codes, with hardly a fight—and with no retaliation. It was amazing I hadn't thought of this before: Johanson was a megalomaniac; revenge was always uppermost in his mind. He'd let us get away only because *we were on the wrong track*. What I'd forgotten, in my concern for Finney, was that the bond of hate Johanson and I had cultivated over the years was stronger than any friendship. He probably knew perfectly well where Finney had gone, and wanted to keep us ignorant. Well, Dawson would dig a few answers out of the computer, but I was certain we had to return to Earth and deal with Johanson.

I stopped. I was half a dozen rungs from a grating, and there was something up there. I scanned, but got nothing. Or rather, I got a block. Whoever it was had a shield. I couldn't pick out any more than an outline. There was an alcove of some sort, with a ramp to the right of this duct. Oh well, only one way to find out. I went up another couple rungs, grabbed the edge and launched myself as I popped the grating. I came up behind the wire screen, then it fell to the floor and I was facing him. He was awfully big. Six and a half feet, two hundred and fifty pounds, with a helmet-hood falling to his shoulders. He smiled at me. He had wet, flaccid lips that gave the grin a demented look. No tricks were going to work here; there was no way into his nervous system as long as he wore that helmet. This had to be punch for punch.

I shrugged and dropped my shoulders, like I was too tired to bother fighting, and let him close the distance between us a little. I did a quick crossover shuffle and hit him in the solar plexus with a side kick, but he twisted just enough and chopped down as I spun. My left arm went numb. I caught him in the neck with a spear hand and jumped out of the way. No good. I'd have to be planted firmly to rock him, and I wasn't sure I wanted to get that close. I shook my arm. Feeling was coming back slowly, but he knew his business. He moved inside, jabbing with his elbow. I blocked it, reversed back on him and took a shot on the hip getting positioned. I wobbled and traded swings with him again, ducked and spun and then I was behind him. Perfect. I hit him in the back of the head, dodged to the side and buckled his knee with kicks, front and back. He staggered, and I landed one on the temple with everything I had. Boom!

I wanted no more of this. As soon as he went down, I moved for the incline, but he got his leg out and tripped me. I stumbled up the ramp. I had no chance against the other guy. He wasn't as big, but he was just as shielded and a lot faster. He hit me three times to my one useless swing, but I only saw the motion of the third blow; the second one knocked the wind out of me. I rolled back down the ramp, drowning, trying desperately to draw a breath, to relax my lungs long enough to pull *in* before it was all over. There were little blue and yellow spots everywhere, and my head was burning. I couldn't hear a damn thing. I felt a blur breaking through the spots, and I got my hand up to meet it as I hit the bottom of the plunge and my diaphragm started the long haul back. I felt something small in my hand go *crack*, but I closed around a boot all the same. Something dull and heavy crashed against my hip, then several more thuds landed all over my body. I kept trying to move and kept trying to breathe. Another something went *crack* along my side, but I rolled away, exhaled my first breath and started another. The spots began clearing. I had hold of something, and there was no way I was letting go. All my concentration was on that hand. I applied a pressure technique and impressed an electrical charge. I wanted my hand to close. Whatever was in it was going to give, like an aluminum can, like an orange. I finished my second breath, caught a tremendous shot to the chin and went flopping to one side, still holding on. Something warm ran down my face and neck. Suddenly, I could see. The first guy was kicking me around. There was nothing wrong with his aim or his delivery. What he wasn't breaking, he was bruising. But I had the other guy's foot, boot and all, and as my ears started working again, I could hear him bellowing. I was crushing his foot. He swung blindly and—hey—I finally blocked something. I had new hope. I let go and rolled. They were in each other's way now. I jumped up, shot a kick at the injured guy's head. Contact! Okay, Mollitor, you're on balance again, you're landing properly. I jabbed, danced away and got behind the guy on the floor, kicked his arm aside. The big man thought he had me, figured I was too busy to see him. He'd gotten used to beating up on me when I was a lump, anyway. So, he came in swinging, wide open, trying to land one powerhouse explosion to put me out for good. I twirled, flashing past his head with one leg and bringing the other up in a spinaround. He walked right into it. I caught him on the side of the jaw, then hooked under his chin and snapped my leg straight. The breaking sound was either his jawbone or a whole lot of teeth. It lifted him a couple inches off the ground and he crashed backward with a grunt. I finished the move by jumping over the second guy.

Big mistake. Lying there with a crushed foot, nearly unconscious, he still managed to throw a punch—there's no delicate way to put this—right into the balls. I staggered a couple steps up the ramp and then I was on my knees, crawling as quickly as I could manage. Any other aches and pains I had were completely forgotten. All my insides felt smashed, no feeling in my legs. Those two were in no shape to follow, but I was sure I was worse off than either of them.

I kept moving, just gritted my teeth and plowed on until I was able to stand. Somehow, I got up the ramp and out that duct, aboveground, out of the ENCOM installation before I collapsed. I spotted a stand of storage tanks, and I stumbled between two of them, my head spinning, hit the ground with both knees at once and held onto the dull, oily, galvanized metal. It seemed the only stable structure in the universe.

I started throwing up.

IX

There's no breeze topside—"under the dome," the locals call it—no cool, night air to clear the head. There's nothing but the flat, invisible circulation of atmosphere, and nothing to see in the sky but the dome itself, five hundred feet at the top.

My cheek got comfy with the dusty gray surface as I lay there; I just hoped no one stumbled on me by accident. I glanced back at the duct. Preventing them from following me was more important than tending to my injuries. I had to cave in the opening to that shaft; no way around it, it *had* to be done. I didn't have enough in reserve to bother with a deflection shield; I was fair game for any sensors they might have. I needed all my strength to gauge the molecular vibration of the metal, to soften the atomic structure enough. I used a pinpoint focus, one section at a time, and slowly buckled it into a tangle of steel. By the time I was done, the air around me was literally humming with energy. The temperature was a good five degrees hotter. I'm not Dawson, though; the effort exhausted me.

I was in bad shape. At least a couple ribs were cracked, a bone in my hand felt broken and there was something wrong with the angle of my jaw. I guessed it was dislocated. I got it back in line while trying not to move around too much. I was still plenty sick from that last punch. I finally could open and close my mouth without too much pain, but, when I turned to my ribs, all of a sudden, my concentration was shot. Something was nagging at me, some sort of pulsing in my head. Fever. There was no strength left in my muscles; I was tired, so damn tired of all this. It was hopeless; there was no way I could escape in this condition. It was just too late—they'd had no business sending an old man like me on this mission—I'd been out of the field so long, I was far too rusty to get it all back so soon. The mission was going to fail because of me. Worse, Dawson was counting on me, and now she was on her own. I'd failed. Pictures were pouring through my head: Dawson trapped in that oscillator field in Paris; Dawson knocking me out of the way and the explosion blowing her across the hallway; Johanson standing there, chuckling, smug, hands on his hips, chiding me for daring to take him on. I shook my head. No! Clear, damn it!

But then the attack started. There were blasts coming from all sides. It was in my head, an entirely psychic assault, but it was very real. If I didn't parry these shots, they would do damage. I'd fought this kind of battle before, with high-level T-paths, but never when I'd started out so weak, and never from so many directions at once. The waves alternated: a smash, then a digging and tearing, a muscle lock, then another nerve smash. The sheer force of the blows unbalanced me; the variety and speed were ruining my concentration. I dodged and countered, but there was nothing to engage, no source to blast back at and weaken. I could neutralize isolated frequencies, but redirecting any of my energy from defense let another few blasts through. Energy fields screamed all around me, crashing into one another as they built in intensity. I tried flashing an SOS to Dawson, but I couldn't shift focus long enough to catch a response.

The attack evened out abruptly, and the pictures began again. Now, in addition to the assault, I had the delirium to contend with as well. I saw Johanson leveling Insight HQ with a nuke burner, screaming people running out with their skin blazing, the Old Man's head rolling out the door. I lunged for Johanson, but missed, and he danced away and fired again. I couldn't move fast enough; I fell. I fell a long way. I saw myself huddled in a corner, my arms chained behind my back, an oscillation collar around my neck, helpless to move or probe. There was Dawson, also wearing a collar, taking a methodical beating from a half-dozen thugs in shocksuits. I couldn't move, I couldn't break the chains. She tried to stand, and took a vicious kick in the stomach, fell back down. One of the thugs grabbed her hair and slammed her head to the floor, then four more held her arms and legs and the other one started tearing away her clothes. *I had to move*. I fired a needle with all my strength. It would strike, it would burn every neuron in his brain to ash, it would—no. I couldn't send anything past the collar. I couldn't stop them from gang-raping her. Even her screams were muffled, overpowered by Johanson laughing, roaring, nudging me with his foot to share in the joke, licking his lips and laughing some more. He could do whatever he pleased, with no one to stop him. Not Mollitor, no, certainly not that worthless old man. He can't even stand up. He can't stop a psi-attack, can't locate his enemy, can't move, can't stop a gang of greasy punks from beating and raping his woman. Hell, he'd be better off just killing himself, ending this foolish life that's gone on far too long already. Go ahead, Mollitor, you trash, you wimp; you don't need a building to jump off, you don't need a gun, your mind is weapon enough. Come on, tough guy, end it. Here, we'll help; take a few more shots like these and you'll break. No? You want to be a hero? You want to be stubborn? You want to go maybe another hundred years, remembering every failure, remembering Dawson lying there, replaying every scene like a broken record? Go on, you gutless punk. You know who your enemy really is, you know where the fault really lies. Let it rip. Go on. *Do it!*

I did it. I screamed and fired everything at once, no aim, no focus, no purpose to it at all. Just to be rid of it. Of everything. It was very loud. It blew through the assault, through the fever, through the past and the present and all I'd ever imagined or feared. It burnt the storage tanks on either side of me black, and crackled the atmosphere right to the top of the dome. It was the kind of blast you could never do deliberately. You would never want to. When it was over, there was nothing left. No voices, no pictures, no energy fields, no frequencies, no strength. Nothing remained but a slow, steady throb. It thudded dully, as if buried in cotton, continuing to push blood out in deliberate spasms simply because it could do nothing else but continue. A tired machine churning on after it had ceased to matter, pounding against a long file of cracked and battered ribs. It was the ribs that I finally recognized; they hurt like hell. They were mine. So was the heartbeat. I felt many things, but victorious was not one of them.

The hum that started then lasted only half a minute. It defined into a murmur and then a voice.

Easy, easy now. Blank straight across, just relax and listen. The voice was a flash at psi-level, no specific wavelength, just a soothing hum. It was a voice I'd come to know quite well over the last forty years of running agents in networks across the world. No verification needed. It was Finney. One of us had found the other.

Just sit tight, he went on. *Relax, don't bother answering. This is a wave-impress; I'm not really here. You listening, Mollitor?* A laugh. *Yeah, I know it's you. The only way to trigger this is to beat the suicide program, and I know damn well you're the only one who's gonna manage that. OK? Listen up. You've just come through the assault, so we'll start with that. It wasn't a choke or a block. If you'll recall, there was no oscillation once it really took off. No wave interception. Tricky, huh? That's because it's simple. It was a straight frequency overload—*

all channels—keyed to your specific vibe. Or rather, attracted to your vibe. Everyone gets hit a little differently, depending on their pressure resistance. Once the overload gets strong enough, you're facing it outside and inside, anyway. The mechanism, as I'm sure you've copped to, is the energy-field pattern. An accumulation precipitates an attack. They're like a drifting electrical storm. They appear at intervals at different geo-coords, but the sequence still looks random to me. The important thing is that they're drawn to any area of heavy psi discharge. The more power you exert, the bigger target you are. Which is why I knew they'd find you, *eventually. All right. You know* how *they operate already, so I'll spare you that. There's a way of detecting and measuring their buildup before they strike, but I don't know what it is. Johanson knows. Maybe he can plot their movement as well; I'm not sure. In any event, if you get out of Paris,* stay out. *Keep away from Johanson until we know more; he's too dangerous for now. He's not behind it, Mollitor, believe me, this is much too big; he's just a couple steps ahead of us in figuring it out. As far as I can tell, we three are the only ones who've beaten the assault directly. You can avoid the fields entirely by blanking at the right moments, but that's not the type of defense which would naturally occur to any of us in this business.*

You still with me? Just keep breathing. Nice and easy. Don't worry about another performance; they won't be back. Which is the next point. These energy fields have no intelligence. Once they hit a target and drain it, they move on. No backtracking to finish off a weak survivor. God knows why. Obviously, whoever's behind it hasn't got control. Someone's unleashed a demon. I can't imagine why any psi network would instigate a force that systematically destroys all higher-level T-paths, but hell, only a high-level operation is capable of it. I don't know. I think Mary was close to a solution. There was something going on with her, Mollitor. Something about Mary holds the key to this thing. What was she doing those three, four years between the time we retired her from operational, and her assignment to Paris? There's a gap. I know it's got something to do with San Francisco. She was using variations of the old Frisco network codes for her subwaves in Paris. That's how she kept dodging the comm block. You check it, you'll see what I mean. Not the new California setup; I'm talking about the old Frisco net, the one Johanson blew in '57.

Dammit, I wish I could anticipate your questions. First of all, stop looking for me; let me stay off the wave. I'll work better from the dark side. Maybe I can find what the hell Mary was up to. What else? Brief Dawson, obviously. I just wish there were a few more old-timers left. It's not simply a matter of experience and ability. I'm convinced this is tied up with events long past; with the reorganization after Johanson's treason, maybe even going back as far as the War and your old Group in Paris. We need people who were there, to brainstorm with. Think about it, Mollitor: Mary, Poli, Basil, LaRue, you, me, Johanson—it's no coincidence we seven were attacked. You include Dawson and the Old Man, and you've got what's left of the original Pool. Hear me, old buddy. You've got *to stay off the main waves. There are too many leaks, too many double and triple agents. Until we know for certain, the most likely suspect is Insight itself. We can't trust anyone who's officially with the Pool. Yes, I know what you're thinking; I'll get a message to the Old Man as soon as I can get one in without anyone else knowing.*

Well, that's it, that's all I can think of. It suddenly occurs to me that I'll have no way of knowing if this message is triggered or not. It's getting a little scary out here. Touch and go. I hope you live long enough to get this, Mollitor, and I hope I live long enough to hear your answer. Good luck, buddy. Give 'em hell.

The hum built back up for a moment, then the vibration faded altogether. It was gone; it was never there. It had been a one-time readout, a flash impress keyed to a random subwave, triggered by the specific frequency of the dissipating energy fields. Ingenious. No one could ever stumble on a message like that. Finney was still out there, still operating behind the scenes as effectively as he ever had.

I stood up and looked around. The radiation filters in the

dome gave the air a slight shimmer. It was eerie. To keep from becoming disoriented, you had to watch the gray dust at your feet, squint if you had to gaze straight ahead. Keeping track of direction isn't easy when every point in the sky looks like the next one and a compass is worthless. What the hell. I'd been up here before. I figured I must remember something. The bar wasn't far from the landing field. I was either going to have to make it there aboveground, or go back into ENCOM and follow the corridors. Not much of a choice, under the circumstances.

I had a lot to think about. I cleaned the blood off me as best I could, stabilized my rib cage and began the dusty trek to the rendezvous with Dawson.

X

The Dobermans didn't look friendly, but then, they never do. The ears went straight back, the eyes glared, brown on yellow, the breath came rapidly. They were both big. They had Dawson pinned in a corner, one facing her from about six feet away, a deep growl through his bared teeth leaving no doubt to his feelings as he matched her, step for step, sideways. The other one paced a few feet beyond, guarding the perimeter, keeping Dawson against two walls. You could see the muscles on all three, could feel the tension in the cautious crouch-and-approach stalking of one another. They were all in black and all about the same size. The only difference was that the human was on two legs and was keeping quiet.

Dawson concentrated on the one in front of her, trying to soothe it, unplug its brain from every conscious channel, but these creatures were too hyped up. They were professional guard dogs. It was a very delicate business here. You don't want to annoy or injure a vicious animal; it only makes them more deadly. She was pretty sure she could kill one of them instantly, but that would give the remaining one the advantage of first attack. On the other hand, knocking them out slowly was going to take far too long. One set of alarms had already gone off when she'd disengaged from the computer. It was a silly trap she'd fallen into. Keying into the system, she'd been careful to bypass or smother any trips. It hadn't occurred to her to do the same on the way out. A rookie mistake; Darby would've been furious. . . .

"Computers," he'd said, "like prisons, are meant to keep things *in*. Everyone knows what a trained psi agent can do. There's no longer any way to block access to information systems. Any static shield can be bypassed, any code broken. So . . ." he dropped the chalk and looked at the roomful of young trainees hanging on his every word, "—you've got to watch your step coming out. No matter how hard it was to get what you were looking for, no matter how rushed you are, don't just grab the prize and run." He turned to her. "Right, Dawson?"

"Absolutely," she said, shifting her shoulders a little against the wall. Her eyes sparkled. She was still infatuated with him in those days. Recovered fully from the accident and newly appointed director of the San Francisco Pool, it had taken only a couple weeks for them to fall for each other.

He was, physically, the complete opposite of Mollitor: short and heavily muscled, a fair-skinned, almost hairless body, ruggedly handsome nordic face with white eyebrows and fine blond hair. Darby had been Finney's partner in South America, the front man to Finney's invisible trick. Darby was the organizer, a born leader with natural charisma and enough common sense to have survived twenty years in the spotlight. He actually enjoyed drawing fire. It created the image of a dashing, reckless survivor that the ladies couldn't resist. This was what kept him alive in the period following Johanson's defection, when every Pool network on the planet was reorganizing and every agent was potentially blown. Chicago could offer little aid to their far-flung operatives, since no one dared use the computer until it was overhauled to find Johanson's trips. Darby had been smuggled out of South America by an underground railroad of girlfriends, and made it to San Francisco only two months before Dawson was assigned to run operations. If he felt any animosity at her being handed the organization over him, it didn't show. Darby, above all, desired a smoothly run network. He was much too high-strung to spend days in back alleys waiting for a break. His type of high-profile activity demanded a vast, multi-faceted safety net in the background. With Dawson's arrival, he simply rechanneled his energy from the network to the director herself.

Of course he'd heard of her. Even before the scandal, Dawson had been something of a legend to the younger agents. Her exploits with Mollitor during the War had been told and retold so often that the actual events were long forgotten, and the principals had a comic-book-hero aspect. All the more so now that Dawson was known to have single-handedly broken Johanson in a probedown. None of this overly impressed Darby, though. He'd been the hero enough times to realize it was nothing more than preparation that got you into the right place at the right time, and little more than luck that got you out. No, what blew Darby's mind was that this superspy veteran of a thousand capers was a beautiful blonde in her thirties. Through all the duplicity and brutality, she'd remained a warm, funny, exciting female. As a dashing superspy in his own right, bored with the years of easy sexual conquests and inferior colleagues, Darby thought he recognized an equal. He didn't say a word. He flirted with her on the wavelengths, incessantly. Their becoming lovers only augmented what was a natural camaraderie to begin with. Eventually, San Francisco became *the* central network of the post-Johanson Pool.

She shook her head. Dammit, she thought, why am I thinking of Darby at a time like this?

The lead dog sensed her momentary distraction and

inched forward, tightening the semicircle, the growl dropping deeper in its throat. Time was running out. Dawson was still poised, but undecided about how to attack. The indecision bothered her. Analyze it. The lead dog would spring any moment now. She had the beast's reflexes slowed enough so that she could dodge the teeth. It would take one blow to stun it and a second one to kill. By then the second dog would have leaped and connected. She'd have to hit a nerve plexus quick and then get behind. So? What was the problem? These were dumb animals. They couldn't sound an alarm; unless she made a horrible timing error, they couldn't kill her. Why the stall?

She watched the second dog with a side glance. He wasn't scared, he wasn't tired, his coordination wasn't dulled. No matter what, those teeth were going to land. She might kill the dog, but he was going to do some damage first; there was no way to avoid it. That was what was nagging her. She remembered all too well the pain of her leg torn open . . .

No! this wasn't the same. There was no bomb, there was no danger of death. She'd been out of the field too damn long; these last ten years as training director had taken a toll. There was no less ability than before, but somehow, the edge had been lost. Okay, forget it. A few seconds of pain and it would be over. It couldn't stop her. Only the anticipation could do that.

She fired a growling blast at the lead dog. It gave the creature the impression that she'd moved. When he sprang, he was counterattacking an animal that had just hit him in the head and jumped back. Dawson stood planted, ducking her upper torso to the left of the snapping teeth, and drove the heel of her left hand into the creature's jaw. His head jerked one way and his body the other, leaving his right flank open. Dawson focused beyond the black fur, swung and spun, driving her right fist through the ribs with a crack and crushing the heart against bone, presenting the other dog with nothing but a shoulder blade to land against. She felt it as she kept spinning, the teeth ripping open the black tunic and the skin below, dragging diagonally up to the shoulder and sliding toward her neck, but by then she'd finished the spin. She jerked her elbow hard into the dog's chest and the teeth let go as all the breath went out of him. She kept on going with the elbow, pushing him over, swung around and landed on his back. The growl turned to a whine as she locked her hands under the dog's jaw and yanked back. A single yelp, then he went limp. It was over. Time elapsed: maybe twenty seconds. Result: two dead guard dogs. Price: who the hell knew? She let go of the dog and probed her wound. No vessels severed. The teeth had gone through mostly skin tissue before hitting the wide plate of the scapula. The bone was bruised, but the bleeding felt superficial. The incredible thing was that there was no pain. She'd been too hyped up to feel anything but the impact. A steady ache was edging over her whole shoulder now, her hands were starting to shake, but there didn't seem to be any loss of mobility. So far. Mollitor would have to look at it. She dropped into their subwave, flashed, *Mollitor?*

No answer. There was some kind of interference in the wave, faint—but still, any fluctuation in their private wave was very odd. No one else could possibly tap into it; the codes would be hopelessly obscure to anyone born after 1970. She smiled to herself. Not even Johanson was an expert on old rock and roll.

Johanson. He was the least of her worries now. The important thing was to get to the bar to meet Mollitor, and to do it without setting off any more alarms. She scanned along the wall, found the wiring, fused it, carefully monitoring for backup systems. So far, so good. She ducked out of the room.

As she passed from chamber to corridor to chamber, Dawson blinked out the lighting ahead of her and stayed close to the wall, keeping a heavy mindscreen up. This was all automatic. In the active part of her mind, she considered the alarm system of ENCOM as a whole. No matter how cautious she was from here on, the fact was a number of alarms had already gone off and were being checked into. She had to prevent the word from being passed along. The entire communications net of this installation had to be deactivated if they had any hope of getting off this planet, this moon.

She sensed movement a couple chambers ahead. No

more run-ins, if it could be helped. She spotted an air duct in the far wall, ran over, popped the grating off. She climbed in gingerly, protecting her back, using a simple kinesis wave to pull the grating back over the opening. She didn't want to rely on psi energy this much—there might be sensors—but with only one arm up to full capacity, there wasn't much choice. Dawson moved quickly through the duct, scanning ahead, still searching the wiring for the central terminus.

After about ten minutes, she stopped. This approach wasn't going to work; there really wasn't time. When she got to the next grating, she came down off the rungs and hopped through the opening. Thirty feet to the floor. Her boots hit lightly and she felt around. It was time for something more than these simple vibration shifts. She put her fingers to her temples, closed her eyes and fanned out a wide, jamming wavelength. It touched the walls and Dawson increased the output until it pushed through the steel. The lights went out. As it passed through chamber after chamber, she sensed more and more electronics sputtering to silence. She keyed alternate waves into the sensors to keep them thinking that everything was running smoothly, and stepped up the output again. Her teeth clenched. After five minutes, she was keying wavelengths faster than she could count; after ten minutes, the entirety of ENCOM's surveillance apparatus was being held up by her mind. It was like an upside-down pyramidal graph, with every two sections supported by the one preceding them, and the whole thing held together at one point. Now came the hard part. It wasn't enough to smother the alarms; they would remain that way only so long as Dawson kept concentrating. She had to transfer the circuitry, *as one unit*, into her brain. Very carefully, she disengaged the control circuits from the master board and realigned them with the overall schemata she held in her head. It was slow going. This was where the alarm system would be most sensitive; she had to be aware of every fail-safe and backup circuit that could tip the computer to what was happening, and she had to do all this while continuing the primary blanking wave throughout ENCOM. By the time she was finished, Dawson was both supplying the power to run the system and exerting the force necessary to keep the system from operating cohesively. There was no sense of *Dawson* left in her mind; there was literally no room. And then, suddenly, she had it, it was complete, so she let it all drop. Everything across the board blanked out. The computer was in no position to figure out what had just happened, so it refused to take over.

Dawson staggered to the wall and held on, breathing hard. She started to empty everything else from her mind, to take a short, meditative recharge, but she heard sounds of footsteps approaching. She ran silently across the room, crouched in the doorway and scanned.

There were two of them. They were a couple rooms away, but there was no way of passing them unawares. She moved her head and felt the pain shoot across her shoulder. It was stiffening up. She had to relax the peripheral muscles. No, more importantly, she had to close the wound. At one point, it went almost to the bone. She thought about it. Mollitor always said, with a deep, wide wound, don't just close it up or an abscess will develop. You've got to knit it together a layer at a time, deepest point first. Infection on the surface can be treated; you want to avoid sealing in an infection at all costs. Remember, this is psi energy, you aren't packing the wound with anything. Take it slow.

She caught a shimmer of light from beyond the archway. The guards had powerpacks. Dawson started across the doorway, but she'd been shifting modes too much these last couple hours. Was this levitation or physical motion? Her feet stumbled. A beam of light flicked across her.

"Okay, don't move," one of them said. She scanned them. God, they were young. One held the light above his head, the other pointed a weapon. After all she'd been through, it seemed quite silly.

"You make a move and I'll drop you," he said, as they slowly advanced. "Who are you? What are you doing here?"

Dawson couldn't see them very well in the faint glow, but her scan told her enough. One was five seven, short dark hair, glasses. He moved with the light, smooth step of a dancer, or a fighter. He had unnaturally long arms. This was the one holding the lamp. The other one seemed about twenty years old, sandy hair and baby-faced. His pulse was fast; he was nervous as hell. Must be new on the job. They both wore the brown and orange uniform of ENCOM's security force. Both their communicators were blanked out. They'd been caught by the power outage and were scouting the area on their own. Good. No backup.

"What are you doing here?" he repeated.

Dawson was tired. Dead tired.

"I don't suppose you'd believe I'm lost and trying to find my way out? No," she said, eyeing them. "I didn't think you would." She laughed. "How about this one: *I* knocked out the power and there's nothing you can do to stop me. Is that any better?"

He motioned with the blaster. "I think this can stop you."

"Quit talking with her," the other one said. "All right, you. Let's go."

"This is so silly," Dawson said quietly. "You guys aren't even shielded. Oh well."

She didn't move. She hit them both with a blanket stun wave, smothering the blaster at the same time. They both fell, but the one with the light stayed conscious. As she walked over, she could see him staring, flat on his back, trying to move his arms. He looked scared.

"Don't worry," said Dawson, crouching next to him, "You'll be fine. You can tell the story to your children."

She increased the wave, and his eyes closed. Dawson pulled his jacket off and draped it over her shoulders. She scanned once behind and once in front, then disappeared into the shadowed corridors.

XI

The room was full of smoke, and the smoke was a dozen flickering colors from the rotating lights in the ceiling. The effect was chintzy, as was everything else about the plastic and chrome decor. A semicircular bar sat against one wall, on a raised dance area that spread out some twenty-five feet before the tables started appearing at random in the smoke. No one ever danced in here; the raised area was where the heavy drinkers hung out. The people moving around in the weird light made up the bulk of the operational staff of ENCOM: panel workers, maintenance crews, guards, people from the landing field, secretaries, computer techs, what have you. Whether they were here, in the only real bar on Luna, to socialize, let off steam or just drink to unconsciousness, the one common denominator was a hellish amount of noise.

Dawson came in cautiously, walked through the door as if she were peeking through a keyhole. The brown jacket she'd taken from the guard was pulled high on her shoulders, hiding the tear and the dried blood on her back. Her hair was pulled tight into a ponytail. As her eyes darted side to side, and the widebeam scan fanned out across the main floor, she pulled the cape together at her throat and held her fist there. She looked down; it was shaking. Too intense, she told herself, you must look like a soldier returning from the jungle. These people are here to relax. Blend in, damn it, cool out.

She dropped her hand, shook her head and let the blond hair fall loose. She tried relaxing her face, but her teeth had been clenched too long, her eyes had been jumping too much. The best she could manage was to look exhausted. She loosened her shoulders and a long needle of pain shot from her neck to the center of her back. Dawson ignored it.

The two men watching her approach the bar were a comic-strip contrast. The one was short and wiry, with little balls of muscle bulging his short-sleeve pullover. Coppery complexion, moustache, every feature small and sharply outlined. His buddy stood about six four, in faded green overalls, with a big belly and arms like tree trunks. He had a huge, mushy face, pale under the eyes, several chins blending into his neck. There was no finesse about him at all; anything he did in this world would always be accomplished through sheer size. The little guy nudged him and motioned at the woman in black.

"Ain't she some doll, huh, Roto?"

Roto widened his eyes in the folds and picked up his drink. He grinned. "Haven't seen her in here before."

The little guy looked up at him.

"That's good, Roto. That's exactly the line I was looking for. Yeah."

He moved down the bar and got within range, snapped his fingers as Dawson ordered her drink. The bartender's face turned.

"The lady's drink's on me, J.J.," he said, then leaned onto one elbow, facing her.

Dawson's head did a half-swivel; corner-of-the-eye glance. "Thanks, but I'll handle it."

"I insist."

"Look, I appre—"

"I haven't seen you in here before. I always buy a new lady a drink. Waddaya wanna do, ruin my record? The name's Danny. What's yours?"

Dawson finished turning her head.

"It's nice of you to offer," she said, "but I'm expecting someone."

"Yeah?" he said, smiling, rubbing his chin. "That

whose jacket you got on? Shift don't change for another couple hours."

Dawson looked around the room, spotted an empty table. "You'll have to excuse me," she said, starting away from the bar.

He grabbed her right arm just above the elbow.

"C'mon, doll, don't be so tough. You got time. You can have a drink with me. Hey—" he said, eyes widening, "that's some muscle you got there for a dame. You keep in good shape, huh?"

"Let go of my arm," she said quietly.

"Roto, she's in good shape, huh?"

The big guy came up alongside Danny, blocking Dawson's path. He looked her up and down, admiring the shape of the black insulsuit. He licked his lips and smiled dumbly.

"Hi."

"This here's my buddy, Roto. We work out on the panels. Roto, this is—what'd you say your name was?"

"I didn't. I'd like to sit down by myself and wait for my friend. If you'd please let go of my arm . . ."

"No problem, honey," he said, not letting go. "We can see you're a stranger here. It gets lonely; I understand. Let's get a breath of air. Hey, Roto?"

The big guy took hold of Dawson with a gentle movement that ended in iron fingers. The slightest touch jarred her left arm all the way up; she winced. All right, she thought, enough. Playing the quiet little blonde just isn't a very effective role. She looked at Roto; he was smiling limply. Just a big, dumb animal. Probably friendly enough on his own. It was this little weasel who needed to be taught.

"Do you intend to let go?" she asked.

"I don't think s—"

The smile didn't exactly die, it just froze. Everything went rigid, every muscle and nerve from the eyes down. His legs locked, his hands remained closed where they were, his chest refused to let his lungs draw breath. Sweat broke on his forehead and the eyes started darting around. Roto, still focused on Dawson's breasts, didn't notice anything amiss. She turned toward the little guy, pitched her voice through the noise for his ears only.

"I'd rather not embarrass you in front of your friends," she said, "but if you don't let go of me, I'm going to break both your arms in several places." She smiled coldly. "You get the message?"

The eyes kept hopping around. His face was noticeably pale, and the edges of his lips were turning blue. His eyes met hers and stopped. Hell yes, he was getting the message.

"I'll assume you didn't mean any harm," she said. "Neither do I. Just *leave me alone*."

Dawson released the freeze and turned to Roto, as Danny collapsed backward into the bar, spilling his drink and clutching his chest with both hands. The breath came crashing in and out, in and out.

"It was so nice to meet you, Roto," she said, patting his cheek, watching his face light up like a happy puppy, "but you'd better see about your friend. I think something went down the wrong tube."

Roto suddenly noticed something wrong and rushed over to smack Danny on the back. A man Roto's size, however, can't really rush anywhere without getting in someone's way. The particular someone in this case was feeling a bit cocky from his alcohol.

"Hey, watch where you're going, you big asshole," he said.

"What'd you say?" Roto yelled, jerking up. The other guy's drink went flying.

"Why, you son of a—"

Roto swung from the knees and rocked him into the crowd behind. One guy caught him, took a look and shoved him away. The guy he landed on grunted, pushed him aside, then hit the first one in the forehead with his glass. Two more pulled objects from their jackets and started moving on Roto, who was just warming up. Danny, still coughing, fell against someone else's leg. It looked like a brawl was going to unwind any second, but J.J., the bartender, was used to these episodes. He clipped Roto neatly behind the ear with a magjack and, as the big man went down, he came up from behind the bar with a scatterstun. Triple-barrel.

"*Freeze*, you mothers!" and freeze they did. At that range, J.J. could take the whole dozen of them with one blast. The room got a lot quieter; Dawson edged slowly away.

"That's enough shit," he growled. "Anybody lost a drink, you get a free one. Anybody throw another punch, you wake up tomorrow. Any questions?"

There were several grumbles, but no one argued.

"Someone get this guy out of here," he said. "Okay, what'll you have?"

Quick and to the point, she thought—nice to have someone competent around. The decibels climbed back up and stayed there. Dawson excused her way through the crowd, keeping the optiflicker high. She got to the empty table when a voice muttered in her ear,

"Boy, you blondes really know how to stir things up."

She spun around.

Mollitor! Oh, God, am I happy to see you. Her good arm grabbed him around the waist, pulled close.

"Verbal, kiddo," he whispered. "Sit down, I'll explain. Just keep the wavelengths blanked."

Dawson leaned away and took his hand as they sat, but she was worried. She forgot the ache in her shoulder. Something serious was going on here. Mollitor looked a lot grayer, almost haggard.

"What happened to you?"

The blood had been cleaned up, but she knew him too well. She could sense his breathing was wrong, his free hand was curled and held close to his body, and there was far too much tension in his face, a tremor along his jawline. His bottom lip was split in two places.

"Doesn't matter," he said. "I had a run-in with a couple unsavory gentlemen. Are you all right?"

She shrugged with her eyebrows. "My back's a little messed up. You can look at it later. What did McIntyre say?"

"McIntyre's dead."

"Suicide?"

He nodded.

"Oh, for God's sake . . ." she said, looking away into the smoke. She squeezed his hand tighter. "Mollitor . . ."

"I know what it is, kiddo."

"What? The suicide assault?"

"Exactly. It's a frequency overload." He gave Dawson the details of the attack. It lacked the immediacy of a subflash but, coming from Mollitor, filling in the details was no problem.

"Finney," she said, when he'd finished. "Well, we found him, in a sense. You think he was here?"

"Who the hell knows? It's a sure bet he's on Earth now, though."

"Wouldn't he have to have been on Luna to leave the impress?"

"That's out of my depth, kiddo," he said, swirling his drink. "It wasn't really an impress. It was a random subwave with a specific sequence trigger. It was there for anyone who survived the attack. I don't know what bearing the gravitational fields of Earth and Luna have to do with it. I never keyed a message like that."

She nodded. "Finney's full of tricks."

"That's why I'm betting he's alive. Hell, he beat the assault, or so he says. What else could—what are you thinking?"

"I'm wondering why I haven't gotten hit. If they're drawn to heavy psi discharge. . . . Smothering those alarms all across the main plant took a heavy load."

"Yeah," he said, scratching his temple. "Well, really, all you were doing was setting a massive blank-out across the circuits. Finney said that split-second blanking diverts the attack. Maybe you hit the right timing."

"More like overkill."

"Whatever. What did you get from the banks? What does ENCOM know?"

She exhaled loudly, shook her head, finger on the rim of her glass.

"Are you ready for this? They had an A-3 priority file on psi collection, going back almost fifteen years. It's been dead the last five."

"Dead?"

"Terminated, 2084. Not only that, but someone wiped the bank. Empty and unused. And if blank storage space isn't silly enough, think about them keeping an A-3 priority lock on a file that has nothing left but a title.''

He thought about it. ''What's the title?''

''You got it, Doctor, that's the punch line. Code name *Maize*. Mary's old field name.''

Mollitor's jaw slowly dropped, his eyes wandered back and forth.

''*Old name?* That was her field name in San Francisco. Before . . .''

''Before Paris. Before she ever approached Elena. While Johanson was still a reputable Pool agent.''

''Hell, Dawson, that was over thirty years ago. Why would they use *Maize* as a code name?'' He stared into the smoke, toward the bar. ''What, in God's name, was Mary doing all those years?'' he whispered. He suddenly snapped back to face her. ''Who wiped it?''

''Don't know. McIntyre?''

''No, it's not his style. He was—'' He broke off, tapping slowly on the table, then faster.

''What?''

''McIntryre.'' He clenched his fist. ''The impress I pulled from his dead mind. Those clouds, the bridge with all that swirling, that's it. It was San Francisco, it was the Golden Gate in the fog. And . . . yeah, the kids. It fits.''

''Didn't Finney say something about San Francisco?''

''Sure. Aside from the false lead in Paris, he said Mary's subwaves were based on the old net frequencies. He also wanted to know about her activities in Chicago, right after the Johanson thing. Damn it. We guessed wrong, kiddo. We picked Luna, but it was really San Fran.''

She didn't look convinced.

''I can't believe Mary was . . . I don't know what. Was she a double? For who? What could anyone have bribed or blackmailed her with?''

''No, not that. She was just running some deal of her own. For her own reasons.''

''That far back?''

''I guess so,'' he shrugged.

''Well, who was in on it?'' said Dawson. ''Who did Mary confide in? Who did the legwork, who squeezed computer time?''

"Like I said, we've got some digging to do in California."

"What was that about the kids?"

"Huh? Oh, that. McIntyre's impress had kids in it. Kids playing. I guess it was a reference to the children's program in San Francisco."

"You think there's anything in that?"

"I don't know. Do you?"

Dawson took a big gulp from her glass.

"I don't know," she said. "Is it just a coincidence that the head of the children's program all those years was also Finney's partner in South America?"

"Darby," he said quietly.

She nodded.

"I think," he said, "that there are no coincidences on this case. I think, in any event, we should contact Darby. The possibility that McIntyre was trying to lead us to him just makes it more urgent."

"He's an old man, Mollitor."

"All the better."

"He hasn't been connected with the Pool for ten years."

"All the better."

"Mollitor . . ."

"What?"

She sighed and looked off. "I was the love of his life, and I walked out on him. You're asking me to go knocking on his door and reopen the wounds. And for what reason?"

"We need information."

"He may not have it."

"You want me to go?"

"Very funny. He'd just *love* to see you."

"Someone's got to. Let's face it, kiddo, we're up against a very heavy psi-assault weapon. As Finney pointed out, the most logical suspect is Insight itself. We can't afford to contact the Pool. If we're going to get help, it's going to be from retired agents, or from old personal contacts like Andre."

"I know."

"I'm sorry."

"Yeah." She nodded to herself. "Is that why we're talking this instead of flashing it?"

"Well, yes and no," he said. "Once we get to Earth, I think it'll be safe enough if we use only our subwave. For now, though . . . well, I was in Ranagen's office for twenty minutes and I'm sure he had me vibrascanned. It wouldn't surprise me if they had sensors in here. You've done too good a job blanking the alarms—I don't want to give us away now."

She smiled. "All right. The sooner we start . . ." She finished the thought with her hand. "Let's get out of here. Which shuttle are we on?"

"Shuttle? I thought you were handling that."

"Me?" she said. "I was going to come running out of the computer with every alarm on Luna screaming. You were supposed to have the getaway car waiting at the curb."

"Oh."

"A fine partner you are. I've got to do all the work around here?"

"What the hell. You're younger than I am."

"No excuse."

"Okay, okay. Come on," he said, standing up. "I'll figure something out as we go."

Dawson got to her feet and took his arm, steadying him.

"I hope there's no trouble," she said. "You look a lot worse than I feel." She took his chin in her hand, stared deep into the gray eyes. "You sure you're OK, love?"

He nodded grimly, but she knew it was more determination than honesty. He'd obviously taken a bad beating, psychic as well as physical, and it would take some time to heal. For the first time in her life, she felt a disparity in their ages. Her own injury hurt terribly, but it was knitting; even now she was healing it, layer by layer. She still felt strong. Her body felt, essentially, just as young as it had that night at the turn of the century, the night they stopped the cellular clock in its tracks. Regenerative tissue control had been discovered, and twenty long years would pass before anyone duplicated the feat. The bond forged that night was the main part of what had carried them together through the last seventy years; merely thinking of it reminded Dawson how precious Mollitor was to her. And now, the gray at his temples white, his forehead pale and full of lines, his injured hand curled tight to his stomach like an arthritic paw, he looked far older than she could recall.

She let her hand drop and he winked at her. Dawson bit her lower lip.

"Mollitor . . ."

"Let's go," he said, touching her cheek.

They started for the door and, suddenly, he stiffened.

"What is it?"

"That guy in the corner," he said. "The little guy with the sunglasses."

Dawson looked over. Sunglasses on the moon?

"Who is he?"

"He followed me all across Paris. I don't know who sent him or how he tracked us here, but it ends now."

The little man pushed up from his chair and started toward them. He was looking at the bar. Mollitor and Dawson both felt the tickle while he was still fifteen feet away.

You need passage out of here.

It was a statement of fact, no inflection, and it was flashed on a very odd frequency, a commercial band. Dawson scanned back, was deflected, then locked onto the guy's shield and began dissolving it.

Please. This is no contest. I've arranged passage for you. Level nine, dock B. Auxiliary has been left unsealed.

He started to turn away, but Mollitor's wave had him, pulled the man closer. His face was full of loose skin, oatmeal-colored, folds hanging from the cheeks to well below his jawline. The nose was just a blob and his upper lip hung over the lower, obscuring the mouth. His collar was turned up against a mottled neck; the hat covered his forehead. He looked like a disease victim.

"Who are you?" Mollitor asked softly.

Please. Someone will notice. You must go.

"Can you speak? Who sent you?"

Dawson clutched Mollitor's arm tightly. The little man's lip quivered and slowly unhinged from his chin; a ragged hole of a mouth began to appear. The breath bubbled out unevenly and a flesh-colored glove touched Mollitor's sleeve, as he croaked one distinct syllable,

"Vox."

Three: King of Lithuania

XII

Everything about the Baron Valimir Otto Xenarie was immense. His estate, just north of Old London, was a sprawling expanse of meadows and forest measuring some hundred acres. The main house consisted of dozens of rooms spread over four stories, not counting the three towers. In all, there were two complete libraries, an art museum, a film studio, a gym, two swimming pools, a communications installation, an observatory and more bedrooms than you'd care to count. His own private shuttle hangar was connected to the servants' quarters. The Baron knew how to live, but then, the Xenarie fortune made it easy. It had been acquired and passed on, like the family title, through nine successive generations, and there seemed no limit to it. There was no real name for the business he was in; it was simply buying and selling. Anything. Everything. What couldn't be bought was probably already owned by one of his friends.

Then there was the Baron's physical presence. *Imposing* was far too small a word. Vox was a giant, six feet seven inches tall, over three hundred pounds, a seventh *dan* grandmaster in the oriental arts. You had to see him in action. It was inconceivable that a man so large could move so quickly, but that speed had saved my life often enough to make me a believer.

I'd met him in China in '58, a year after the Johanson episode. Dawson was still in bed from the accident and I was going crazy with frustration. There was nothing I could do for her and no way to settle my vendetta with Johanson. All my contacts overseas were blown; I didn't dare return for a shoot-out in the streets. The Old Man agreed I'd be best off seeing what I could reorganize of our Southeast Asian networks. Everyone was being reshuffled. We were putting old Euro agents into South America, Darby moved from Argentina to Frisco, Finney shifted to Africa, Mary came back to Chicago to dismantle Insight's communications system (Johanson's communications system) and build another in its place. Was that the time period Finney was worried about? Hard to tell. I wasn't in the States much during the '60s.

I met Vox in Canton, where he stood out even more than usual. He was ignorant of the Pools operations, but the upheaval caused by Johanson's defection was creating serious enough repercussions in the business world to gain his attention. I was involved in a touchy double-cross game with Intertel, and that was enough for him. The Baron hated Intertel. He had a grudge against the Soviet Empire going back to before his birth, to the Energy Wars in the '20s. It seems that one of their early rocket volleys misfired and landed just ten miles offshore in the Baltic. The resulting detonation vaporized most of Estonia and all of Lithuania, leaving the Xenaries—who, among others, were fortunate enough to be elsewhere at the time—without a homeland to return to. Vox inherited the formal title of Baron, but, privately, he always thought of himself as King of Lithuania, the last avenging son of a proud people.

For ten years we worked together, setting up networks in Pacifica and on the mainland, ultimately dueling with Johanson across Europe and Africa. Most of my current European contacts were made during the '60s, while Dawson was running her own Pool in San Fran. We're talking twenty-five years, though. I still didn't know how Vox had found me now, or what had prompted him to start looking in the first place. Maybe Finney.

I thought about this, and a lot more, all the intrigue and adventure of twenty years past, lying on a massive four-poster staring at the ceiling, somewhere in the Baron's mansion. The creepy little guy from Luna (from Paris?

From God knows where) had made all the necessary arrangements. We'd avoided Customs in London entirely, caught a private hover waiting for us and now . . . Well, we were guests of the Baron. Knowing him, he wouldn't even make an appearance until we were cleaned up and rested. There was a timetable to everything in Vox's world, and it was all precisely automatic; everything from before-dinner cognac to the security shield blanketing the entire estate. In the world he had carved out for himself, Vox truly was King. I felt safe for the first time in days.

I flashed a signal to Dawson, in the shower.

How long you going to romp in the water?

Quiet. It's such a relief to be warm, I never want to move.

You're gonna get all wrinkled.

So what? I'll finally look my age.

No chance of that. You're turning amphibious on me, though.

Oh hush. Just because you jump in and out in two minutes . . . I swear, Mollitor, your attention span is regressing. Or maybe it's your patience.

I haven't had any patients in years.

Ugh. Horrible. With that, I sign off.

Wait! How's . . . Dawson?

But she'd blanked. Touchy, touchy.

The water stopped running. Then the bathroom door nudged open and thin trails of steam came sliding out the crack. Dawson was humming. Something vaguely familiar; certainly not modern. Jefferson Airplane? Steely Dan? Names that had no meaning whatsoever anymore.

"Hey, kiddo?"

"Just a sec," she called from behind the door.

I stretched and held onto the headboard, stared out the window. The fog had rolled away with the morning and it looked like the sun was going to win round one today. I felt a lot better. My ribs must be getting tougher as the years go on, I thought. More leathery. They crack, rattle and bend, but everything stays intact. Only my left hand required more healing time. The metacarpals are tricky little bones. I still couldn't make a tight fist. Other than that, I felt in pretty good shape for a hundred-and-forty-year-old man.

"So? What is it you want, old man?"

She stood in the doorway, towel knotted at her shoulder, falling to mid-thigh. Her hair was almost dry.

"What I want," I said, rolling onto my side to face her, "is to know how you pulled out that piece of thought without my knowing?"

She cocked her head, smirking. "I don't teach you all my tricks."

"Uh huh." I snapped my fingers, and her towel unknotted and fell to the floor. She looked down quickly and back up, eyes surprised. "And I don't teach you all of mine," I said.

She laughed, shaking her head, bit her bottom lip and put her hands on her hips.

"So?" she said. "What exactly is it you want?"

"I think what I want has changed."

"Oh?"

"First things first. Come here, let me see your back."

She walked over and sat down on the bed. I sat up, felt along her shoulder.

"Tell me if it hurts." I scanned the tissue under the skin as I went. "Christ, Dawson, you were lucky. It cut into the trapezius. If it'd gone all the way through, you would've been in big trouble."

"Isn't that my middle name?"

"You can joke about it now, but, I'll tell you . . ."

I continued along the muscle, to where it attached to the scapula. The scar was still raw, about four inches in a curve, but there was no swelling and only slight redness in the surrounding area. There wouldn't be any complications. Another month or so, and it'd be just one more brown line to add to the dozen others. I looked at some of the older ones; I could remember how she'd gotten them. Christ. What a story our bodies told. The knives, the bullets, lasers, the crashes of metal and glass, the scars we wore as reminders of eighty years in a lethal business. My medical knowledge and our psychic control of tissue had saved us so many times . . .

You did a good job, kiddo.

My back's beginning to look like a road map.

My hand fell to her waist. I ran it over her hip, my fingers feeling the top of the wide scar that ran down the side of her leg; the only wound we could never completely repair, the explosion. I rolled my hand past it, over the top, felt the soft skin of her inner thigh.

Don't worry about the road map. You're still beautiful. You always will be.

She leaned back against me, tilted her head up. I kissed the long neck, chin, quickly on the lips, then on to her cheek. I took her earlobe in my mouth, humming softly, and moved my hand up. She slid forward onto the edge of the bed, her legs spreading, and I kept going as far as I could. I had my other arm around her, my injured hand on her stomach gliding up to her breast. Nothing that soft could do me any damage. She shifted a little to the side and brought her lips to mine. The circuits were all linking up, automatically. Being in total psychic contact with each other only intensified the physical contact. More than watching and feeling each other move, we could literally sense our chemistry interacting, could feel the tingling from both sides at once. She pulled my robe open and twisted herself off the bed, leaning over, our lips still locked, running both her hands down my chest. The surge of power alternated one to the other and back again. We were enveloping each other's vibrations and I could almost hear the energy hum. Our lips let go and I stared into her eyes.

"You know what's incredible?" she said in a shaky voice. It had to be verbal; all the wavelengths were full.

"Hmm?"

"That we never outgrow this."

"Lucky us."

She growled and smiled, then blinked, and the threads of my robe fell apart.

"You'd better lie down," she said. "My back's in no shape to play missionary."

XIII

Three o'clock, teatime. Always has been, always will be. The room was full of brightly colored tapestries and paintings, columns on either side of the fireplace. It was a huge place, but then, all the rooms Vox built for himself had to be. The furniture was antique, tastefully expensive, a touch lost on Dawson and me, since we could remember when this same stuff was called Scandinavian Modern. I ran my hand along the grain of the wide tabletop, began counting the repetitions in the stone pattern surrounding the fireplace. Which brick would I pick for an impress? What clue was there that Vox would spot? I always thought this way when I encountered the Baron. We'd played cloak-and-dagger espionage so intently for those ten years that I instinctively fell back into old habits at the prospect of working with him again. Silly, I supposed. Vox must be almost seventy by now. Without regenerative control, he was well past the age of fieldwork. It was hard to tell, though. The man, after all, *was* a championship fighter in his time. God knows what tricks he learned in China.

"Well," said Dawson, turning away from the window, cup in hand, walking back toward the table, "do you know what happens now?"

I shrugged. "We wait for Vox. This is his show."

"I know that," she said. "It's just—well, I want to get to San Francisco. I want to get this over with."

"What? Darby?"

"Yeah." She set her cup down and stared at the wall, tapping her foot quickly.

"I don't know what the hell you're so nervous about."

"It's not nerves. I'm just impatient. I hate making decisions I can't act on immediately."

"Oh? You get the feeling that we made a decision?"

"Didn't we?"

I smiled. "We wait for Vox. He has information for us or we wouldn't be here."

"Right," she exhaled loudly, and sat down. Drank some tea. Frowned. "Shouldn't I at least book a shuttle?"

"Dawson . . ."

"All right, all right."

The massive oaken door on the other end of the room swung open silently. Dawson stood up. The strange little man walked in and proceeded directly to the window without looking at us. He had his sunglasses on, the collar of his housecoat turned up. He drew the curtains and perched himself on the windowsill, then he stared at his black-gloved hands and announced, on a strong wave,

The Baron Xenarie.

I heard him before he appeared. He was saying something to one of the servants in the hall. The voice was a little raspier, but the resonating boom was unmistakable. It was the speaking voice of a trained operatic baritone. I could recall times that voice had shouted sudden warnings to me over the cacophony of a dozen blasters firing, buildings collapsing, lasers shrieking, psychic attacks throbbing in my head. It always rose above the din, loud and clear.

He was definitely older; I could see it at a glance. His hair was thick silver, deep lines creased his cheeks and around his eyes. If I cared to scan, I would undoubtedly find his vibrational wavelength changed as well. But he still walked with the light step of a fighter, his body erect, big as a goddamn house.

"Val . . ." I said, getting up.

"Mollitor."

He closed the distance between us and stopped, held out his hand. I took it and squeezed with everything I had, just to keep from being crushed. He wore a brown coat and vest, with a white silk scarf knotted at his throat. Same square jaw, clean-shaven, which was where my head came to. None of Vox's immense bulk was fat, never had been, and it was apparent that he'd kept working out all these years. I stared up into his eyes, those brown and gold pools, full of merriment, yet unable to ever forget the pains of the past. The pain of his people. Christ, it'd been ten years. I'd forgotten the intensity of those eyes.

"So," he said, "the warrior returns to his old comrade. It has truly been a long time."

"The warrior is summoned," I replied, smiling. "Thanks for the lift off Luna."

"Think nothing of it." He let go. "Dawson, my dear, you look lovely. You become more beautiful as time goes on." He took her hand, kissed it.

"Time goes on for all of us, Baron. I don't feel more beautiful. Thank you."

"Come, come," he said, spreading his arms. "Sit. Drink. More tea?" He clapped his hands loudly. "More tea," he boomed. "We have much to speak of."

We all sat.

"I trust you had a relatively easy time of it at ENCOM," he said. Dawson and I looked at each other. "Yes? No?"

"We made it," Dawson said. "It feels a little more difficult these days, but I guess we're still effective. Thank you for getting us out."

He smiled. "I wish everything were as easy as arranging transport."

"How did you find us?" I asked him.

He had a mischievous look on his face. A tall, thin butler came in with a tray, refilled our cups and asked if anything else would be needed. The Baron waved him away. He waited until the door shut, then turned to me.

"I've had you tailed since Paris. As you were well aware of." He reclined in his chair. "I suppose guarding your back is an automatic reflex for me, Mollitor."

"Did Finney tip you?"

He looked puzzled. "Finney? The little Irishman? Why, no. I haven't heard from him since, Lord knows how long. The '60s, I imagine. What makes you think that?"

I took a deep breath. "Val. How much do you know of what's happening?"

"In the Pool?"

"In general. Do you know what we were doing on Luna?"

He shrugged and shook his shaggy head. "Would you care to tell me?"

"Why was I tailed in the first place?"

"I told you. I was covering you."

"But why? From what?"

"Hmm," he said, stroking his chin. "Perhaps I was mistaken. I received word you were in Paris. It was so soon after LaRue that I assumed—"

"What about LaRue?" I interrupted, with a side glance at Dawson. She was sipping her tea, watching us.

"LaRue is dead," he said.

"Yes, I know that."

"He was assassinated." When I didn't respond immediately, he looked at Dawson, then back to me. "Surely, your agency doesn't believe he jumped out that window. You don't believe it was suicide, do you?"

"No," said Dawson softly. "We don't."

"Well, then . . ."

"Baron," she said, "are we to understand that you were investigating LaRue's . . . death, on your own, and your man simply spotted Mollitor?"

"That's correct. I had no idea you two were even in the field any longer."

"We weren't," I said. "You didn't contact the Pool in any way?"

"In Paris? That Pool?" He snorted. "Certainly not."

"You just stumbled on me."

"Yes. At Andre's. Of course, there's more to it." He looked at me, long and hard. "You mean you weren't—you *aren't*—working on LaRue's murder?"

I sighed. "As you just pointed out, Val, there's more to it than that. I—" I was suddenly aware of the fourth person in the room, the creature at the windowsill. I scanned without turning, but he was shielded. I jerked my head in that direction. "What about him? This subject isn't open to the public. I'd rather—"

Vox waved me away.

"Don't worry about Iorg," he said. "He's my most trusted servant. He's my psychic eyes, my connection with your *wavelengths*. Iorg cannot speak and, in any event, I am his King. He would never betray me."

I nodded. It made sense. Vox had no psychic powers to speak of. No aptitude for it at all. I'd taught him how to receive messages, and how to block simple thrusts, but that was it. A mute servant who was a psi-transmitter had obvious advantages.

"You know about Poli?" I asked Vox.

"Yes," he said. "Shot to death."

"And Basil in Munich. And Avery in San Francisco. And LaRue. They're connected. The Old Man sent Finney to investigate. He vanished, the day after they got Mary Z."

"They?"

"We don't know. It was a psychic assault. They nearly got me on Luna. Finney claims he was almost killed too."

"You've talked to him?"

"No. He left me an impress. Johanson's been attacked also. He beat it."

"Johanson," he said, eyes widening. "This becomes involved. The attacks are not his doing?"

"Not as far as we can tell. Why? Did your investigation lead you to believe they were?"

"Not as such," he said. "I was unaware of any psychic assaults. I recognized the possibility that LaRue was killed by Johanson. I've seen enough of his tricks. And anyway, he holds Paris in his grip."

"Not for long. I got hold of the codes to nullify his communications scramble when I was there."

Vox's face lit up. "Excellent! This may flush his silent partner out into the open."

"What silent partner?" asked Dawson.

He sipped his tea. "Perhaps I know something you don't. Johanson's in league with someone. There have been too many unnecessary contacts and re-routed transmissions for it to be otherwise. I assumed that LaRue had discovered the specifics and was killed because of it. But that means it's very big."

I didn't have to ask why. LaRue was a heavy; he'd been

with Insight since the War. It would take a lot to get the best of him.

"Who do you suspect?"

"At first?" he said. "The Pool. Or some faction within. LaRue was distrustful of this Tanner gentleman, the one who runs operations in Paris. But I also suspected ENCOM. They have the means. When the two of you set off for Luna, well . . . I didn't know what you'd found, but I was willing to follow the master."

It was laughable. What a merry-go-round.

"To be honest, Val, none of that involved us. All I think we accomplished in Paris was breaking Johanson's comm block."

"You didn't discover anything pertinent to the murders?"

I scratched my head. "Not really, not in Paris. We went to Luna to—"

Hold it, Dawson flashed at me.

"Baron," she said, "how were you involved in this to begin with? What was your connection with LaRue?"

He ran his big hand through his hair, rubbed the back of his neck. "LaRue was gathering data. I was helping him."

"Here?"

"In London. In Old London. The past six or seven months. That is precisely why the suicide explanation is inane. We were just getting somewhere. LaRue had to go to Paris for a couple days. We were to continue, but, well, he never returned."

"What sort of data?" I asked. I had a funny feeling, like something very far away was about to creep into my life.

"We were looking through archives, doing simple detective work. LaRue wanted information on psychic experiments done in the '30s."

"Done by whom?" Dawson said, but my breath was already frozen, my chest had already tightened up. I knew damn well what he was going to say.

"LaRue talked about a man named Weatherly. British, died in '45. There weren't many people still alive who—Mollitor, are you feeling well?"

"I'm fine, fine. Just go on."

"You knew this Weatherly?"

Christ, what a question. Gil Weatherly had been one of my closest friends. He was the one who'd suggested to Dawson, Elena and me that we seek out other potential T-paths, that we actually pursue this whole business of developing psychic powers. He was the brains behind the operation, the computer wizard, the man with the outrageous ideas. Gil was the experienced one, he was twenty years older than I, he was—well, he was dead. Dead almost fifty years now. There was nothing to say.

"What was LaRue looking for?" asked Dawson. "I mean, specifically. Did you know?"

Vox held onto my arm and answered her.

"Something about psychic power. I never really understood the details; that's not my area. Mollitor, are you sure you're—?"

"Don't worry, Val. It was just a shock." I turned to Dawson. "He was working for Mary. LaRue. It's all . . ."

She saw me fumbling for words and immediately shifted us out of verbal. My mind got very clear.

What about Poli? she flashed.

Don't know. Stands to reason he knew what was up. He was Europool coordinator. But this was Mary's baby. Off the record.

So she sent LaRue to dig up Gil's info.

Right. And worked with Elena personally to cover all bases.

I don't get it, Mollitor. Why not contact us? *We knew Gil. And Mary must've known we'd thought along these lines before.*

We were too closely connected with HQ and the Old Man.

The ones who'd farmed her out.

Don't know. Was this just her plan for a comeback?

I guess so. She didn't see it as dangerous.

Even after Avery? And Basil?

She didn't see the connection.

But why, Dawson? They got Poli next, then LaRue. Why didn't she catch on?

Maybe she did. Too late. She only lived a few days longer than them.

"Val," I said. "Think back. Did LaRue ever mention

why he was digging for this stuff? Was he on a case for the Pool?"

"One moment," he said, fingers at his temples. "I'm not used to this. And Iorg can't transfer it as fast as you can flash it."

"What?!" I looked over at him, sitting on the window-sill, very still, head on his chest.

"You see why I need him?" said Vox. "All right. No, this was not Pool business. LaRue was very angry, very discouraged with your headquarters. He openly suspected traitors. He said this was a personal inquiry."

"Uh huh. But he went to Paris. More than once?"

"Oh yes. Every few weeks. But then, I assumed it was necessary."

"Why?" said Dawson.

"Well, he was obviously working with *someone*. How else did he keep acquiring new leads? He couldn't send any messages, though. There was Johanson's communications block and, anyway, LaRue didn't trust his own organization's wavelengths. So he shuttled between London and Paris."

"Anywhere else?"

"Not that I know of."

"And he never mentioned Mary?"

"Don't be silly. He mentioned her a good deal. She was one of the few people in your hierarchy he respected. But no, he never admitted to working with her on this specific case."

You've got to finish it, Mollitor.

What?

You've got to pick up where LaRue left off. It's the only way.

What did Mary do that last week, though?

Finney knows. Or no one does. That's out of our hands.

And Darby? And San Francisco?

Nothing's changed. I'll leave immediately. But you've got to dig up Gil's research. It'll tell us how they do it, and how to combat it.

Back to they *again.*

That's what I'll find out. The answer's in California.

Why? Because McIntyre left an impress?

No. Because they killed Avery. Because everyone else was an old-timer, worried about this psi-collection business. Avery was just in the wrong place. I want to know what makes San Fran the wrong place.

"Did you get all that, Val?" I asked him.

His face looked strained. "I heard it," he said, loosening his scarf a little. "I certainly don't understand it all, but I heard it." He turned to Dawson. "You'll need transport to the States. Perhaps weapons?"

She shrugged.

"It *would* be better if we kept this among ourselves," I said. "No commercial flights. No equipment from the Pool."

"There will be no difficulty," said the Baron. "I have ample supplies. And I have a transcon shuttle. You may depart when you wish."

Dawson was staring at him intently. He finally noticed, and raised an eyebrow in question.

"You know what you're getting into, Baron?" she said.

"Of course," he boomed, lifting both arms. "I fought beside this man for years. Anyway, I owe it to LaRue."

"This is different," she insisted. "It's twenty years later and you're twenty years older. This is psychic warfare. It's out of your league. I don't know if you're really fit to be—"

"Oh, come now—I can't call you 'child' because you're nearly twice my age—but, please, don't be concerned. Mollitor taught me all about shield deflection many years ago. They can't kill me with one blow. And rest assured, my dear—" he pushed up out of his chair so fast that he blurred, stood towering over us both, laughing. He rolled his shoulders and spread two massive hands before his chest. "Rest assured, one blow in return will be all I ever need."

Dawson and I looked at each other quickly. Our smiles dropped and our eyebrows raised. It did seem our concern was misplaced. It was the enemies of Valimir Xenarie who were to be pitied.

XIV

Dawson left that evening for San Francisco. We ran a scan on Pool wave reports right before the shuttle was launched. Apparently, Chicago was just discovering our trip off-planet. There was no official news of McIntyre's death, but then, there wouldn't be. That wouldn't go far past the Old Man. Dawson and I were officially nowhere to be found. Nor Finney. Tanner was keeping busy, bucking for the Europool coordinator job left vacant by Poli's demise. He was pushing a little too hard, a little too fast, in my opinion. It wouldn't have meant anything, except LaRue had been suspicious. I was inclined to trust his instincts. LaRue had, after all, been head of the Paris Pool at one time; he and Poli had coordinated the entire European theater until Johanson's treason in '57. It stood to reason that he would stay in contact with Mary, his successor in Paris. There was still something wrong with the scenario, though. Poli would have let the Old Man know, if he'd been involved in Mary's research, and the Old Man would have, almost certainly, clued me in. This meant that either the Old Man didn't trust me, Poli didn't trust him, or Mary didn't trust Poli, but confided in LaRue anyway. It was complicated, much too complicated for me to figure out, now that three of them were dead and I was out of contact with the fourth. Maybe Dawson was right, perhaps California offered a simpler solution.

Vox, meanwhile, was acting like a happy puppy. I'd

never seen him so animated. He, apparently, had spent the whole night puttering around, arranging, preparing, anything but sleeping. I found him in the gym the next morning. He was running through some *katas* and lifting monstrous weights, taking short breaks to sing bits of arias. He looked considerably less than his sixty-plus years.

"Mollitor," he said, letting go of the bowed bar and jumping back as the weights crashed to the mat, "good morning." He dropped into a half-crouch. "Want to test the old man's reflexes?"

"Which old man?" I laughed. "No, Val, I'll pass, thanks. I don't tangle with guys your size if I can possibly avoid it."

He looked disappointed. "No?"

"One of the secrets of living this long."

"Very well," he said, picking up a towel and wiping his forehead. "I'll have to wait for the real thing for a workout."

I walked over to the equipment rack; Vox followed.

"What makes you think this is going to be strenuous?" I asked him. "We're just looking for old papers."

"Hah! Looking for papers, indeed. You think we go to a flea market?"

I shrugged. "You didn't have any trouble before."

"No. And LaRue was alive then. As were the remainder of your top agents in Europe. Someone is making this more dangerous. We must be prepared to respond in kind." He passed his hand along the rack, glanced at me. "I see you've found yourself a pair of boots. Good. I have extra insulsuits, if yours is damaged. For the rest . . . any weapon you desire is yours."

I didn't bother looking over the assortment; the expression on his face was much more interesting. His eyes had a sharp edge to them. Anticipation. The cheeks were ruddy, his mouth set in a hard line. The scar he'd gotten in Nairobi was invisible to anyone who didn't know exactly where to look. I knew because I had the matching one below my own jawline. It was one of the simpler things we shared. Temperament was the big thing; our attitudes meshed well. Vox had always taken this business quite seriously. He was a man who knew his strengths and his limitations, who underestimated neither his opponents nor his ability to deal with them as necessary. If it came to killing, he was prepared to accept that duty with efficiency, and his expertise covered all types of weaponry. It had been a long time since the '60s. In the intervening years, I'd grown used to thinking of him as a big teddy bear; his grim seriousness, now, was a little startling. But this was a frightening business; you've got to deal with it in your own way. I patted him on the arm.

"Nothing for me, Val."

"As you wish." He took a broad double belt from the rack, fastened one loop around his waist and the other over his shoulder. The belt was lined with shurikens, flat, palm-sized stars of razor-sharp steel. He zipped his insulsuit the rest of the way, pulled the belt snug, then put his vest on over it. He scooped his coat and scarf off the table, draped them over one arm and turned to me.

"We're ready, then?"

"Like old times," I said. "This actually isn't much of a mission, Val. An attic in London." I laughed. "I hope you don't get bored."

"Have no fear of that, my friend. Any intrigue at all is preferable to this wretched life as a country squire. Come," he said. "Iorg informs me our hover is waiting."

I looked at him. How come *I* didn't hear anything.

"He does?"

"You're surprised?"

"I guess not," I said. "Nothing that guy does should surprise me. He's not flying with us, is he?"

He gave me a tolerant look. "Of course not. It's a two-man hover. I have special clearance for the bypass route into the old city."

"You seem to have all the angles covered."

He laughed. "As you would put it, Mollitor, this is *my turf.*"

"And Iorg?"

"Oh, have no fear. He will be available when I need him. He always is. Come."

Somehow, that wasn't very comforting. The guy gave me the creeps.

"You drive," I said.

* * *

He "drove." Vox was a great hover pilot; he had the light touch and quick reflexes so crucial to maneuvering on air cushions. He was born to it, I reminded myself. I, too, had been able to perform all sorts of vehicular acrobatics in my time. Getaway chases or afternoon rush hour. I had to admit I missed the thrill. What the hell. The age of the combustion engine was long past. The only place you could still see a Jag XKE or a V-8 Camaro was the museum in Chicago.

In the last weeks before LaRue's death, he and Vox had been tracking down old associates of Weatherly's. In many cases, these were children or grandchildren of the people who'd actually known Gil. It was clear that LaRue was getting the names from Elena, via Mary. It was a wonderfully complicated setup, in that no one knew how all the threads connected except Mary Z.; no one could ever guess the true scope of her plan.

LaRue made his final trip south in March. Vox received word later the same day of papers left in an attic that Gil might have used as storage space. It was the best lead they'd gotten in months. Vox agreed to buy the contents of the attic, sight unseen. He had no intention of checking it out until LaRue returned. Two days later, though, the big Frenchman was dead, and the timing seemed more than coincidental; the attic appeared significant. So Vox bought the house. He also bought the buildings on either side and placed guards in a discreet manner. Then there was nothing to do but wait. When his man spotted me in Paris, Vox figured I might as well be who he was waiting for.

We docked in the hoverport above Trafalgar and walked the eight blocks to the house. The streets were plain, very no-nonsense British, with rows of red and yellow flowers the only decoration along the cracked sidewalk. This area was one of the oldest still standing. It was a matter of pride to the residents to keep everything intact in its perpetually declining state. The tourists found it adorably quaint and that was, after all, the main business of the old city. London, like most other population centers, had been nuked in the Energy Wars. It had gotten off luckier than some. New York, for instance; Tokyo, Leningrad, Los

Angeles, Detroit, Montreal, Rio, Mexico City, Havana, Rome—the list was incredible to someone who'd known these cities as something other than craters. London had survived its attack. The two blast sites were big tourist attractions, and the rest of the Old City catered to the crowds on holiday, while Metro London spread in a circle around the dying nucleus.

The crowd thinned as we rounded the last corner. No one but students of classical architecture would be interested in this street. Aside from the little card shop, the buildings were all old townhouse apartments, most of them boarded up, in varying states of disrepair. A lot of the lower-story windows were broken. I heard noises coming from the alley behind, gravel kicked up, a couple dogs. Vox walked beside me, taking long, slow strides, his head upturned, glancing side to side at the building tops. The sky was brilliant.

I sensed something between two of the houses, and only then realized that I'd been throwing a light scan out automatically. I stopped, touched Vox on the arm.

"What?"

"I don't know." My eyes darted. "Something . . ."

Two dirty faces peeked around the corner of a porch and ducked back, giggling, feet scampering back to the alley.

"Kids."

"I suppose," I said. "It felt like a heavier footstep, though." I scanned both the houses. Nothing. "Forget it. Come on."

"It's that one ahead," he said, pointing.

I looked up at a three-story Imitation Victorian. The paint used to be cream, the trim used to be dark wood and the steps used to be in one piece. It sagged in all the appropriate places. The boarded windows resented the useless shards of glass that still clung. It was a house that just wanted to be left alone.

I followed him up the steps. Most of the condemned structures on this street were padlocked. When Vox bought this one, he'd had E-tron locks put on. They were expensive, but the Baron had money to burn. He pulled the descrambler from his pocket and attached it to the silver plate beside the doorknob. *Click*. I scanned.

"There's someone in there."

"I hope so," he said. "I'm paying them enough. There should be two, one upstairs and one in the cellar."

"Nope, just one," I said, double-checking.

He looked at me. "Are you concerned?"

"Not if you're not. Lunch breaks have been known to happen. They didn't know we were coming today, did they?"

"No." He thought about it. "You feel like being over-cautious, Mollitor?"

"Not just yet," I said. "What the hell. Let's go up."

Vox led. The main room in front was cavernous. Sheets made every stick of furniture look alike, lumpish gray ghosts renting space from the spiders. The chandelier hadn't seen a light bulb in years. Dust lounged on everything. The only light came from a single, bare bulb hanging at the top of the winding staircase. There was nothing eerie or ominous about the place at all. No vibes. If anything, it was depressing.

Vox touched the railing and rubbed the dirt between his fingers. He looked over at me.

"Your guard's in the cellar," I said. "You want to notify him?"

He shook his head. "Already done. I signaled him when I descrambled the lock. I see no reason to let him know who I'm with."

I shrugged, waved. "Lead on, Baron."

We went up one flight, creaking, but not rickety, then the second. The wood got worse the higher we went. Vox descrambled the lock on the attic door and I peered up, past him, into the black.

"Any light?"

"We'll use this for the moment," he said, pulling a small tube from his vest.

He flicked the end, and a soft orange radiance appeared. He held it above his head and I followed him up. He was feeling along the wall with his free hand, then stopped as he came to the top landing.

"There should be a window somewh— Ah, here we go."

He gave a jerk with one arm and the board splintered

free of the nails. The sunlight crashed through the cobwebs before hitting the wooden floor in patches. I blinked a few times, swept one huge web away and stepped past Vox.

The vibration was overwhelming. Every rafter and floorboard, the chair, table and both boxes were full of Gil Weatherly. I just stood there a moment, too stunned to move, while Vox inspected the room. It was very peculiar. I could almost see Gil sitting behind the table, unhooking the wire-rim glasses from his big ears, running a hand through his hair, that long, tight smile of his greeting me while he flashed a *long time, no see* into my mind.

Incredible. Vox had been barely 16 years old when Gil died, here in the same city. He was 115 at the time, at the limit of his regenerative control. Dawson, Elena and I had come to London for the funeral; the last surviving members of *L'Escouade,* come to honor its founder. Christ, the vibrations. The twentieth century; a whole other world. I walked over to the table. Vox was watching me with a puzzled look on his face.

"You and LaRue were looking for a man named Weatherly?" I said softly.

He nodded.

"You found him. In any event, you found his legacy."

"You're sure?"

I sighed, untied the box closest to me. "I'm sure." I pulled the compuscanner from my belt and began adjusting it for read-in. "Val," I said, glancing up, "would you mind?"

He lifted the huge box and turned it upside down, depositing the pile of papers on the table. I began passing each sheet over the scanner before dropping it back into the box, while Vox prepared the rest for recording. A lot of the pages were computer readouts, other were notes and letters, some were stapled reports. "Autonomic Vibrational Kinesis" was the title of one. "Endogenic Synaptic Reconstruction" was another. Weatherly had covered the gamut of psychic application in his lifetime. He couldn't *do* everything, his own personal power had been at a level below Dawson's and my own, but he'd had the scientific discipline to extrapolate theories well beyond anything *anyone* was going to achieve. He'd stayed far away from

Insight, regarding us sometimes with tolerant scorn, other times with open resentment. His only contacts with the Pool had been an occasional lunch with Dawson or myself.

I finished the first box and moved to the next. I was getting faster at transferring papers, one-hand-to-the-other-and-drop, when my eye suddenly caught the title, "Linear Transfer Modalities of Non-Integrating Energy." I held it in my hand; it felt about thirty or forty pages. I folded the report longways, and slipped it into my inside pocket, zipped it. Then I went back to the recording.

"What was that?"

"Don't know till I read it. It might be what Mary and LaRue were after. I think it'll give Dawson and me a big clue to this case."

"The suicides?"

I frowned at him. "We'll see. All the victims are being hit with a massive vibrational overload. Much stronger than any one person could direct."

"And that report . . . ?"

"It offers a theory of how someone could utilize more than their own native power," I said. "At least, I hope that's what it's about."

"A vibrational overload . . ." he said, hand at his chin. "You've fought that kind of battle for years. Granted, this supposes a quantitative boost in sheer energy, but the method—"

"No, Val, it's more than that. It's—it's hard to explain. There are whole other levels to this attack."

"I don't understand."

I thought about it. I wasn't sure I did either. As an assault from the *outside* it made no sense.

"It's something like despair. It taps your fears. Every sense of guilt or failure comes to the surface. It feels hopeless. You're so busy fighting an impossible overload that you can't cope with the terror, the inevitability of your life confronting you at the same time. It was like nothing I'd ever faced before. I'm not really surprised that these people killed themselves. It was that or insanity."

I could see him turning it over in his head.

"*You* defeated it, though."

"I'm one hell of a psychic manipulator."

"Indeed," he laughed.

"No brag, just fact. After a hundred and forty years, I figure I'm entitled to a little self-confidence."

He laughed again. "You're alive, that's what's important. And it means they aren't infallible."

"I don't know, Val. I think it's a mistake to think of a *them,* of a person or group of people directing an attack against us."

"Oh? I thought you and Dawson agreed that everyone connected with this research of Mary's was being systematically eliminated."

I moved over to the next pile of papers. "Not exactly. Avery wasn't connected, as far as we know. Actually, neither were Basil or McIntyre. And Dawson hasn't been attacked yet. Nor you. No, I don't buy it; it's too arbitrary. Even if you figure it's only high-level T-paths getting hit, that doesn't explain why it skipped Dawson and the Old Man. Or Darby or Ballantine, or other retired agents. No, I don't believe any intelligence is sending out destruct rays."

"Then what is behind it?"

I glanced at him. "Maybe Weatherly knew," I said, tapping my pocket. "Maybe he foresaw it years ago."

"Or allowed someone access to some very dangerous information," he mused.

"No. If there is a *someone*, he's simply the beneficiary of a coincidence. What's involved here is psychics, the science or art itself. We've been playing at this business a long time, Val, and we've never completely understood it. We perform all sorts of tricks, but we're not any closer to knowing *why* they work the way they do than we were a hundred years ago. Do five decades of heavy psychic output produce some kind of overwhelming feedback? Are we accidentally tapping into some collective, cosmic mind that's too strong to channel through our nervous systems? Who knows? Maybe your basic human psyche, complete with all its urges and delusions and neuroses, is just unequipped to utilize a significant portion of the available brain without eventually cracking. Maybe we've been biting off more than we can chew for a long time, and it's finally catching up with us." The sound of my own voice suddenly bothered me. I looked back at the scanner and the flow of paper across it. Vox just watched me.

"You really believe that?" he asked.

I sighed. "No. But I haven't read the report yet. It may make a believer of me. There have been a lot of swashbucklers like Finney and Darby, but damn few scientists like Weatherly. That's why these papers are important. Hell, it would've been better if Insight had never gotten involved in spying; if we'd just set up a research foundation, I might actually know what I was doing by now."

"You didn't have much choice," said Vox. "I seem to recall hearing about a war."

"Yeah." I glanced at him. "There was a war, all right. You were damn lucky to have missed it."

I finished the recording, slipped the device into my pocket. "That's it," I said. "Let's go."

He shook his head sadly. "Some adventure."

"Keep your chin up, Val," I laughed. "Someone may try to kill us yet."

"I certainly hope so," he said. He locked the door and led the way back down the stairs.

I scanned the rooms on the upper floor. Doors were all open, every knob something to hang the dust on. One level down, the rooms were closed and the hallway was recently swept. Spiders looking for webs, no place to call home. Poor spiders; they should be agents. We got to the landing with the light bulb, and I checked on the guard in the cellar.

"Hey," I touched Vox on the arm. "Your guard is gone."

"That's impossible. I would have received a signal." He took the descrambler from his pocket. "Maybe it's broken?"

I gave him a look. I didn't like it. I took a couple steps down, deepscanned. There was nothing in the front room, no vibration but ours anywhere in the house. I still didn't like it. Vox squeezed past me, stopped a couple steps below. He stared out over the rail into the dusty room, his neck craned forward, eyes moving side to side. I got the impression he was *smelling* for something. Arms bent, hands curled.

"You think, maybe—?" I started to say, but that's as far as I got.

Vox lashed an arm across my chest and took me down with him, flush to the wooden steps, as an explosion hit the wall behind us. Plaster rained. Another blast hit the railing. Thermal. The first one had been laser.

"Behind the sofa," he hissed in my ear.

I looked. A blaster peeked over the top, a hand, the edge of a hood. I crushed the hand in a mental vise as it fired, and I saw a glint of light leave Vox's hand out of the corner of my eye. The man behind the couch screamed once as he fell over, into full view, a shuriken imbedded in the hood at forehead level.

A long beam raked the wall above my head, a high-pitched whine shrieking in my ear. Another blast took out the step right below us; I felt it sear my arm. They were getting too close; we were sitting ducks up here.

"Get the light."

I popped the bulb, and we slid down a couple feet. Another blast erased the step I'd just vacated.

"That one came from the front door," I said. "Two behind the sofa. Maybe one more laying back. That's four, tops. How do you want to work it?"

"They're well-armed. We have to get out."

"Agreed." I listened. Someone moved behind the sofa, edging for a clearer shot. Did they have infrareds?

"Do you want to get the door?" said Vox.

I gauged their positions in the dark. I had three pin-pointed. "Not enough light for your stars," I said. "You take out the door. I'll cover you."

Vox smiled. He loosened his scarf and crawled down a couple more steps. He crouched and grabbed the rail. I could barely see his outline. I took a deep breath.

He swung his entire bulk up and over the railing, and I ignited the sofa. The air in the room went *boom!* Both guys jumped back from the flames with a yell, one of them swatting at his chest. Vox landed and rolled for the door. A guy came out of the shadows, firing, and I snapped the supports on the chandelier. It shattered all over him. There was plenty of light now. Vox got to his knees and whipped two shurikens into the one guy at the sofa. Then he jumped up. He planted himself before the door, rolled his shoulders and snapped both fists into the heavy wood. Through the wood. The whole wall shook, the frame splintered. He jerked his arms back, pivoted, and threw a thunderous sidekick, crashing the door off its hinges onto the front porch. The room was flooded with sunlight.

The other guy at the sofa finally got his suit to stop burning as I leaped to the floor. He aimed with both hands, point-blank. Vox flashed another shuriken into the gun butt, taking off three of the guy's fingers, and I hit him on the chin with the heels of both hands. The shot went wide, over my shoulder. I carried him ahead of me, onto the porch, half through the force of the blow, half levitation. Vox dodged out of the way.

"Look out!"

I rolled into the doorframe, and the guy coming out of the kitchen caught his buddy on the porch dead center with the laser. Vox and I looked at each other as the body hit the post and slid down. No more games. I ignited the entire kitchen. The concussion shook the house, blew the guy forward like a rag, into the doorway at our feet. Vox lifted him from the belt with one hand, and tossed him off the porch onto the walkway.

"Any more?" he said.

I scanned. I was still getting nothing. If Vox's guards were in there, they were dead anyway. So were the two thugs by the sofa. I could see that.

"I'll get the guy under the chandelier," I said.

He nodded and crouched behind the porch railing, searching the street. There was no way I was walking back into a burning house, no need. I knocked the chandelier away and levitated the guy out, dropped him on the cracked steps leading down to his partner. Vox looked up at me.

"Not quite the psychic warfare Dawson cautioned me against, is it?"

"I think she meant California."

"Well, that's good news, eh? We're not in California."

"Oh, we will be, Val," I assured him. "We will be."

"Very comforting. Meanwhile, could you put out the fire, please?"

I looked over my shoulder. "Dawson puts out fires," I laughed. "I just start 'em."

"You're joking."

"No, really, I can't."

"Some agent you are," he said. "I'll bet you couldn't even pass the training exam."

"Hey, watch it. I *wrote* the goddamn training exam."

"Well, you know what they say . . ."

"Yeah, I know what they say. Let's get out of here."

"Different 'they.' You'd better notify the fire department, at least."

I keyed a signal into the alarm box on the corner, then went down the steps. The guy from the kitchen was definitely out for a while. Concussion. I knelt beside him and started easing his neural rhythms, keep him from going under. He didn't mean anything to me, but that was no reason to let him die. I've been in this business a long time; I've done my share of killing. I don't need any extra blood on my scorecard, not if I can help it. His breathing leveled out. He still gave off no vibration, but now I knew what it meant.

"Mafia," I said to Vox. "That's why I didn't pick them up. They've got implants."

His eyes widened. "All five?"

"I guess so. I didn't get a peep in there."

He whistled softly. "Someone paid very dearly for this."

I had to agree. Antivibe implants shield thought, nerve impulse and natural vibration. It's the ultimate in clandestine equipment for the non-psychic. The problem with it, besides being phenomenally expensive, is that you can never remove the device. Over time, the frequency wears down the central nervous system, your fibers go and you're through. Mafia torpedoes often used them. Not a job with a future. The astounding thing was that they'd sent five Imps on a single hit. Someone had indeed paid big money.

"ENCOM," I said, without too much thought.

"Why?"

"I imagine they didn't appreciate the job we did on their computer. Ranagen figured I made a fool of him."

Vox was going through one guy's pockets.

"Congratulations, Mollitor," he said. "Once again, you have a contract out on you."

"Fifteen years since the last one. Hmm, I wonder how long they've been tracking me?"

"Not on the shuttle. And not at the estate. I can guarantee that."

"Maybe not," I said, "but they knew I was with you. They knew I was coming to this house, today. They did their homework."

He tossed aside a set of keys, thumbed open a couple maps of London, tossed them, handed me a photo. It was about five years old, good angle. A nice shot, if I did say so myself. I put it in my pocket.

"What about this?"

I took a box of matches from him. French. Then a napkin. I unfolded it. Andre's. Their method of operation was becoming clear. I spotted the address written in blue pen on the napkin, and my heart started pounding. I must've gone white.

"Mollitor . . . ?"

"Oh no."

"What is it?"

"They went back and traced me from Chicago. Val, they followed us through Paris all the way to Luna and then here."

"So?"

"The address," I groaned. "My God. We've got to get to Paris immediately. Elena. My God, Val, she's a hundred-and-thirty-year-old woman. We've got to—"

"Come on," he said, taking my arm. "The hover can make it across the Channel."

"You're sure?"

"Of course. I'm piloting it, aren't I?"

"It's a rough ride in a thing that size."

"Big deal."

We locked eyes. It was like old times.

"Let's go."

We trotted back down the street toward Trafalgar, while the house crackled behind us. A slow, rising wail of sirens broke the morning.

XV

I was thoroughly spooked every step of the way. That was the bottom line. Sure, I was angry, and concerned, and in a hurry but, mostly, I was jumpier than I could ever recall being. Every bird that crossed our path over the Channel was a tracer, every radio clearance was a deception, anyone on the ground who so much as glanced at us was a hit man for someone, every sound from every alley was a tail. I had it bad.

I threw a shield around the car at the Étoile Hoverport, then keyed an impact trip. Anyone stupid enough to break through the shield and touch our hover would fry. I was in no mood to play around. The cabbie's accent made me nervous, so I blanked his mind and took over motor control. His body stayed in the seat, but it was me driving.

Vox understood my caution, but he kept trying to calm me down.

"Be reasonable," he said, watching the streets go by. "You had no way of knowing someone would tail you after the fact. It's ridiculous. You may as well reconsider every mission you—"

"That's not the point. I had no business going to Elena's when I was on the run. It wasn't safe and it wasn't smart. I just needed somewhere to let Dawson recharge, and the streets were full of Johanson's thugs."

"There you are, you had no real choice. Mollitor, you should listen to me. You're too good an operator to hamper yourself with guilt. You actually make remarkably few mistakes. Now, that time in Bangkok,'' he laughed, ''—that was a mistake. You remember that girl at the hotel? Lord, what a line. If I hadn't shown up, you'd still be swimming in the China Sea. You know, it's a shame . . .''

I smiled along with his laugh. I appreciated what he was doing, but it was no use. We crawled through the late-afternoon congestion in spurts: three blocks clear, then an intersection snarl. I knew the alleys and back ways almost as well as the cabbie, but you can only move so quickly in Parisian traffic. I tapped into the Pool wavelength for something to do. Tanner had an all-points out on Dawson and me. Said it was official from Chicago, but I didn't buy that. There were many fools in Insight's hierarchy, but the Old Man wasn't one of them. If Finney's disappearance troubled him, then Dawson and me following suit must've been a relief. It meant we were on to something. And anyway, by now, Finney would've made contact. He'd been the Old Man's personal rover for the past seven years; they surely had systems I wasn't privvy to.

In any event, if the Old Man wanted to find me, he wouldn't put it into the hands of Tanner and the other second-rate directors of the Euronet. I didn't like it, I didn't like all the commotion Tanner generated. In a city where you're fighting Johanson and Intertel every day, you don't broadcast all your information over the main waves. You keep a low profile, maintain limited access to your operation. That's what you do, if you're playing it straight. Tanner. Finney didn't trust him, Mary never liked him, LaRue openly suspected him. I had no opinion; I barely knew the guy, but I didn't like the feeling I was getting. Hardly enough to indict. Until I saw Dawson, I just planned on avoiding him.

Vox tapped me.

''Don't mean to disturb you, but we've crossed the river. We should be fairly close, no?''

I smiled at him. ''How many years since you been here?''

''Paris?''

''No. The cafe.''

''Ten. Maybe more. I never forget a place. Listen,

Mollitor, I think we should approach on foot. More room to maneuver. Anyway," he jerked a thumb at the front seat, "I see no reason to get his taxi blown up. It would ruin the fellow's entire day."

We got out at St. Germain and started walking. Almost dusk. The stone lions in the courtyard looked very gray in the fading light. You had to know they'd been lions in the first place to even attach a label to the faceless, shapeless lumps of rock they'd become.

The sky was dirty white. It obviously planned on holding the threat of rain over our heads all evening. The wind whipped off the river and swirled through the streets as we walked. Everyone's collar was turned up. They all looked like spies.

I felt something hit my shield suddenly, a probe of some sort. I spun around and locked onto the wave, met a shield on the other end. Two guys were back a couple blocks, at a magazine rack, staring at us. Vox's shoulders started twitching. He shook his head, held one fist to his chin and shook again. I slipped a needlethrust around the shield I was already engaging, and scanned along the wave attacking the Baron. The guy got his shield up, but I blew it away with a flash overload and nervethrusted him. He clutched his head and fell against the kiosk. The first guy flashed a needle at me, and I deflected, fired one back. He blocked, and attacked Vox. The Baron gave a grunt and stumbled a couple steps, his teeth clenched. His fingers reached for a shuriken. I caved in the guy's shield and blew him backward. The other one grabbed his partner's shirt and pulled him around the corner. The wavelengths went clear. Vox had a star in his hand, staring back down the street. He glanced at me.

"They're gone," I said. "You all right?"

"Yes," he said. He was more than a little pale. "I'd forgotten what that was like. Who were they?"

I kept scanning. They were blanked now, wherever they'd gone.

"Maf' would've stuck around," I said. "They could be anybody. Lucky for you they were small-time."

He smiled. "If that's small-time, I think I'll skip the big

operators altogether." He put the shuriken back into his belt. "What do you think? Should we split up?"

"Come on, we're almost there. They don't matter. They're probably Johanson's."

Vox looked back once more, shrugged. "They'll continue to follow us."

"Let them. I meant it when I said they were small-time. They'll keep their distance from me, if they know what's good for them."

I could smell it as we passed the Jusseau Metro-stop. Damp ashes. Charred, wet wood. It's a sickening smell. It's only fires that should have never been started that smell like that once they're put out. I bounded around the corner. The street didn't look any more derelict than it had, but the cafe at the top was now rubble. No green awning, no etched glass, no Elena. I deepscanned. They'd blown the place last night. Thermal, not nuke. No residue. The force of the explosion had probably been augmented by breaking through the protective shields. I walked closer. No trace of Elena's vibration. I keyed to the city files. There was nothing in the police or fire department reports to indicate a body had been found. It didn't mean she wasn't dead. It didn't mean anything. If she were still alive, more likely she was hostage than loose on her own. Although . . . Christ. I remembered her last week, hobbling along, and that was on *familiar* ground. What had she said? "Anything strong enough to break my shield is going to kill me anyway." I felt sick. Elena was so fragile.

I continued scanning the ruins, and forced myself to think it through. The Maf' didn't go in for kidnapping. They extracted information and eliminated targets. They were businessmen who had an image to be concerned with. Incinerating a cafe on a deserted street just to get information from an old woman constituted overkill. So, if it wasn't the Maf', what was the torpedo in London doing with her address? The details were piling up. I was a walking target as long as ENCOM's contract on me held. Now that Weatherly's papers were destroyed, the recorder in my pocket was very valuable. I had to get it to the Old

Man in case something happened to me. *Before* something happened.

"Mollitor!"

I turned. Vox was at the bottom of the street, against one wall, his coattails whipping about in the wind. His eyes met mine, darted left, right, up, then five fast blinks.

"Right," I shouted back. We were surrounded by five of them, but they were giving us room. I threw a shield around the rubble and jogged back down to the intersection.

"Moving?"

"Not yet," he said, brushing his silver hair away. "They're simply watching. Why? Do you want one?"

"I don't know. What would I do with one?"

"Interrogation."

I looked at him. He'd been getting younger all day. The years hadn't changed him; not really. He was still a tough cookie.

"No, I think we should get going," I said, giving the block a visual once-over. "As long as they keep their distance, we—"

I broke off, as my eyes fell on the scrap of the street sign hanging by one rivet to the corner building. A piece of green paper was barely visible. I reached for it, unfolded it.

Jeux sans frontière, written in spidery black ink. There was something terribly familiar about the phrase, but I couldn't remember what. Something very long ago. The handwriting was a lot easier to place. I finally felt a little relief. In a world of telepathic relays, oscillator blocks, vibrational impresses, coded wavelength trips, leave it to an old woman to think of tucking a note behind a street sign. No one—not Tanner, not Johanson, not the Maf', not even Finney—would notice. It simply *wasn't* done that way, anymore.

Let me conspire once more with you, eh, Doctor?

"I see we have a clue," said Vox. "This is what you were looking for?" He leaned over to read it. "What does it mean. Mollitor. The old lady, she is alive?"

Jeux sans frontière. It was a clue, but what? There was no impress in the paper at all, yet, somehow, I knew my path led across the ocean. Something just *felt* like America. Damn! Where did that phrase come from?

"She was alive when she wrote this," I said. "And she was able to leave it for me. That means she got away." I stared off, down the boulevard. "Which is also our next move."

"What is?"

"There's nothing more we can do here."

Vox snorted. "We can confront this Tanner," he said, "and get to the bottom of these murders."

"No, Val. Tanner is small-fry, at best. It's not worth it."

"Not worth what?" he said, hands on his hips.

"Blowing our cover."

This time he laughed out loud. "Mollitor, for God's sake, look around. What cover? Johanson has you tailed, the Syndicate has a dozen Mafia torpedoes pointed at you; half of those guys"—he waved—"are probably reporting to Tanner as well. And you're worried about blowing your cover?" He pulled his coat back around his waist, held it there against the wind. "Let us finish one battle at a time. We should have followed up on those men in London, found their contact point. You know that. All right, I accept that you were worried, had to leave for Paris immediately, save the backtracking for later. So, here we are. We should immobilize Tanner right now, find out what he knows, and then pinpoint Johanson. It's going to be important, Mollitor. I mean, my God, he's having us tailed for *some* reason. Look at it logically."

I just stood next to him, a thin cold rail beside the mountain, the wind blowing viciously through my hair and my clothes. *Games without frontiers*. It was a game, all right, only I didn't know the name of it, and Elena was using rules I'd forgotten. There was no time to do all the things you were supposed to do. Nailing Tanner, fighting with these street hoods, the Maf'—they were all distractions. Anything that diverted my attention from the main track was a mistake. I knew what I had to do, I could sense it on every level.

"I'm too old to play it by the book, Val, and I'm too stubborn to be logical. I need your help." I looked him in the eye. "I *need* your help, but we've got to play it my way."

He sighed. "Have no fear, Mollitor. I trust you implicitly. I was just making observations." He cleared his throat. "Where to?"

"We'll need a transcon shuttle, fast. We have a couple stops to make and thousands of miles in between."

He thought about it for a moment. "I know just the place," he said. "There's a banker here who owes me several favors. Monsieur Roche."

"He has a transcon?"

"The bank does. Don't worry, he knows better than to refuse me. Very delicate position, bank president."

"Great," I said, laughing. "Lead on."

There was a mischievous look on his face.

"Shall we see what we remember from Canton?"

I followed his glance—a semicircle around us.

"Sure," I said. "Double-X pattern. Four on three."

We crossed the main boulevard, ducked into a side street and separated. I ran down an alley. We'd crisscross in four blocks. Johanson's tails were rank amateurs, that much was apparent. We'd have no trouble shaking them.

Four: San Francisco

XVI

It was four in the morning and very wet. Not raining, just wet. A salty wind cut through the mist, and every streetlight was a diffused glow in the watery atmosphere. Not even halogen stood a chance in this fog. Dawson couldn't see ten feet in front of her.

It didn't matter. Even without those ten feet, even without the invisible powers that let her sense curbs, vehicles, winos or assassins with only the barest effort—were she totally blind—Dawson would feel secure in this place. She could still draw, from memory, a map of San Francisco, detailing every alley, every omnishuttle route, without missing a squiggle. That's what ten years had done. The intervening twenty meant nothing; they could've been a century. For ten years, this had been her city, her turf to defend, and what she'd come to share with this place, time could never take away. It was something Mollitor never understood. For him, the universe existed in his head, and whoever he came into contact with, wherever he spent time, these were simply allowed access to that universe. When he moved on, what stayed behind became something of a ghost.

Until the accident, until her appointment as head of the San Fran Pool, Dawson had adopted much the same attitude. It was easy. Coordinating the Europools with Mollitor all those years was more a supervisory role, and their exploits took them to every corner of two continents. There was never time to acquire roots, no reason to attach special importance to any of the dozen bases they worked out of. That all changed in the '60s. San Francisco was her home, and any malady, any crisis striking this city would always feel like an attack upon her own person.

Dawson walked along the Embarcadero, remembering, scanning, thinking. She thought about Avery. It was, after all, the real reason she was here.

Paul Avery had been one of the brightest prospects Insight ever fielded. The son of a Pool agent, he'd approached HQ when he was only fifteen, and asked to have the powers he'd noted in himself trained to precision. He recruited himself. And he was a phenomenon. Telepathy, levitation, cloaking—he mastered all the details of psychics quickly and, in the process, showed a natural aptitude for leadership. Upon graduation from the Academy in '62, he was assigned to San Francisco. Dawson gave him as much responsibility as he could handle, and it wasn't long before Avery was chief of field operations, which meant he was coordinating agents across North America.

When she resigned the directorship in '69, Dawson felt secure leaving the position to Paul. The old-timers scoffed, but Insight's youngest director lived up to his mentor's expectations. Dawson had often felt a certain vindication in this; she was proud of the way he'd run her Pool. Their Pool. It made the news six months ago all the more painful. She knew the dangers of this business, but, somehow, you always assumed that you could go on dodging fate, that you could continue to avoid the big mistakes. You never figured anyone could blow up your apartment. When the investigation concluded that the blast had been psychic, and that it had come from *inside,* well, that posed more questions than it answered. And nothing she'd discovered since, in Paris or on Luna or from Vox, changed that. Not even Finney, Mr. Know-it-all, could explain it. There was no reason for Avery's death. He wasn't involved with Mary, he wasn't old Pool, he wasn't a high-profile operator at all.

Dawson felt around—she was close to the wharf. She smiled to herself. Vox's transcon pilot had offered to drop her anywhere in the city, almost insisted. There'd been no way to explain that she really had no preference, that walking aimlessly, one foot in front of the other in the fog, was exactly what she wanted to do at four in the morning. She stopped, faced west, listening to the waves rolling into the docks. Somewhere out there was Alcatraz, island of the pelicans, former prison, tourist site, always The Rock. Beyond that, the waves, and yesterday's sunset, and the gulls gliding in the Japanese wind. San Francisco was eternal. The War hadn't leveled it; the perennial earthquakes left only wounds.

Her scan began picking up signs of life, outlines. Two guys sleeping against a wall. Much lighter sleep waves of a dog down on the strip of sand. Here at the wharf, she could hear scattered activity: fishermen readying their boats, the rattle of lobster traps, the muffled chink of galoshes, metal slapping on leather, puddles splashed, the wooden docks creaking and groaning with footsteps. She smelled tobacco burning, just a wisp, then it was lost in the salty fog. The wooden post she stood next to was notched in dozens of places, chunks missing lower down, but it was still sound. She smiled, pounded the post lightly with her fist. It was good to be back.

She was purposefully avoiding any thought of Darby, she suddenly realized. Her first course of business here was obvious, and she knew the direction of the house, but it wasn't something she wanted to face just yet. Silly. She hadn't wanted to face it for twenty years; did she really think the feeling would change by morning? As if on cue, the first hint of light diffused through the mist. Dawson started walking again, to the end of the wharf, then to the left and up Van Ness. This was business, she told herself again, and she had to impress that upon him. Sure. First, *she* had to believe it.

It *was* business. She was here to find out what Darby knew about Avery's death (though he'd long been retired by then), and what he could tell her about the children's program. She was here to bounce ideas around and see where they led. And that was what was troubling her, because they would ultimately bounce away from business and back to Darby and Dawson. After ten years of the city, ten years of each other, she'd picked up and left, resigned the directorship, abandoned the relationship. To Darby, it would always be because Mollitor showed up, fresh from the battles in Europe; Darby had always seen it as having lost Dawson to a rival.

It wasn't simply the fear of continuing the misunderstanding. Dawson felt sure she could explain it now, that it had been less a choice of Mollitor over Darby than of renewing the continual risk and excitement of the unknown over a secure and peaceful directorship. After ten years, all the action in San Francisco fell within specified parameters. She'd tried, but you don't wait until you're a hundred to decide to settle down. No, what was frightening was the physical reality. The year was now 2089; the Darby she remembered was from twenty-five years ago, a man in his early forties. She remembered a handsome blond, a dynamic personality, rippling muscles; she remembered an intimate confidante and a wonderful lover. The thought of this man, this *image*, having become a seventy-year-old retired agent living on his pension was terrifying. It meant she couldn't correct the past, couldn't possibly make amends. The years had sealed their history.

Dawson took a deep breath, kept walking. It was a problem she and Mollitor had faced for years. The world went on, friends grew older, everything bore the mark of time—except them. It was only after the War that she'd started noticing. So many people had been killed; the friends that remained were valuable. And yet, the years kept rolling by, and, one by one, whether by natural timetable or by their own psychic clock, everyone steadily wore down; they withered and passed on. No one else ever perfected regenerative control. No matter how close she drew, no matter what she shared with others, the horrible attrition continued, until you were afraid to get too close, until the ephemeral nature of it all shut you off for good. It was unnerving. Dawson was fully prepared to die by any means in battle—laser, radiation, acid-gas, torture—rather than let her flesh feel the weight of her actual years.

She knew it was irrational. Vox was almost as old as Darby, and look at the shape he was in. Then there was Finney. He'd been Darby's partner in South America for years, and he was still in top form. He had to be close to ninety.

The bottom line was life. You continued beating the game until the moment it beat you. Frail and wrinkled, Elena kept the fire burning at a hundred and thirty. No, Dawson wasn't really afraid of wasting away to a shell. The fear she felt involved intimacy. Certain things weren't supposed to erode. People falling to the winds of time was one thing, but there was something eternal in what lovers shared. The sensations, the total reality should never be altered or denied, should always be exactly as—

No, she sighed. She was wrong. Nature wasn't arranged to deal with her. It was Dawson who was the freak, the mutant, it was she who remained young. It was silly to expect everyone else to as well. Nothing could change her memories of Darby, in the field or under the sheets, just as nothing could change Darby growing old or Dawson refusing to. You had to live your life as it unfolded. The present mattered; not the past, and barely the future.

All right. This was now. People were being killed.

Every psi agent on the planet was in danger, and this was no time to get mushy or scared or resigned. The fog began to lift. Her destination just a few blocks away; Dawson was ready to face it. The walk had done her good. The world was a barren, frightening place, but she would continue to be Dawson until the bitter end. She was too old, and too stubborn, to do otherwise.

XVII

She could've knocked, rang a doorbell, but somehow, it seemed absurd. If he were asleep (not a bad bet at five in the morning) she'd have to make a racket, and if he was awake, well, banging your knuckles on wood was a bit crude. She engaged the psi shield enveloping the house and flashed, *Jack? You there?*

Hello, Dawson. Come on in.

The door unlatched and swung open. The first thing she saw as she walked in was the fire, burning low in the fireplace, one end of a poker lying in the coals. The room felt very warm and dry after an hour on the foggy streets. The man sitting in the big chair against the wall had his hands folded in his lap. He wore a blue sweater and a pair of old work pants. His hair was white, but then, it had been almost white thirty years ago. He did look a lot older but, somehow, it wasn't at all frightening. The strength was still plain to see on his face. He seemed wide awake, as if he'd been expecting someone. He showed no particular emotion at seeing her, just shifted his hands in his lap and nodded. The eyes hadn't changed a bit; the clear blue was as penetrating as ever. The front door swung shut.

Welcome to an old man's humble abode.

She laughed nervously.

You look great, Jack.

Why not? A few wrinkles, a little arthritis. We Vikings never really get old.

What are you doing awake at this hour?

A ragged smile curled on his lips and Dawson's shoulders relaxed a little at the sight of a familiar mannerism.

Waiting for you, of course.

How—?

Simple. The magic Irishman paid a visit.

Finney?

My partner of old. Apparently, we're all back in business, beautiful.

"I—well, I mean—what do—"

She raised her arms and smiled sheepishly. She was confused. You don't grope for words when you're not using words in the first place. The transmission just goes blank and you stammer what you have to say on verbal. She took a deep breath and tried again.

"Can you bring me up to date? About the suicides. Wha—what did Finney tell you? When was he here?"

"He's here now. He's in the old HQ records department at this moment, if the bypass codes I gave him still work. What is it you want, Dawson?"

Her arms dropped to her sides and she stared at the floor, then at the fire. She'd been expecting something intense. This matter-of-fact attitude threw her.

"Actually," she said, "I'd like a hug."

"The all-purpose solution," he said with a laugh, and stood up slowly.

Dawson rushed over to him and held tightly, her head against his chest. She felt the tension fall away with the physical contact. It was all right, nothing to worry. He was an old man, but it was still Jack. They were partners again.

"That coat's pretty wet," he whispered. "Why don't you get out of it and I'll build up the fire."

He squeezed her shoulders, then moved away toward

the fireplace. Dawson shrugged out of the coat, watching his back. He moved a little stiffly, but it seemed natural. It was a relief that he was taking this so nonchalantly.

The poker lifted out of the coals, poked once or twice, then remained suspended while three small logs rose from the brick tile and slid onto the grating. Puffs of wind swirled the coals around until flames began licking the edges of the wood. Then the poker rested in the fire again. Darby's broad back relaxed. He unfolded his arms and half-turned toward her.

"Come get warm."

"I'm not cold, Jack."

"Come here anyway."

Dawson walked over, took his hand. They looked at each other for a moment, then turned and stared into the fire.

So, what are you doing here, Dawson? Backup for Finney?

No. I haven't even spoken to him since this business began.

I wonder when it did begin?

I mean the suicides.

Of course. He thinks it's Pool-generated.

That seems likely. You know what his angle is?

Something about Mary Z. She wave-locked a lot of research before she left San Francisco. Never been noticed.

What's he think?

He figures Mary either set time-delay codes or primed sleepers among her agents. When the time came, she triggered them and the psi-assaults began.

Do you buy that?

What do I know? I'm not on the case. Any theories of mine are based on information ten years old.

Dawson looked at him.

"It doesn't make sense," she said, switching to verbal. "Mary didn't mean us any harm. If she had, well, she set up the new computer system in Chicago. She helped re-build the whole operation. Insight was vulnerable enough at that point to crumble at the slightest tampering. There was no need for anything as devious as a coded death assault. Certainly not one set to engage in thirty years. It's ridiculous."

"I don't know. Maybe this wasn't intentional. But she was involved in some sort of secret program, and she was banking it for the future. The fact that it killed her suggests that she lost control of it."

"She never had control," said Dawson quietly. "Mary was on our side to the end. If the facts seem to indicate otherwise, then we're just reading them wrong." She shook her head. "It doesn't matter. I still want to know who killed Avery."

Darby nodded to himself and squeezed her hand.

"I tried to dig up what I could, but the Pool chased me away. No interference from retired operatives, they said."

"Who's they?"

"Fantello. He ran through the investigation and psi-autopsy as fast as possible."

"You think he's covering something up?"

"What's to cover up? The place was demolished. I got the same energy fields that Finney tells me he found around the others, but so what? You expected that."

"True," said Dawson. "Damn it. What about the kids. The children's program?"

"What about it?"

"I don't know if there's a connection. Our mole at ENCOM was killed by the assault. His final impress was full of references to San Francisco and the children's program. That's what led me here, in fact."

He held out his hands. "I don't know what to tell you. They used me as a consultant for a few years after I retired, up until they graduated the kids I'd begun training. I suppose—wait a minute . . ."

"What?"

"Well, it's a long shot. But if you want to continue ignoring what the facts seem to indicate—that is, that Paul killed himself, induced or not—then there *is* a possible suspect."

Her eyebrows went up. "Really?"

"Sure. The Rat. San Francisco's own bad boy. You haven't heard of the Rat?"

She shrugged. "No. Should I have?"

"Not necessarily. Local politics. Come on, sit down," he said, moving to his chair. "I'll tell you about the Rat—Lupu."

"Wait a minute, I know that name. Lupu. Wasn't he—oh damn, I can't place it. Pacifica? Was that it?"

"You're thinking of the old man. Carl Lupu was a Pacific operative in the '40s. Retired '56, died of a heart attack in '67. This is his kid, Eric. They put him in the children's program as soon as he could talk. Trained by yours truly." He gave a short laugh, shook his head. Dawson sat down. "The kid was a whiz," said Darby. "He didn't even have to try. When I left in '78, he was, oh, thirteen or thereabouts, and he was running through every simulation drill we had in record time." He sighed. "He was good, but what a bastard."

"A thirteen-year-old?"

"Oh, absolutely. He was cruel. He'd purposefully try and injure people during training. That's when they started calling him Rat. He had this long face with thin, greasy hair, and no one dared turn their back on him."

"So what is he now?"

"Now he's a gang leader in the city. He dropped out of the program when he was nineteen and spent a few years as a petty thief up and down the coast. Finally came back to his roots. He's got one hell of a grapevine. First-class operation."

"And he's fighting us? For how long? Why hasn't Chicago been—"

"Take it easy. Lupu has virtually nothing to do with the Pool. He runs guns to the islands, smuggles dope, a little extortion, some currency scams—your basic criminal setup. No intelligence department to speak of. No espionage. He's just interested in making money and pulling the wings off flies."

"Oh, lovely. A man with a purpose."

"It's what you get when you combine power and immaturity."

"So why would he be after Avery?"

Darby leaned back. "Paul filed a report on Lupu's activities the end of last year. I don't really know what was in it—Paul and I hadn't kept in close contact and Fantello never talked to me about anything—but I would guess it was pretty detailed. I do know that he'd been worried about Lupu's psi activity for some time."

She thought about that for a moment.

"He's strong, you say?"

He nodded.

"Strong enough to kill Avery like that?"

Darby spread his hands. "Who could know that? I left Insight when he was thirteen. Based on where he was then—if he kept gaining power at that rate—hell yes, he could blow through any shield by now. I just don't think he had the technical know-how to get to Paul in the first place."

"Who, in the Agency, had contact with him last?"

"Fantello took over the children's program from me. He would know. But good luck getting any answers from him."

"You don't like him much, do you? Fantello."

"What's to like? He's a stupid, egotistical lout. He owes his appointment to some favor he did the Old Man. Just like everyone else these days."

He sounds so bitter, she thought.

"Why not?" he said, glancing at her sideways. Then he grew quieter. "The whole Pool's gone to hell. It could've been great once. Even after the mess Johanson caused, there were possibilities. We had a fine operation, right here in San Fran, before we thoroughly botched it."

Dawson stared at him, bit her lip. "Because I left?"

Their eyes met.

"Partially. Paul was capable, but he didn't have the experience with people. Snakes like Fantello kept working their way in. I was in no shape to help him, anyway."

"Look, Jack, I— "

"Save it, Dawson," he said softly. "It's over. It doesn't really matter anymore. For now, it's enough that we're friends, and I don't want any of that old bullshit to get in the way." He held out his hand to silence her. "I don't want to hear it. No, I haven't forgotten, and no, I don't forgive you, but that's my business. Let's just bury it and go from there."

Dawson didn't say anything. Her eyes moved around, searching for something to rest on.

Come on, Dawson, he flashed. *Are we here to plot strategy or not?*

After a few moments, she sighed.

Okay. What does Finney want to do about Lupu?

I only mentioned him in passing, to Finney. But it wouldn't matter. In Finney's one-track mind, it's all Mary. He wants to unearth whatever it was she was planning, and to hell with any side tracks.

It's ridiculous. Avery and Mary had nothing to do with one another.

That's what it looks like, but who knows what Paul discovered. He was *director.*

So was I, right after Mary. And you were interim director before I showed up. If there was some bizarre time trip lurking around, we would've spotted it the first few years after she left. It wouldn't sit around to be found by Paul thirty years later.

You don't know *that, Dawson. We weren't looking for anything. Paul may've been.*

Why? There were no suicides at that point. He was the first.

You've got a point. I don't know.

Dawson blanked the wave and thought to herself. Behind this whole business was some superpsychic force randomly attacking psi energy surges. Here was Lupu, a potential superpsychic in his own right, and Finney was ignoring him. Well, to be fair, maybe Darby hadn't impressed the full scope of the threat. Maybe Finney was just searching for a way to neutralize the Rat's power before tackling him. In any event, it seemed that Dawson's next move should be to confront Lupu herself. She hadn't faced the assault that Finney and Mollitor had; she therefore lacked their reservations toward meeting the source.

"How would someone get in contact with Lupu," she asked Darby.

He squinted at her. "It would depend on what someone had to sell or wanted to buy. You?" She nodded. Darby shook his head and chuckled. "Lupu doesn't book social engagements. It's got to be business and, to meet the boss, himself, it's got to be big."

"And if it were?"

"Grapevine. Just leave word in the right places and he'll find you."

"No good. I'm not giving him that kind of edge." She tapped her foot, thinking. "Where would *you* look?"

"You mean, if I wanted to take him by surprise?"

"Right."

"I'd have to find a back way into his hideout. That means information, and that means calling in some old favors."

"Got any lying around?"

Darby got up and walked across the room. "Chinatown," he said, spreading his hand on the wall next to the window. "It's probably not the best shot, but I've been out of circulation for a while. Wan Lee's. It's a grocery; there's a tearoom in back." He cocked his head to one side, kept his hand flush to the wall.

"What is it?"

"I'm not sure. I felt something disturb the shield out there."

Dawson's eyes darted around the room. She fanned a widebeam scan through the walls into the street, the alley in back, through the houses on either side and a hundred feet up for hovers.

"Nothing," she said. "You're sure?"

"Something pushed on the shield and jumped back when it met resistance." He turned around to face her, raised his eyebrows. "Oh well. I don't sense anything, either."

"I don't like it. No one should be snooping around here. You have no connection; you're not even an agent."

"Who's your backup?"

"Nobody, this soon."

Darby put a hand on her shoulder. "Forget it, Dawson. Whatever it was, if it's afraid to show itself, I'm not worried. And if it does—well, I'm not completely helpless, you know."

She looked at him. "No, of course not. I'm just—this has been a crazy week. I'm a little jumpy."

"You should live in the land of earthquakes. It does wonders for the nerves."

"You're no indication," she said, smiling. "You were always the calm one."

"Okay, so what's the plan?"

"Plan?"

"You want Lupu, that's obvious. Okay, we'll get him. Just tell me how you want to work it: Hard scam, soft scam, hit and lure, push-pull? I don't care. If we're back in business, you're the boss. What do you look so shocked about?"

"Jack, I—I don't know—I'm not sure you should be . . ." She stopped, dropping her hands to her sides, shook her head slowly. Darby's eyes narrowed.

"No, don't finish the thought. Don't even play with the idea. If I've let myself get so feeble that one lousy mission will kill me, then fifty years of work have been for nothing. Or maybe this is what all the years have been training for, one last burst. Either way . . ."

"Jack, we're talking about a force that's sweeping aside agents who *are* in shape. It's just . . ."

The lines in his face relaxed. "So maybe I'm not a superspy anymore. If it's all the same to you, I'd just as soon die trying." He smiled. "What do you want from me, Dawson? This has been my entire life. And anyway, someone's got to keep you out of trouble."

"Okay," she sighed. "How would *you* prefer to work it?"

He scratched his chin. "Back to the basics. Can you do Finney's shadow trick?"

"Close enough."

"All right. I'll run profile on the outside. We'll hit Chinatown and you can watch my back while I get the info. Once we're inside, you lead and I'll cover."

She smiled. "That's a switch."

"Hey, I am aware of some realities. Lupu could blow me away without half trying at this point. Okay, do we need equipment?"

Dawson tapped her temple. "As long as our timing's right, we shouldn't need anything else."

Darby took a long green cloak off the hook on the door,

handed it to her, then went to the closet and pulled out a tan trench coat. He draped it over his shoulders and turned to Dawson.

"Let's go. Chinatown opens early."

He held out his hand, and the tweed cap jumped off the mantle. He caught it, then clicked open the door.

"Show-off," said Dawson. She snapped her fingers at the fire, and the flames immediately died to a smolder.

He took her hand.

"So are you, which is why we get along."

XVIII

Grant Street smelled of fish. All sorts of articles were unloading from transports up and down the street; dull plastic antigrav cases floating down from hovers, reusable slat-and-chicken-wire crates tossed from the back of trucks by burly delivery men. Fish was, by far, the most pungent merchandise being delivered. Smoke rose from the alleys in back, giving the salty air an added thickness. The activity was sporadic and noisy along the narrow street. The soft chatter of Chinese was accentuated by coarse shouts in English, a little Spanish here and there. A few kids milled about, waiting for an orange to bounce free of a crate, a grocer to take his eye off a smaller case for just long enough. Some of the teenagers sidled up to the trucks, offering to help unload for a few coins. Dogs sniffed at the curb, ducking away from tires and ladders and vicious feet. Horns honked. Good morning, Chinatown.

"Surprised?" asked Darby, as they came out of a side street into the middle of it. "It hasn't changed."

Dawson looked up and down the street, nodding, smiling. She felt a tingle run down her back. "That's truer than you know," she said. "Take away those hovers and it was exactly like this a hundred years ago."

"Same shops, huh?"

"Same buildings, anyway."

"What else?"

"Same high prices."

"Fish?"

She nodded solemnly. "Fish."

They turned up the street.

"What about Fantello?" Dawson said, kicking a pebble off the curb. "They didn't really make him director, did they?"

Darby buried his hands in his trench coat.

"Acting director, they called it. He's the boss of the children's program. As far as Chicago's concerned, that's the city's main purpose. Very few missions originate here any more. The Pool keeps its eye peeled for any Intertel or ENCOM activity that arises. If nothing shows up, then our illustrious agents leave messages for each other in obvious drops, putter about the office and collect their paychecks. Fantello was simply the most logical nonentity to fill a useless position."

"Ugh."

"Been that way for ten years, progressively worse." He smiled. "I did quit for a reason, you know. Creaking bones aside."

A blond-haired kid, about ten years old, fell into step next to Darby.

"Got any spare change, mister?" he said, holding his palm out. Darby's hand started out of its pocket.

"But it was precisely that vacuum of activity," he said to Dawson, "that allowed the Rat to dig in here and set up shop." His empty hand came out and tousled the kid's hair. The kid jerked his head away and stopped, letting them walk on. "Who knows?" said Darby. "Maybe he would've done it anyway."

"Thanks, asshole," the kid called at their backs.

"You're not going to give him anything?"

"I've gone the limit until Monday," he said wearily. "I hand out twenty bucks a week, that's it." He looked at her. "Believe me, Dawson, there isn't enough spare change in the world to take care of all of them."

They walked the next block quietly.

"Okay," said Darby, hand on her shoulder. "It's a hundred yards ahead."

Flash it.

"No. Be careful with the waves. The oriental edge to this city has grown since the '60s. You understand? There are a lot of marginal telepaths around."

"I thought you said the Pool has nothing to do these days."

"Petty crime is currently very big. Trust me. Low polarity on the shield, pinpoint scans only."

"The place is on the right?" She glanced across the street and back, then up along the roofs.

He nodded. "Opens onto an alley in back. Little path, ends at Kearny. Down the block's the Pyramid."

"I remember the streets quite well, thank you."

"Sorry, it's been a while. I'm excited."

She was all business now. "Let's just find Lupu."

She kissed him quickly and turned the collar of the cloak up. She walked close to the storefronts, and then the walk became a shuffle and the blond hair seemed muddy, and she pushed through a crowd of men arguing over a broken crate and then Darby couldn't pick her out at all. He sighed, and started up the block for Wan Lee's.

Dawson walked the extra block to the end of Grant Street and made the sharp right onto Kearny. Everything opened up, a wider road, buildings a little newer and larger, much less sidewalk traffic. Only the storefronts that backed Chinatown had that red-brick-and-bay-window look. She stayed on that side of the street. Four blocks ahead loomed the old Transamerica Building, a huge, three-sided pyramid some twenty stories high. Halfway to the Pyramid was the Clock. Dawson smiled. She *had* forgotten. She made her way to it, moving quickly past the parked cars, optiflicker high, alarm shield up, autoscanning the alley a hundred feet through the buildings to her right, as she came to her favorite San Francisco landmark.

The Clock was dark green, twelve feet high, imbedded in the sidewalk, with heavy double-pane glass over a face marked in big roman numerals. It had been placed here somewhere around the late 1800s. Dawson had stopped now and then, during the '60s, just to look at it, to touch the green, flaking metal, to stand in the presence of something far older than she. When you're a hundred years old yourself, there are few things that give you a sense of actual history. The War had decimated a good many of them. The Kearny Street Clock was a relic, much more personal than, say, the Golden Gate Bridge, that she cherished, if only for its longevity. She held the base and looked up, sighed. Ten to seven.

Darby.

She cut down the path, between stores, through one deadend alley into the next. She scanned, found the back of the tearoom and leaned against a big dumpster a few yards down, opposite the door. She moved some gravel and glass around with her foot, felt the stubbly wall next to her. No impresses. A dog walked by, then a wino, singing in a soft slur. Neither noticed her.

Dawson pinpointed a probe into the tearoom, hooked onto Darby's vibration. He was excited, metabolism up, but his movements seemed perfectly normal. A professional, she thought, even ten years rusty. She scanned along the soot-darkened roofs lining the alley, picked up one light shield set around a rickety wooden balcony. Nothing suspicious in it; even without Darby's warning, she knew that the Chinese had always had random power. Then something nudged her leg, just above the knee, and she jumped to the side.

"Hey, take it easy." It was the little blond kid from Grant Street. She stared at him. Faded corduroys, sneakers, torn quilted windbreaker. How the hell did he sneak up on her?

"What do you want?" she snapped.

"You already know what I want," he said, rubbing his thumb and two fingers together. "But *you* want the Rat. It's easy. All you had to do was ask."

Her eyes got large. Who was this kid? She shot a probe at him and, unexpectedly, hit a heavy blanking shield. The kid felt it, pivoted and sprayed gravel as he dodged back up the path. Dawson put a hand on her hip and stood there. The kid's head peeked back from around the corner.

"Don't do that stuff, lady."

Dawson held out both hands in a peaceful gesture.

"I want to talk to Lupu."

He nodded, but didn't say anything, didn't move. She got the uncomfortable feeling that he was stalling for time.

"Can you take me to him?" He still made no move. Dawson reached into her pocket and pulled out a few bills. The kid's eyes registered the offer. He glanced back over his shoulder; she scanned. Two medium-sized dogs were coming down the path. She deepened the scan, puzzled. My God, it dawned on her—he's in contact with the dogs.

"Sure," he said, "follow me." He squinted for a moment. "Only no more of that stuff. Stay away from my shield."

"I've got to let—"

"No!" he said, eyes flashing. "Leave him out of this. You come now, alone, or forget it." The dogs appeared, flanked the kid, one a shepherd, the other a black lab mongrel. They both looked streetwise and efficient.

Dawson glanced once more at the tearoom door, then back to the kid. No use blowing a lucky lead. She impressed a vibration into the dumpster, a trail for Darby to follow.

"Let's go," she said.

The kid took the money and stuffed it into his jacket. He and the dogs turned as one and led the way back out to Kearny Street.

They made their way quickly to Market, then left to the bay. The kid resisted all of Dawson's efforts to converse. Once or twice she thought he was transmitting, but she had to pick it up peripherally, so she couldn't be sure. It seemed low-frequency anyway; he was probably just talking to the dogs. She left sidewalk impresses for Darby until they got to the Embarcadero.

The kid looked up and down the wide, curving street. Then he glanced at his dogs and dashed across. Still a ways from the pier, he hopped over a dirt mound and grabbed an iron rung set in the ground. Dawson and the dogs stood a few feet away, watching. The kid looked up at her.

"Can you help me?" he asked, tugging on the ring to no effect.

"You can't move it?"

He gave a sarcastic snort. "C'mon lady, how strong do I look?"

"Get out of the way."

He frowned and stepped back. Dawson clenched her left fist with a jerk, and the cover rose four feet off the ground and hovered there. The kid's eyes went wide.

"Wow."

"You want me to pull it back in after us?"

"Sure. Thanks." He started in.

"How will you get back out?"

"Don't worry, there are other openings." He looked over at the dogs. The black mongrel trotted over and jumped into the hole. The kid lowered himself. "There's a ladder . . ."

"Go on," said Dawson. She climbed in after him, stopped with her head still aboveground and looked back at the German shepherd. He wasn't going anywhere, just standing guard. She scanned him; he was shielded. Weird, she thought, closing the opening behind her.

The passage was ten feet high, five wide, very dull light coming from yellow bulbs spaced every fifty feet along the ceiling. She scanned through the walls. More rock, water farther back, a network of passages ahead. No one else in the vicinity. She started toward the network.

"Hey, where are you going?"

She turned. "You want to lead?"

He looked upset about something.

"I told you to stay off my shield."

"How am I supposed to know your shield includes the dogs?"

"Well, it does."

"You want to lead?"

"Sure," he said sullenly. He and the dog slipped past her.

The corridor was smooth concrete, surprisingly well insulated from the wet. Dawson gauged the layout of the city above from their direction. They were cutting across the warehouse district, headed roughly for the Bay Bridge. She didn't recognize the passages, though. This had to be an old maintenance tunnel, abandoned long before Dawson's tenure in the city. It didn't seem as deep as the present sewer system, certainly not as far down as the transport lines. All the same, someone had kept this place up; the light bulbs had to be changed periodically.

"Do you work for Lupu?" Dawson asked. The kid didn't answer, just kept walking ahead with the dog. "How close are we?"

He pointed. Twenty feet ahead the passage widened, and several paths converged. Dawson was getting a little tired of this. She stopped walking and dropped a physical force shield five feet in front of her guides. The dog immediately froze and growled low in his throat. The kid spun around.

"What's the—"

"Get this through your head," said Dawson, pointing. "I have no intention of walking into a trap. Now I want some answers, and I'm going to get them. Do you understand?"

The dog's growl grew louder; he bared his teeth.

"Don't play with me," she said. "I don't want to hurt you or your dog. Tell me if you're working for Lupu."

The kid glared at her. "He pays me sometimes. Depends."

"Does he know we're coming?"

"Not yet."

"When will he know?"

"Depends."

She glared back. This was pointless. She was better off immobilizing them both and finding her own way. Suddenly, she sensed movement beyond the kid, at the intersection. *Don't take chances*. She blew through the dog's shield with a quick thrust and froze his muscles, brushed the kid aside and leaped past him, scanning ahead. She hit a heavier shield than expected. As she locked on to dissolve it, a hooded shape jumped from around the corner and stood in the main passage, hands up submissively.

"Chill it, lady," it said. "No tumble. Loose up the wave."

The voice sounded female. Dawson stayed locked on the shield, shifted her stance to keep one eye on the kid.

"Drop your hood."

It fell away with a shake. She was a girl, fourteen maybe, straight black hair to her shoulders, high cheekbones, tanned complexion, slightly slanted eyes. She looked sort of American Indian/Chinese.

"Ease the dog, hey?" she said. "Ragaloo, you proper?"

"Target," said the kid, then he turned to Dawson. "Leave the dog alone. He won't bother you."

Dawson released the freeze, but stayed ready.

"Who are you?" she asked the girl.

"One sec." She met the kid's eyes. "Book. I'll straight it from here."

"Who floats the coin?" he asked.

"You'll get. Chill it. You'll get a wave."

He nodded and took off, back the way they'd come. The dog growled at Dawson and followed. The footsteps died away. The girl slouched, cocked her head, sizing Dawson up.

"You glim?"

"I'm sorry, I don't know what you're talking about."

She gave Dawson a sour look. "Okay, no glim. We talk flat."

"That would be nice. What's your name?"

"Feena. You want to ease that wave, or what?"

Dawson let go of the shield. "My name's Dawson. You can take me to Lupu?"

"Target. Let's go." She started up one of the passages.

"One minute," said Dawson. "You work for Lupu?"

The girl laughed. "No one works for the Rat. Keep clear. Float a favor and he doesn't twist you too bad. You coming?"

"I'm coming. No tricks, though."

The girl had an odd smile on her face.

"No tricks. You seem proper, lady. We'll see . . ."

XIX

The further they went, the more difficult it became for Dawson to gauge direction. There was something in the walls that kept her scans from fixing on the city above. At first it seemed the walls were treated, or lead-lined, but, eventually, it occurred to her that there was nothing actually stopping the scans; they were just being misdirected. There was something ominously familiar about it.

Feena consistently avoided all the larger routes, preferring roundabout paths that doubled back in confusing loops. They moved steadily downward. When Dawson came to a corridor she felt sure they'd already intersected twice, she stopped and engaged the girl's shield.

"Why are we avoiding certain passages?"

"You primed for a head-on with the guards?"

Dawson was puzzled. "You're not one of the guards?"

"The Rat's guards don't straight strangers. They just freeze you, drag you by your hair for a pervert session. 'Specially you," she said, regarding Dawson's body. "Come on. Keep on step."

They began walking again.

"How do you live down here?"

"Got a nest," said Feena. "Swing contacts with some of the topsiders for food. Ragaloo's proper."

"The kid with the dogs?"

"Target. Pass people and stats by the vine and the Rat floats coin. Pretty proper contract."

"And the guards don't bother you?"

Feena gave an involuntary shudder. "Already been through a couple sessions. Been a while. They want fresh faces, anyway."

Dawson looked at the girl. If she'd had no personal grievance against Lupu until now, she was acquiring one quickly.

"Who does? Lupu?"

"Bad wave. We just say 'the Rat.' You're funny, lady; you flash a tough wave."

"Tell me about the Rat."

Feena stopped, looked at Dawson, then stared off at a blank spot on the wall.

"It's bad. It's all his choice. When he tangles you, it's body and mind. Like ice, you glim? We're sparklies, what do you name them?" She thought about it. "Toys, all toys."

Dawson's eyes were large. "Why, in God's name, do you stay down here?"

The girl shrugged, began walking again. "Nowhere to vanish. I book topstreet and the Rat would glim, flash me dead. It's pretty proper down here."

Flash me dead? Was that a true representation of his power, or just the exaggeration of a terrorized girl?

"Listen. Feena, this doesn't have to go on. If you can get me to Lupu without his knowing, I swear I'll put him out of action."

"You're funny, lady," she said again, "—not even a blankshield."

Dawson thought about that. Both the kids *did* have strange shields. They were basically just vibration suppressors. They did no scanning, and had no real defensive power. The shields were easily as strong as Mafia implants, though. There was no way to sense the kids until you saw them.

"Okay. How do I stay invisible?"

"Chill the heavy scans. It's a giveaway."

Great, thought Dawson, how am I supposed to sneak up on someone if I can't scan?

"You'll help me get in?"

"You are in, lady." Feena pointed ahead at the wall.

"That's a sneakhole." She looked around. "You glim to skate the guards, you straight it that way."

Dawson lightly probed the grating. No sensors. She jerked it loose and looked down at the girl.

"Would you come with me?"

Feena looked worried. "Don't know. Maybe I shouldn't've glimmed you to it. They tangle me, I'm twisted bad."

"I'll protect you. Wait, watch, I'll show you."

Dawson spotted a loose brick on the floor, levitated it four feet and clenched both fists. Her arms trembled. She snapped her eyes shut and the brick crumbled with a sharp crack. Dust sprinkled the floor. Feena's mouth dropped open. There was an awe in her eyes that shifted to excitement.

"Okay?" said Dawson

"Target. It may connect proper. I'll take the bet."

The duct was just tall enough for Feena to walk upright; Dawson had to crouch. She shot light pinpoint scans every few minutes, nothing long or strong enough to trigger a sensor. As they passed into a second and then a third series of ducts, Dawson began to get a fix on their location. The insignias on the wall were the giveaway. These tunnels connected the old U.S. Navy base on Treasure Island with the city. The installation itself had been closed after the War, but Lupu had apparently excavated the bunkers and passages for his own use. It was a pretty smart place for a hideout. No one bothered anymore with the island, certainly not belowground. If you knew the layout of the tunnels, you could maintain access to most parts of San Francisco without ever showing yourself on the streets.

They were nearing some kind of activity. Dawson could see a soft radiance ahead; it felt warmer. Feena put her mouth to Dawson's ear.

"Wides out ahead. Guards, maybe."

Dawson nodded. She crept up a ways, one hand on the wall, sensing. She picked up one vibration, then a second. Twenty more feet and she could hear two men talking. A hoarse laugh. It came from around a left curve, maybe fifty feet total. She put a finger to her lips and motioned Feena to stay put. This had to be quick and to the point. No footsteps. Dawson levitated a couple inches and glided around the corner. One of the guards happened to be looking her way. Oh well, she thought, so much for surprise.

She filled the hallway with a massive vibe overload and leaped at them. The one who'd seen her brought up his arm to meet Dawson's, but momentum was working against him. He fell backward, went into a roll and jumped to his feet as the other one reacted. Dawson didn't even look. She hit him in the temple with her heel, and his head bounced once on the wall before he slithered to the ground. Then she faced the first one. They were both crouching, fingers curled, matching shift for shift. She could see he was a trained fighter, but it didn't matter. He wasn't going to send any transmissions through the overload, and, eventually, when he closed to strike . . .

He did. He feinted with a hand and shot a kick at head level. Dawson spun under it and chopped across on his knee, reversed a backhand to his nose. He stumbled back a step, and the cracked kneecap couldn't hold the weight. She dodged behind as he fell, put her knee against his spine and yanked his head back, two fingers at his throat.

"You keep very quiet now," she said, "or you're dead. Where's Lupu?"

She ripped away his shield and probed. There was no way for him to keep from thinking of the answer. *The main hall*, wherever that was. She dug deeper.

Who's with him?

Bruno and the old guy. That didn't tell her much, but at least she knew how many. She pinched a nerve at the base of his neck and let go as he passed out.

"Dyno, Lady," said Feena. "Total dyno. You're the zippest twister I ever saw."

"Where's the main hall?"

"Dead on," she said, pointing ahead. "Told you this was a sneakhole."

Dawson got up. There was no way to check if any autosensors had registered the disturbance, not unless she wanted her scan to trip them anyway. The passage went a couple hundred yards before ending at a circular hall. She could tell it was circular because there were arches cut into the inside wall every thirty feet. Looking through the one ahead, she could see a row of them across a wide open space. She glanced back at Feena; the girl had a hand to her mouth and a terrified look in her eye. This had to be the place.

Dawson moved silently into the arch and peeked. The ceiling was fifty feet above and the floor about the same distance down. The whole room was a big concrete circle some hundred feet straight across. Shelves of books and a huge databank took up half the far curve. The floor space was furnished as comfortably as possible, considering what they had to work with. Two large oriental rugs, several armchairs and endtables surrounding one massive rectangular worktable in the center. It was wood, and covered with papers, maps, pens, calculators and the like. Two men stood at it. The bigger of the two was dressed in a tee-shirt and jeans. He was nearly as big as the Baron: huge shoulders, barrel chest. He had a tiny head topped with a mass of brown curls. The guy next to him stood about three heads shorter. He had a long thin face, lank black hair to his shoulders, a wiry body dressed in jeans and a red jacket. He was pointing at a map and talking softly to the big guy without looking up; the big guy kept nodding. There was a cough from the armchair nearest Dawson. Whoever sat there was hidden by the high back of the chair. Another cough, then a hand reached for a tissue from the box on the endtable. Dawson's eyes went wide. "Bruno and the old man . . ." It hadn't occurred to her that Lupu could be the silent partner Vox had mentioned. The pieces were falling into place. *Johanson.*

He spun around, half out of the chair, stared up along the wall.

"Lupu! There's someone here."

Dawson blanked, motioned Feena, at the next arch, to silence. Lupu looked up from the table.

"Really?" he said. The voice sounded breathy, hoarse. "I pay these guards good wages. Must I do everything myself?"

Dawson watched him closely. He was scanning. She felt the vibration touch her shield, and quickly readjusted her frequency to remain invisible.

"Why yes," he said, "there is someone there. Come here."

Feena started backing away.

"I said *come here!*" he shouted, clenching his fist. Feena gave a cry as her body jerked forward, and she flew through the opening, fifty feet down and thirty across in a straight line, crashing in a heap at Lupu's feet. "What do we have here?" he said, turning her over with his foot. "Ah, little Feena. What games are we playing today? Hmm, no answer?" He reached for a handful of hair, wrenched her head to his waist. "Shall we simply tear it from your little mind or shall we first allow Bruno to make you a bit more . . . pliant?"

"That's enough, Lupu," said Dawson, stepping into view high above. "*I'm* the information she has. I forced her to lead me here."

He let go of Feena's hair and stepped past her. Johanson, at the sound of the voice, jumped up and stood, frozen, next to his chair.

"*You*," he said in a whisper, then turned to Lupu. "Do you know who this—?"

"Silence!" said Lupu with a wave. "This is my domain. Will you join us, my dear, or shall I bring you as I brought the other?"

Dawson said nothing. She stepped out of the arch into midair, dropped lightly to the ground. She and Lupu scanned simultaneously, testing each other's shields. No effect.

"I know this one, Lupu," said Johanson. "She's far more dangerous than you think."

"You don't know how dangerous I think she is, do you?" he said. "In any event, she's a guest." His eyes didn't waver, didn't blink. One solid color. Dawson had never seen eyes like that; a totally black sheen coming off them. "An uninvited guest. We have procedures for dealing with such guests. And Bruno *is* growing weary of these children. I think he would appreciate a mature woman, wouldn't you, Bruno?"

No one said anything. Lupu's voice, for all its hoarseness, had a calming effect. He could announce a dismembering with the same equanimity as ordering a cheeseburger and fries.

"Well, my dear, how do you like Bruno?"

"I came here to talk to you, Lupu," said Dawson, not taking her eyes off him. "Seeing Johanson with you makes me wonder if there's any point. Still, it's worth a try."

"Indeed. To talk. Now that is interesting. I've always thought of myself as a man of *action*."

He slammed through Dawson's shield and a white flash exploded in her head. The sheer ferocity of the attack took her by surprise. She staggered to her knees and locked onto the vibration, dissolving the frequency. She parried his next blast and felt a big chunk of her shield crumble. He was incredibly strong; she needed to distract him for a second. She focused, and the big table exploded into slivers, throwing Bruno across the room. Lupu crashed into Johanson and they both went down, but his attention wavered for only an instant. He flashed another thrust. Dawson met it with one of her own and grabbed her forehead, wincing at the recoil. The dust was settling; she got to her feet. Lupu stood up, blinking, holding his head. She had the second she'd wanted. Her nerve probe slithered around his shield and lanced into his motor center. Got to slow him down, she thought. He grunted, shoulders twitching, then dissolved the frequency before it could solidify. Their shields locked. Dawson knew hers was no match.

"Quite a fighter," said Lupu. "You've fought Johanson before?" He didn't seem aware of the damage her nerve probe had done. Dawson said nothing. "And you let him live? Truly a humanitarian."

"Damn it!" said Johanson. "Don't play with her." He stood up, brushing himself off. "Kill her now. If you need my help . . ."

"When I need your help, old man," he snarled, "it'll be for planning. Not execution." He glared at Johanson.

Dawson threw herself ten feet into a flying kick aimed at Lupu's chest. He flashed an overwhelming psi-thrust, and she felt her shield rip away and the white light sear her brain again. Lupu started to twist, but he had no chance. He folded in two as Dawson's foot slid off his sternum. The half-twist had protected his heart. He couldn't stop his ribs from cracking, though, and couldn't keep from being driven back into the bookshelves. The entire rack collapsed on him. He was out.

Dawson rolled on the rug, trying to clear her head. The force of that blast was still ringing, and her eyes couldn't focus yet. A hand grabbed her by the hair, lifted her clear off her feet and a collar snapped around her neck. She recognized the vibration; one of Johanson's oscillators. She opened her eyes, and there was Bruno, leering at her. He spun her around, slammed her between the shoulder blades and she hit the floor face first. Her arms were jerked behind her back, metal snapped over the wrists.

"Turn her over," barked Johanson.

Dawson was flipped over, wincing as her body came down on the cuffed hands. Blood flowed from her nose. Bruno sat on her legs as Johanson fastened the ankle cuffs. She couldn't send anything; the collar kept scrambling the vibrations. She struggled, and Bruno punched her in the stomach. Dawson gasped for breath. Then Johanson was leaning over her face.

"I should kill you now, princess," he hissed, "but I don't wish to anger my partner. Consider yourself on reprieve." Bruno slapped her, smiled, slapped her again and began squeezing her breasts. "None of that, now," said Johanson. "Take her to a cell."

Bruno looked up. "What about the Rat?"

"I'll see to your precious boss. Just take her away and leave her. Understand? We want her intact."

Bruno looked down at Dawson and growled, "C'mon." He grabbed her by the shirt and stood, lifting her off the ground. Dawson hung backward like a limp doll. Johanson hurried over to Lupu and began untangling him from the rubble.

"Just drop her and come right back," he said. "I'll need your help with him."

Bruno went out one of the doors and along a curved corridor. Dawson was helpless. She couldn't move her arms or legs and couldn't transmit. Nothing to do but stare at the ceiling and grit her teeth. He came to a door and kicked it open, walked in. He stood her up and looked at her, the front of her shirt still knotted in his hand. The green cloak clung to one shoulder, and there was blood on it, from her nose and mouth,

"You're a real mess," he said, and straight-armed her in the face with his free hand. The front of her shirt ripped away as she flew across the little room, hit the wall with a thud. She slid to the ground, still conscious. Bruno dropped the scrap of material and licked his lips.

"You're lucky, bitch, that we got no time for this, now," he said, patting his groin. "But I'll see you later."

He turned and slammed the door with a boom.

XX

Dawson squirmed into a comfortable position against the wall. One thing was certain—Darby had exaggerated neither Lupu's power nor his viciousness. That was one evil punk in there.

First things first. The collar had to go. Johanson had obviously forgotten that they'd cracked the code. She ran through the frequency series and the oscillation cut off for five seconds. She severed the leather. Next, the cuffs. She popped the locks and began massaging her wrists and ankles. Lucky this isn't Johanson's hideout, she thought, he'd have another of those psi-tombs ready for me.

Johanson. He wasn't the focus now. She remembered how Lupu had talked to him. Yeah, it was just like Johanson. Sitting in Paris, having beat the suicide program himself, how could he pass up an opportunity to get close to the source of this power, to protect himself? But for what?

What could Johanson offer Lupu? Wealth, sure, but Lupu was doing fine on his own. Technology, most likely. Johanson was still the wizard. With his know-how, and Lupu's strength, they could easily have blown up Paul.

Dawson's nose was still bleeding. She set an impact shield on the door and removed the cloak and ragged remains of her shirt. She tore the bottom half of the cloak into strips, put the top half back on and tied it together in three places. No fashion plate, but what the hell, she was clothed. She held the old shirt to her bloody nose.

What had Lupu said to J? ". . . I need your help for planning . . ." It was Johanson who knew the ins and outs of psychic espionage. It was Johanson who knew about Weatherly's power-transfer theories, Johanson who probably wiped that computer file at ENCOM. Johanson, as always, was the invisible brains of the operation. But, so what? Dawson knew the limits of *his* power. Lupu was the unknown factor. She thought about the fight. All of his attacks had been direct, just straight, overwhelming waves. He'd dissolved her nervethrust only after it hit. Obviously, he was limited in his handling of variable frequency. This wasn't really surprising; finesse came with experience and, for all his power, Lupu was still a twenty-five-year-old novice. There were ways to beat him, if she played it tricky. The hard part was going to be surviving his attack in the meantime. Dawson dropped into a deep meditative wave, recharging her energy while running through the frequencies and intensities of Lupu's vibration. Everyone psi-attacked according to a set pattern, although only experienced fighters recognized this. Next time, she'd be ready for him.

Two hours later, she felt a lot better. She considered the loose ends. Darby might or might not find his way in here. She'd left vague impresses; he'd have to beat the guards on his own. Mollitor and Vox could get to San Francisco at any point. It would depend on what they found of Weatherly's and what sort of follow-up had to be done. No help there. Finney would eventually make his way down here, but God only knew what his timetable and priorities were. And Feena. That poor little girl. Maybe she escaped during the fight; Dawson could only hope. The concrete in here was treated; she'd have to open the door to get an accurate scan.

So, she thought, why not? Lupu wasn't the type to patrol the halls himself. The worst she could run into was Bruno, and that was just fine. The bastard. In any event, it was better than waiting for them to come to her.

She crept to the door and listened. Nothing. Okay, spring the lock, push open the door. No one in the hall. She started away from the main amphitheater, scanning the layout. There was a stairway around the next curve that opened onto a higher level of passages leading back to the circle of arches. She went up the stairs carefully, scanning for sensors, keeping the wave as wide as possible. The Rat Lupu would guard against pinpoint vibrations. Wide, general waves didn't threaten him, so he wouldn't key alarms to them.

She passed several rooms on the upper level, scanned the atmospheric vibrations in each to spot any of the Rat's thugs. It was interesting. Everyone she'd sensed down here had nothing but one of those blankout shields. Obviously, this was all the competence Lupu wished his servants to possess. She placed an impact impress on each door, muffling it against detection, and kept moving in a wide curve back toward the main room. The idea was to remove potential reinforcements before the fight ever started. She still wanted to talk to Lupu. If he had unwittingly figured out the key to energy transfer, she wanted the information. The next battle with him was bound to be to the death, anyway.

The hallway ended abruptly in a double arch. She scanned inside. It was a medium-sized room filled with electronics: monitors of the installation, vidlines to the outside, databanks. The stuff she'd seen in the main hall must've been the control console. There was another arch at the far end of the room. Someone was standing in front of the monitors. Dawson's jaw set. It was impossible to mistake the shape; Lupu couldn't have two guards that size.

She stepped into the room. Bruno turned around, the surprise on his face breaking into an evil grin.

"You got out," he said. "Good. I'll notify the Rat"—he moved away from the board—"right after I get finished."

Dawson probed him. Just the same blanking shield.

"I could make this easy, Bruno. I could pull your brains out and hand them to you." She dropped into a crouch. "But it would give me far more pleasure to beat you at your own game."

"That's a lot of talk, bitch," he said, circling. "You don't know what pain is. I'm here to teach you."

Dawson let him circle, kept facing him. She shifted onto her right leg, saw Bruno note the shift. Doesn't matter, she thought, let him make the move.

He came in on her right and reversed to the left with amazing speed. The hand blurred just past her cheek, and she jabbed two fingers into the shoulder joint, leaped past him and drove the heel of her hand into the base of his neck. No effect. He backhanded, and she deflected the blow partially. It still grazed her head. Bruno caught her leaning away, buckled the slower left leg with a sidekick. She stumbled. The big hand lashed down and Dawson caught it, rolled onto her back, legs extended, flipping Bruno high into the machinery ten feet away. He crashed off the console, glass shattering, his arms busy regaining balance, and Dawson was on him with four fast jabs—nose, throat, solar plexus, groin. The shot to the nose drew blood, the one to the groin got a grunt, but that was it. The guy was just too heavily muscled. He straight-armed her again, and the best she could do was roll with it, skidding along the floor on her bottom. He lunged. Dawson pushed off with her arms to meet him, legs locking around his head, and twisted sharply. Bruno slammed to the ground, but she didn't hear the wind go out of him. Damn it, how strong was he? He grabbed Dawson's leg, tore it from around his head and, with one arm, swung her entire body over his, *smash,* to the ground next to him. He flipped himself on top of her, grabbed a handful of hair and bounced her head viciously against the concrete. Dawson saw stars, almost blacked out. She felt Bruno force her legs apart and grab her pants at the waist. She brought both fists up, hard, against his ears, but he only grunted again, and ripped the front of her pants down. Oh well, she thought, I guess I really *can't* beat him hand to hand. She tore away his shield and locked his motor center. Incredibly, he still resisted, his muscles continuing to spasm, pawing at her. She flashed a mindthrust, enraged, and gripped his throat, flashed another thrust. The neck muscles gave way; his eyes rolled. Dawson snapped his head back, forced him off her, kept the pressure on until he lost consciousness. She crawled away and leaned up against the computer table, panting.

She felt the back of her head, gingerly. An egg-shaped lump was rising. She looked down; what a mess. This son of a bitch was really intent on raping her. He had single-handedly destroyed every stitch of clothing she had. And this was who she decided to trade punches with? "That's just like you, kiddo," she could hear Mollitor say, "—always doing things the hard way."

She stood up, shaking her head. Well, now what? She couldn't very well walk around with her pants ripped to her knees. She looked around; not much choice. She pulled Bruno onto his back and got his jeans off. She tore the legs down to size and used a strip of her own pantleg for a belt. Wonderful. She now looked like an adult version of the kids from Grant Street. Leaving Bruno lying there in his underwear, she hurried through the door. It occurred to her several rooms later that she really should've broken his legs, for insurance.

Back to the circle of arches. This time she was on the opposite side, right above the bookshelves. The debris from the exploded table was all over the room, the papers and whatnot pushed into one big pile in the middle. Feena was nowhere to be seen. Lupu sat in one of the armchairs, smoking a cigaret, watching the smoke trickle out his nose, while Johanson paced back and forth, gripping his hands rhythmically behind his back.

Dawson watched him. The mannerisms hadn't changed; he still walked with a nervous shuffle, the same compulsive swallowing bobbed his Adam's apple and—even from this distance she could see it—the twitch in his right eye. He was older, though; he looked it. He'd gone grayer, his face growing leathery tough. It was actually a big improvement; Johanson, in the old days, had looked more like a sick fish than anything else. It was interesting, though. The years were finally having their effect. He was already over a hundred. The drawback to *partial* regenerative control was that, once the psychic infrastructure started giving out, all the years you'd been hedging came crashing down in less than a decade. It made for a scary final few years. Darby knew it, Finney knew it. It was just one of those things you didn't think about until you had to.

Dawson smiled grimly. On no account could she ever feel sorry for Johanson. She felt nothing for him, not hate or pity or nostalgia or even revenge. Too many years had gone by. He was simply her opponent, always on the opposite side of anything she believed in, and she came away from each encounter hoping it would be the last.

"Damn it, Lupu," he was saying, "then what *is* it you want to do with her?"

The Rat removed the cigaret, flicked ash on the rug. "I'm not exactly sure. She just seems too valuable to dispose of."

"She's too dangerous not to dispose of."

"Perhaps. She certainly knows a lot."

"Yes, there is that. Well, look, you've got a chance—"

"Your problem, my dear Johanson, is that you've grown old in spite of yourself. Everything is such a serious proposition to you. Vendettas, secret deals, sabotage—you really are the old school. When was the last time you got laid?"

Johanson looked at him sharply. "That has nothing to do with our current problem."

Lupu laughed. "How do you know? Maybe I want this little blond morsel, maybe that's why I'm keeping her alive. God knows *you* could use something. I'm telling you, you discount the mundane too quickly. Perhaps if we both gave her a tumble, we'd feel better. At least we'd stop arguing over details."

"You're hopeless, Lupu. You can't behave like a child and expect to form an empire."

"Oh, of course, the Empire," he said, waving the cigaret in disgust. "Please don't start that again." He sighed. "There's no chance of her joining us voluntarily, is there?"

"You must be joking. Even if you hadn't attacked her

immediately, even if your big brute hadn't started tearing at her clothes, my presence here alone would make it impossible. You saw the way she favors that left leg? I did that to her, long before you were ever born." He shook his head. "Forget it."

"Well then, answer me this: Why is she here?"

The old man shrugged. "I found you. Why couldn't she, as well?"

"Because, you old fool," he snarled, "there was nothing to point to me. They were all busy tracing that crap in Paris, that business with the fat lady. Right? Or why did you bother creating the impression of a fifteen-year-old file on the moon that'd been wiped? And why pay that simpering jackass Tanner all that money?" He dragged once more off the cigaret and stubbed it out. "He's going to have to go, Johanson. He knows too much, or thinks he does, anyway. I don't like leaving potential blackmailers around."

Johanson held out a hand. "If you wish to remove him, that's no problem. I can have it done, or . . ."

"Or what?"

"He could commit suicide."

Lupu smiled. "You don't fool me for a minute. Ever since you got here, you've been egging me on. You want to see it done. You want control of it yourself." Johanson said nothing, but he stopped pacing. "You can't stand being in the dark, but you'll stick around waiting for your chance. What you really can't bear is the suspicion that I might not be behind it, either, that I'm just leading you on." He laughed slowly. "Go on wondering, old man. I enjoy it."

"Why?"

"Because you're the most interesting toy I've ever come across." Lupu leaned back in his chair, stared at the wall. "Until this one," he whispered.

"You're making a mistake," said Johanson.

"That may be. The advantage of the strong is that we can afford to make mistakes now and then. Power has a way of rectifying errors before it's too late."

Dawson stepped into view.

"It's already too late," she said, floating to the ground.

She took two steps forward; they were both up and facing her. "Shall we talk now, Lupu? We can always fight afterward."

"Of course," he said, bowing slightly. "Please, have a seat."

"I prefer to stand."

"As you wish. I must say, your new taste in clothes leaves something to be desired."

"I make do."

"I'm sure you do."

Johanson gripped the back of the chair, knuckles turning white. He just glared at her; Dawson ignored him.

"Exactly what is it you're after?" she asked. "What's the purpose of all this?"

Lupu put a hand to his chin. "I would think it obvious. Wealth, power." He smiled again. "I wouldn't mind ruling the world but, of course, the administrative duties become so . . . tedious. I should ask you as well—What is it you want?"

"That's hardly the point."

"But it is. Just because I have people killed while you simply maim them, just because I draw a larger salary—no, there isn't that much difference. We're both talented mutants in a world of insects. What are you asking me that you can't ask yourself as well? What does this world offer you?"

"You have no comprehension of my life. I'm more than a century older than you."

"Oh, ageism, is that it? You're older—that somehow makes you nobler?"

"If you're responsible for the deaths of my friends, I want to know why."

He nodded. "Understandable. It's a big 'if.' If I am responsible, what if I apologize?"

"You're being ridiculous. You have no intention of using your power for anyone's benefit but your own. You have to be stopped."

"Then kill me."

"I hope I don't have to."

He laughed. "Then I'll have to kill you."

"If you can."

"Well, that's academic. We'll know the answer soon enough, if we can't reach a compromise." He turned toward the middle of the room. "I *do* wish you hadn't destroyed my table, though. Do you have any idea how difficult it is to get a table that size all the way down here?"

Dawson glanced at Johanson. It was horrible, but, of the two, she felt infinitely closer to him. Lupu actually was like a rat, an unfeeling and confident carrion creature, feeding on anything he could overpower. Johanson, at least, had a history; he longed for the fulfillment of his destiny as he saw it. Lupu could care less. He wanted nothing more than the joy of watching the victims squirm. There was nothing to ask him. Even if he was the source of the suicide assaults, it was meaningless; it could have nothing to do with power transfers. He had no desire for empire, no misguided rationale of a master race of telepaths, no theories to explore. These were simply the machinations of a sick kid with far too much power. Compromise was out of the question; the stakes were too high and he was too vicious.

With that thought, Dawson made the first unfair attack of her life. She struck him from behind, with enough intensity to kill. Lupu wheeled around with a scream, locking his shield against the wave, and tried to flash one in return. Dawson deflected the thrust, closed her eyes and ignited the oxygen in the room. She was the only one of the three prepared. She rolled with the blast, leaped to her feet, probing. A thrust hit her shield, locked on. It was Johanson. She rocked him with a needleflash and peered through the smoke. Then she felt her shield cave in and the white light tear across her head. She fell back against the bookcase, dissolving the frequency, snapping her shield back into place. It punched through again, still unmodified; the damage was minimal. She locked waves with Lupu, slipped around him and scored, but he reacted quickly. He pushed her out and lanced into her nerve center. Dawson's left side spasmed, dropping her before she neutralized it. Johanson locked on again and held. The smoke was clearing. She saw Lupu over to one side. She flashed a thrust, shifted the frequency as he blocked. It got through for some nerve damage. Then he really blasted her.

The force was concussive. It blew Dawson's shield in on her, scrambled the waves she was using for attack. For a moment, she was wide open. Johanson was still holding on, so she reversed directions on him, yanked his shield into the way of Lupu's next blast. It crumpled, and the old man fell down with a groan. Her own defenses snapped back to deflect the needle.

This wasn't working so well. Dawson was able to continue scoring on Lupu by shifting frequencies on him. He was figuring it out, but it would take time. The problem was, she couldn't stop his blasts; neither dodging nor shifting seemed to work, and her shield wasn't going to take much more. Johanson, meanwhile, was crippling whatever chance she had. She could blow him aside, but he kept coming back, like a pit dog, and there was steadily less and less opportunity to remove her focus from Lupu to shake him off. Well, there was one method of attack she was better at than either of them. She exploded the concrete at Lupu's feet and flashed a huge force wave at Johanson, knocking him aside. She started edging toward the door, refocused to block the Rat's thrust. He was advancing on her, trading shots. She took two for every one she scored, but Johanson was back on his feet. He was no slouch at explosions, himself. The doorway caved in as she reached it, and another white bolt flashed across her brain, knocking her into the rubble. Lupu kept coming. He brushed her shield aside and locked onto her motor center. Dawson's muscles froze. She tried pushing against his wave, but it wouldn't budge.

I've got you, you little bitch, he flashed at her, and she felt her strength smothered. Damn it, she thought, if only Johanson hadn't been here . . .

Suddenly the back of Lupu's jacket exploded into flames. He shrieked, throwing his hands crisscross to his shoulders, slapping furiously. Then something hit him hard, blowing by his shield and knocking him to the floor.

"Get him, Dawson!" a voice shouted. "I'll take Johanson."

It was Darby, high up in one of the arches. Dawson felt

Lupu's lock release as Darby smashed him back into the floor. She was free. Jack to the rescue, like old times. He came gliding down, coat flapping, arms outstretched, locked tight onto Johanson's shield, crackling the air all across the room.

Lupu was just a few feet from her. She rolled, and kicked his legs out from under him as he tried to stand. He rammed his way through her shield as she slipped by his. They had hold of nothing now; just two waves locked head to head. She'd finally pulled even. When it came to thrusts, she couldn't match his power, but now, in a dual grip neither dared ease for an instant, they could both feel the balance. It was like two heavyweight arm wrestlers straining against the other's immovable bicep, each waiting for bone to snap.

Dawson's advantage was their proximity. She grabbed his forearm and forced it back to the shoulder, held the other wrist tight. The intensity of Lupu's wave gained the edge, but Dawson accepted the trade off. With sixty years of combat experience behind her, she was breaking his arm. Across the room, Darby and Johanson were trading mindthrusts. That won't last long, she thought; neither of them enjoys that style of fighting. She was right. The room started to fill with explosions, electrical charges, books and loose debris flying all around. Darby ducked behind an overturned chair, peeked out.

"Hey, Johanson," he taunted him, "the odds are even. Come and get me, asshole."

The floor in back of Darby blew up, throwing him down, but not before he launched the chair. It hit Johanson in the legs, tumbling him over the top, and they locked shields again. Now Dawson could feel the energy level building in the room, the force of four powerful waves straining against one another, vibrating the air. The walls trembled. The concrete wouldn't last long, she could sense it. She suddenly released Lupu's arm and backfisted him in the face. He fell into the rubble and twisted around in time to block her next swing. She kicked and he deflected. She shot a spear hand to his throat and he broke two of his fingers blocking. He got to his feet and dodged another jab, stumbling over the debris. Dawson spun with a combination and landed the kick squarely into his chest. The Rat crashed into the hallway, wincing at the pain in his ribs, and rolled to his knees. They were still bearing down, wave to wave. Although he was gaining steadily, Lupu didn't dare shift to a thrust. He was just trying to stay in one piece. She advanced on him again.

Lupu wasn't throwing any punches. He seemed to know that Dawson could counter anything he came up with. He didn't want to get that close. But his speed was proving quite sufficient at defensive maneuvers. He took a number of blows, bruising and bloodying him, but few were hitting for full power. He kept retreating along the curve, and then they were at another arch leading back into the main room. Dawson feinted left and came in hard against his right shoulder. He stumbled, and she kicked him through the door. He hit the floor with a gasp. She leaped in after him, and heard Darby shout, "Look out!"

Dawson ducked instinctively, and Bruno's fist crashed into the wall. He loomed above her, completely exposed. What a stroke of luck. She pushed off with her legs, bringing both fists up under his chin. Caught off balance, he went straight up and over, stars spinning in his head, and slammed to the concrete next to his master.

"Some tough guys," she said, looking down at them, but Lupu wasn't out of it yet. He let go of Dawson's wave and lashed a savage needle at her. Her wave crashed in on him, squashing his shield to nothing, but, at the same time, Dawson's brain reeled. Vision went black, ears picked up nothing but a muffled ringing. She never even heard the explosion. Somehow, she knew that Darby and Johanson had pushed the vibrations to the breaking point, that the room was collapsing. She knew it was exploding because her body was thrown into the hall by the concussion. But she didn't actually feel herself hit the wall, and she had no idea whether anyone else was blown out as well. It was a long, lonely way to the other side of consciousness. Nothing existed but the throbbing in her head.

Five: Insight

XXI

A hundred years ago, we knew less about the interior of Greenland than we did the surface of the moon. Today, people live on Luna, and what they haven't excavated, they've at least mapped. Kids are born. Agents are murdered. Business thrives. We still don't know diddly about Greenland.

Vox aimed the shuttle in a lazy arc across the tundra, cut our speed to about one-quarter and flipped on the autocruise. He pushed back in his chair and rubbed his eyes, got a gold-tipped cigaret out of the vest pocket and started patting himself for a lighter.

"Mollitor . . ." he muttered from around the cigaret.

I swiveled in my chair. "A light, Baron?"

"Something less than a fireball, please."

I laughed and flamed the tip. Vox took a deep drag and sighed.

"You're sure the transmitter is out here?"

"It was still there six years ago," I said, watching the long white sheet of land ripple by.

"At those coordinates?"

"Latitude and longitude don't shift. I planted that transmitter myself during the War. Before you were born, old man. Never used it much but, lemme tell you, it's nice to have an out-of-the-way transmitter when you need one."

Vox exhaled and shook his head. "Well, if Chicago isn't safe . . ."

"I don't know if it is or not. With the Maf' on our tail, I'm not going to chance it. The Old Man would personally shoot me if I embroiled the agency in my political problems. Anyway," I said, leaning back, "the fastest way to Frisco is over the pole. I'll key this stuff to the Old Man's private file, and we should get to California by noon."

"Indeed. What about the report?" He glanced briefly out the front window, adjusted a dial. "Is it what you thought it was?"

I shrugged. "Yes and no." I picked up the sheaf of papers, tapped it on my knee. "It poses more questions than it answers, but it does clear up a few puzzles."

"Spare me the puzzles. I wish only to avenge LaRue's death. Are we any closer to knowing who it was?"

"Don't worry. By the time we get there, Dawson will have had a day and a half."

"You make that sound like a lot of time," he said, laughing.

"It is."

"Hah. You expect results quickly. I can see why you aren't chief of Insight."

"What?"

"Slavedriver."

"Oh, c'mon, Val, give me a break. I—"

"No, no, it's all right. I forgive you. But I'll know how to handle you from now on." He glanced back out the window. "What about the old lady?"

I felt a tremor in my stomach. "I don't want to think about that yet," I said softly. "She left me a clue, but I can't figure out what it means. Dawson will know."

"That's some faith you place in your partner."

I looked at him, then swiveled back and stared at the batch of papers.

Hell yes, I had a lot of faith in her. I'd been acting on wild hunches for years, and Dawson always had a way of making me look good in the end. This time would be no different.

The papers. Weatherly.

The key to psi power, as I'd told Ranagen, is energy flow. Learning to control it takes a lifetime, but you have to be aware of the flow, have to keep the stream moving through your head. What was revolutionary about Weatherly's theory was that the energy involved was *non-integrating*. You appropriated it from outside the flow and stored it somewhere in your mind, separate from the energy you were using to tap it in the first place. It didn't have to be regulated, so the quantities could be limitless. The problem was that the transfer mechanism itself had to work flawlessly. That much energy *couldn't* be controlled, and it had to be transferred directly into a computer processor. Let it leak into the normal flow and it'd rip your mind to shreds. Elena had outlined the difficulties very clearly, but Gil's equations pointed up one last problem:

Most people's psi energy is latent, a sequence of impulses that just never get fired. Those people who learn to utilize the energy get stronger and more precise with it over time. We always assumed this was due simply to practice. Not so, said the intrepid Mr. Weatherly. You've got to think of psionics as operating not only within certain frequencies of your mind, but within a certain band of the planet's atmosphere as well. The more people who become aware of their power, the more psi energy is released into the psychic ether, and it actually becomes increasingly difficult to channel the flow. You're fighting to send signals clearly through a field of psi static. You get steadily stronger from working against this field, like a weightlifter using heavier and heavier weights. The static builds geometrically, though. It makes it increasingly tough for a beginning T-path, even with improving training methods.

Energy transfer posed the big dilemma. A group of agents gathering latent power and turning it, in effect, into usable force, would falsely inflate the level of psi static in the background. This would produce a damping effect and would, ultimately, make it impossible to channel normally for any but the most powerful T-paths. It wasn't clear to me how this damping effect related to the lethal energy fields—one seemed passive, the other active—but I felt sure there was a connection somewhere. The agents getting hit *were* the most powerful T-paths operating.

What *did* seem clear now was the cause of Mary's death: the holding energy had leaked into her mind. This was an important point. Mary hadn't committed suicide;

the drugs in her body had been her way of keeping the psi reservoir under control. In the end, even that hadn't worked, but it meant that Mary had actually been performing energy transfers. God knows where she got the information.

The panel began beeping.

"Ten miles," said Vox. "Nine a.m. The middle of nowhere, Earth."

"Advance and be recognized?"

"You know it, Mollitor."

He dipped a wing and roared into a sharp curve, both of us pushed back in our seats, the hills whizzing by on either side, the birds jumping out of the way. It was great. There's nothing like cruising in a fast machine.

As we approached the coordinates, Vox dropped the hover into a circular pattern, a hundred feet off the ground. I could see the top twenty feet of tripod antenna jutting out of the ice.

"Okay, Val. Have you got the relay set?"

"Any time."

I punched in the Old Man's private transmit code, keyed the scramble frequency. "Do it."

Vox hit the button, and two boxes of Weatherly's papers zinged into the transmitter below. A bunch of electrons buried in the snow; they don't make safer hiding places.

That done, we took off, north, skimming the top of the globe, then southwest across Canada. We were about three hours out of Frisco, and I figured I could get a little sleep. Silly me. Trouble waits for me to close my eyes; I should be used to it by now.

"Company, Mollitor," said Vox. I jumped forward. There were two hovers a mile or so ahead of us, eleven o'clock and a little up.

"Who?"

"Maybe Mafia. Maybe your friends from ENCOM." He smiled. "Maybe Royal Canadian Police, but I doubt it. There's a third one below us. You'd better buckle up."

I snapped the belts on. Vox tapped a button on the console, gave the stick a quick flip and we veered off to the right. The two in front matched our move.

"No clouds," I said, looking around. "Just great. Is this thing armed?"

"Not exactly. It has defensive features: force shield, mag-deflectors, things you would expect on a bank-owned hover. No lasers, no missiles."

"Tremendous. How do we get out of this one?"

"I suppose we become inventive. I wish I had *my* shuttle. Then you'd see some weaponry. I could blow these three out of the sky like—"

"Val! For crissake, they're almost on us. What can we do?"

"Can you short out electronics on their ships?"

"Yeah. You've got to pass them first; I need to scan the schemata."

He squinted right and left, gauging position, adjusting trajectories.

"This ship is faster than theirs. A lot faster. You can orbit in this thing. That will be what saves us."

Going into orbit?

"So save us already."

"All right, Mollitor. Hold on and watch some fancy flying."

We jerked down and away, and the two approaching hovers veered. Not fast enough. Vox reversed toward them and we were in a line of three crafts. Only the lead one could shoot. A flash of light left its belly, and Vox slammed us hard right, then up and straight in on our attacker. It shifted to face us and Vox left my stomach behind as he dropped us to the left and blurred by the underside of the two ships. Both fired; I scanned. The second shot deflected off our shield.

"Third one coming from below," said Vox. "Hold tight."

We did a backward loop, blocking ourselves with the other two as number three fired and missed. Vox was, literally, flying circles around them. I finished my probe.

"Got it. Let's get some distance."

Vox wheeled us away as numbers one and two fired. Two hits. The field buckled with the deflection; our left wing was now unprotected. Vox circled, got one behind the other again, and I shorted out the firing mechanism on the laser. We zoomed past, looped back and it launched a missile. I scrambled the heat-seeker and fused the gyro on the ship at once. Hover and missile both plunged.

Two and three were on our tail. Vox dodged and weaved, slamming us every which way, but he couldn't shake them. They were blowing our shield away. The mag-deflectors could take a little sting out of the blasts, but they were meant to deflect metal, not beams of light.

"We need a diversion, Mollitor." He was leaning over the console, stick in hand, perspiration running down his face. He kept shifting our little bit of force shield to different parts of the hover, glancing quickly from console to window to scanner screen. "We need one rather quickly."

"Okay," I said. "Bank left. Ready . . . *now!*"

I ignited the sky behind us into a sheet of flame fifty feet square. Vox rolled us into a tortuous loop, ended right side up and swerved back toward them. The two hovers had separated by some forty feet, trying to reorient themselves.

"Beautiful. You scared the hell out of them."

"What are you doing?"

"What they least expect."

We charged them. Vox aimed us at a point exactly between the two and caught a couple more blasts getting there. Our left wing was smoking. As we entered the space between them, they both wheeled and opened fire: three lasers and two missiles apiece.

"Bang," said Vox, slamming the stick forward and firing the orbit booster.

We dropped. Boy, did we drop. The safety straps cut big welts into my shoulders and all the blood slammed to the top of my skull. We won't even discuss my stomach. Of course, that wasn't the worst of it. We were only a couple thousand feet up when Vox fired us into orbit downward. We still had to pull out of this dive before we hit the ground at some ridiculous miles per hour.

I imagine that's what we did. When the blood reversed flow and went running back to my toes, I passed right out. However many Gs hit us was one more than this old body could take.

I woke up, and the sky was whizzing by, long ribbons of cloud strung across the blue. I looked over at Vox, who was leaning back with his eyes closed, patting his forehead with a wet handkerchief. The hover was on autocruise.

"You call that flying?"

He opened one eye and looked at me out of the corner of it. Then he smiled and closed the eye.

"Call it what you want. We're here, and they're not."

"They got each other, huh?"

"It was a beautiful sunburst, Mollitor. Too bad you missed it."

"Yeah, well, I lost you at the second turn there."

He laughed. "I nearly lost myself. I never tried that before. I'll tell you, Mollitor, someone wants you dead very badly."

"Long as I've got Mama Xenarie as a babysitter, they'll go on wanting."

"Of course. Keep counting on a seventy-year-old karate master, and you know where you'll end up."

"Yeah? Where?"

He shrugged. "San Francisco?"

"Sure. The Emerald City. Fast as lightning."

He looked over at me, puzzled.

"What does that mean?"

"Never mind," I said, closing my eyes.

XXII

Traffic in the city was awful. I mean, I wasn't wild about traffic jams a hundred years ago, when transportation was a two-dimensional process: right, left, forward and back. Stack the same tie-up three or four levels high, and driving begins to resemble a bad cartoon. At least we were on the top level; I'd refused to let Vox take us into the middle of this mess.

"So, where do we go?" he said.

"Who the hell knows. I'll tell you, Val, this city was made for cable cars and bicycles."

"Indeed. You want to visit the museum?"

I gave him a nasty look. "How am I supposed to find Dawson in this?"

"You're always having that problem, aren't you?"

"I mean, finding her *now*, not eventually. She's undoubtedly gotten herself in trouble. Hell, it's been a day."

Vox's shoulders twitched suddenly. He rubbed his neck. "I believe we can find her rather quickly."

"How?"

"Iorg tailed a man named Darby. Dawson was with him. They went underground."

"How long ago?"

He closed his eyes. "Yesterday."

"Val, how does this guy keep contacting you without my knowing? I mean, I *am* a pretty good receiver."

He laughed. "Iorg's frequencies are not mathematically based. It's a language code."

"So? I'm familiar with language codes."

"The language we're using is Old Estonian."

I just stared at him. Why are all my friends so strange?

"So, where shall we go? Iorg will meet us."

Where to, indeed. Hmm, Vox's ethnic contact gave me an idea. It couldn't hurt.

"Pine Street. A pub called the Irish Rose. It's the only contact point in this city I ever used with Finney."

"Finney?"

"Sure. I've got a hunch."

"All right," he said, looking out at the lines of hovers. "It's going to take some time, though."

"Like hell. We're on top. Veer off."

"Mollitor, it's against the law to break off from—"

"Oh, come on, Val. With your money and my security clearance—what can they do to us?"

"Not much, I suppose." We pulled away and shot over the buildings. "You'll teach me to be an American yet, Mollitor."

"I shudder at the thought."

Parking on the roof was clearly illegal. Let them sue me. Both wings on our hover were smoking, anyway. The first thing I scanned as we walked in was the moose head on the wall. Sure enough, there was an impress. It was open-line. I keyed the response vibration on an emergency frequency and joined Vox at the bar. New bartender, new waitresses. Same mahogany counter, though, same stiff drinks. I ordered an extra double irish on the rocks and set it down next to our glasses. Vox paid.

"You always carry American currency?"

He tapped a fat wallet on the bar. "And French, and German, and Swiss and a couple others. You never know what will be necessary."

"Not Soviet, huh?"

"Bah. From them, I take what I want."

I took a sip. "You had some trouble with those psi-attacks in Paris, Val."

"Please," he waved, "don't worry about it."

"Who's going to worry, if I don't? I need you alive,

and effective. It has been twenty years, you know. Do you remember how to deflect?''

He sighed. ''I remember. I relax my mind when the tickle feels thick and then sort of growl when it thins out for a second.''

Christ, what a way to describe needlethrusts.

''I taught you that?''

''I believe so.''

''Well, if it works, keep doing it. Just stay calm when they—''

''*You're* telling *me* to remain calm?''

''Oh. I forgot. You are the calm one here, aren't you?'' I stared at the clock. ''So? Where's Iorg?''

''Oh, he won't come in here. Too many people, too much activity. He's nearby.''

I got up from the stool. I was getting impatient.

''Maybe we'd better just find Dawson and forget about—''

The door opened and Finney shuffled in. He had on a long dirty raincoat that looked like it'd been slept in for the past two weeks. He kept his eyes on the floor, mumbling to himself like an old wino. He hadn't shaved in a week. He sat down at the stool next to me and picked up the drink, stared into it for a moment. Then he tossed half of it down his throat and set the glass down lightly on the bar.

About time you got here, he flashed.

You send me on wild-goose chases and it takes a little longer.

You really went to the moon?

It seemed logical at the time.

Finney broke into a slow laugh, pounding the counter and shaking his head.

''What's so funny?'' asked Vox.

''He is. He takes clues so damn literally. How are you, Baron?''

''Just fine, thank you.'' He turned his back to the bar and folded his arms. ''You two take care of your business, please, and we can depart. I'll watch the door.''

Finney made a face.

What's with him?

He's got the coming-out-of-retirement jitters. People keep trying to kill us. He doesn't like standing in one place too long.

Yeah? Who's trying to kill you?

Maf. Ranagen sicced 'em on me for messing with ENCOM.

What'd you get from Luna?—besides my message.

Old file on transfer and collection. Wiped clean. Where the hell have you been?

Hiding. Making Johanson, or whoever it is, nervous, I hope.

You contacted the Old Man.

I let him know I was alive. Listen, why would the file on Luna be wiped?

Who knows? McIntyre's dead, though. Suicide.

Energy fields?

All over the place. Dawson's been here in town since early yesterday. You seen her?

No. I've been sneaking through old Pool files for three days. Darby got me in.

Let's have it.

To begin with, I was right about Mary. She was heavily into transfer, as far back as the early '50s. Someone must've put her on to it.

You really think so?

He shrugged.

It was a big leap in thinking, that far back. You want to lay it all to intuition, fine. I've got no proof. It just seems funny to me.

Funny indeed, I thought. Weatherly had the basics figured out years and years earlier. A simple file logged surreptitiously before he died; Mary could easily have found it.

Don't fret over it, Mollitor. It's just an idea. She was into very simplistic aspects anyway. Shunting power back and forth, using agents' minds. Probably hypnoblanked them. That way, she could keep sole control.

Why, though? Why not let anyone else in on it?

Back then? You're forgetting your history. Experimentation was frowned upon; we were at war with Intertel. Then Johanson made a mess of everything. When the Old Man called her back to Chicago, she code-locked what she'd gathered and buried it deep in the Frisco files.

Don't tell me. You found it.

I haven't seen a code-lock done like that in thirty years. It stood out, once you knew what to look for. The Old Man put a personal nix on any more experiments, so she never retrieved the info. Didn't need it anyway.

No?

It was simplistic, Mollitor. We've been doing it with the computer for the past twenty years.

All right, so forget twenty years ago. What about now? Poli and LaRue both died. Why didn't she come to us?

He frowned.

What could we have done, at that point, that we weren't already doing? She'd have had to spill the whole can, to Tanner and Johanson and Intertel and all. It was unnecessary. And it was still her experiment. She had her pride.

You saw her that last week?

Once. She stayed shielded, played cat-and-mouse. But she didn't trust anyone at that point. Whatever she knew went down with her.

It killed her, Finney.

What, the assault?

Not in her case. She overloaded herself. You'll have to read the report.

What report?

Thing on energy transfer Gil Weatherly wrote in the '20s.

Where the hell have you been?

I get around. Go back to the storage areas in the '50s. Where are these agents now?

Dead or retired. There were only a handful to begin with.

Who de-primed them?

How's that?

You know, cleared them. They had all this reservoir energy in their heads when Mary went rushing back to Chicago. Who emptied it?

I suppose no one did. Is it important?

I thought about that. If Weatherly's damping effect was for real, it could be very important. Leaving all that surplus energy on the total band could've gotten the ball rolling to where— Oh, who the hell knew? Why clouds of assault energy? Why should the static congeal like that?

Mollitor? What's up?

Never mind. What else about these agents?

He gave me a funny look, but kept flashing.

Nothing out of the ordinary. Maybe she picked them for some specific trait or another, but they all look like regular hard-working spies.

Damn it. Finney, we need an angle.

He smiled.

I know. We got one. One of the agents Mary used was Carl Lupu. Remember? The real tall guy? Worked the islands?

I remember him. So what?

Well, what's interesting is that his kid, Eric, was trained here in Frisco, by Darby and the crew. He dropped out at eighteen and now he's the local godfather.

Maf'?

Independent.

All that means is that he's an unusual alumnus of the program.

It would, Mollitor, except for two things. First, there's no record of him in the program files. No school progress notes. That means Fantello was paid off. And, secondly, Avery logged a report on Lupu's activity two weeks before his apartment blew.

What was in the report?

That's the weird part. I couldn't decode the wavelock. There was some kind of random interference band around it.

My head jerked up. *He was here.* That son of a bitch was here. It all fit. We have to—wait, I wasn't sending. I tried scanning Finney but got nothing. He noticed it too. There was some massive blank-out wave covering the bar.

Vox tapped my arm. He touched one finger to his nose, two to the cheek, a fist, then shifted the thumb and patted his chest. He was watching the front door. The bar was surrounded. Two at the front, one outside the window on the sidewalk, an indeterminate number behind the kitchen door. Vox was telling me to cover the rear.

"Mollitor—" Finney started to say.

"Skip it, we've got company."

These guys had no finesse at all. The kitchen door swung open with a crash and two guns fired. Everyone in the place started diving for the floor. One blast caught my leg as I rolled away from the counter, the other splintered the wood right under our glasses. Finney pulled a big pistol and dropped to one knee, fired with both hands. The first guy out of the kitchen flew back with a six-inch hole in his chest.

Vox upended a table to guard his back and flashed shurikens at the front door. One guy took them in the throat and chest. The doorway was blocked for a moment. Finney and the other two in the kitchen were trading shots. I was on my side, with a leg that felt on fire and no weapon to fight with. The blank-out smothered all psi energy in the room.

"What now?" said Vox. "They can't get in." He scored with another star.

"Unfortunately, we can't get out, either," shouted Finney, blowing the rest of the kitchen door off its hinges. Another shot hit the kitchen wall, from above my head. The bartender was peeking over the counter with a big .30–06. Antique weapons; what the hell, it was an idea.

"Give me a bottle of whiskey," I called to him.

"Mollitor," shouted Finney, "where have they got the blank-out device?"

"Don't know. Somewhere in the room."

The guys at the front door made their move. One jumped through the opening, while his buddy fired at Vox. The Baron snapped his head to the side and flicked two stars into the first guy, chest and thigh. He skidded into the stairway with a scream, as Vox went down in an explosion of light. From my angle, it looked like he got hit in the head. I stuffed a handkerchief into the half-full whiskey bottle and lit it, then hurled the bottle at the doorway as three more started through. The whole front wall burst into flames.

"They got Val!" I shouted to Finney, moving toward the Baron.

"I'm all right," he said, getting up. His head was all

bloody, his coat was ripped. He glanced at the burning wall in front, then at the kitchen wall, finally at the side window. "Follow me."

He lowered his head and ran right at the checker-board-framed glass. I hobbled after him. Finney got up, backing toward the window, firing at the kitchen doorway, the stairs, the front door, the kitchen again, wheeling, swerving, the pistol clutched tight in two hands, spraying the room with thermal blasts. Vox sprang, crashed through the glass and into the street. I leaped after him, hit the pavement and rolled. The blank-out was gone. I didn't even bother looking around. I fired a thousand needleprobes in a circle around me, taking care only to miss Vox. There were lots of painful shouts. I got up as Finney came flying out through the shattered wall. People were lying all around the intersection, rolling and clutching their heads. Four of them were plainly armed. Finney kicked the guns away, tossed me one. I caught it and looked at him.

"I don't use guns."

"Oh, that's just dandy. Instead you incapacitate half the city. Look at this mess."

He waved both arms at the people lying around. Cars were stopped, some squashed into one another. Two hovers had crashed into the three-story building across the street. The bar was burning, people running out, shouting and sobbing. Sirens rose in the distance. Finney stood in the middle of the street with the pistol in his hand, turning this way and that, like the sheriff in an old western after the shootout. Vox was off to the side, staring down the block.

"You all right, Val?" I asked. No answer.

Finney was just warming up. "I mean, for God's sake, some hoods shoot at you, you shoot back. You don't throw a fucking molotov cocktail and blow the place up. You don't knock a hundred honest citizens on their asses just for being in the way. I mean, *look at this mess!*" He waved his arms again, spotted another one of the thugs coming out of the hole in the wall, gun leveled, and he blew the man's legs away without breaking stride. The laser cracked the sidewalk, and the guy pitched forward onto the broken concrete.

"Sorry I'm not a cowboy like you, Finney."

"Damn right you're sorry."

A hover dropped to street level and stopped. Vox opened the door and motioned the driver to the back seat. He climbed in and called to us, "Let's go."

Finney got in back.

"Who's the little gnome?"

"Watch your mouth," I said. "He's the best shadow you'll ever see."

"No fooling? Pleased to meet you, Jack."

"Mollitor," said Vox, "perhaps you could look at my ear. I believe I'm wounded. I can't hear a thing."

I pulled my leg in and slammed the door, and Vox launched the shuttle like a bullet.

His ear was fine. I poked around and scanned until I was sure the hearing loss was temporary. The beam had grazed his skull just above the ear. A bloody scalp wound. My leg was another story. The bone was unbroken, but there was a half-inch hole through the right thigh. A steady throb. I stopped the bleeding and concentrated on repairing the muscle damage.

"Where we headed?" asked Finney, in back. "Hey, Baron," he shouted, tapping Vox's shoulder. Vox looked at me. I hand-signaled the question.

"Treasure Island. The east bay. Apparently, Dawson is somewhere belowground."

"The old civil-defense tunnels?" said Finney. "That's strange. Hey, Mollitor, doesn't this guy ever talk?"

The console began beeping. Police. Vox glanced at me, motioned to the communicator, fired the booster and veered off toward the island. I punched in my security code and muttered some nonsense about active pursuit, life and death. Let the cops chase us if they wanted. I had better things to worry about.

There was something going on in this city that was very important. It was important enough for Johanson to have left Paris at the very moment his enemies were being killed. It was more important than making sure Dawson died in that psi-tomb, so big that the loss of his communications block seemed trivial to him. Johanson, the man who trusted no one, who'd sold out Insight and the Mafia, who even double-crossed ENCOM when it suited him, had entered into a partnership with a local ganglord. The stakes had to be incredibly high. He was undoubtedly after the same thing we were: the secret of energy transfer. I couldn't imagine how Carl Lupu's kid was mixed up in this; he couldn't know a thing about Mary's experiments, much less Weatherly's theories. Still, Dawson had headed unerringly in his direction. It wasn't even what she'd come here for. Had Darby tipped her?

"Finney," I said, half turning in my seat, "did you get any details on Avery's death?"

"Depends what details you want. We know what he did the week before and what his calendar looked like that day. The actual hit . . ." He spread his hands. "The apartment was rubble. There wasn't much to scan."

"What did Darby think?"

"He was mad. He offered to do the follow-up, analyze the field impresses and all. Fantello told him hands off, told him it was none of his business."

"I don't know. Something about it bothers me. Doesn't the explosion strike you as strange?"

"How so?"

"LaRue leaped from a window. Poli and Basil used guns on themselves. So did McIntyre. Isn't it odd that Avery just overloaded? I'm sure he had weapons on hand."

"What are you getting at? You think he was dabbling in transfer? Like Mary?"

"Why not? He could've found her old research."

"I don't know, Mollitor. You think an overload can cause that kind of damage?"

"I *know* it can. You didn't see what happened when I was assaulted."

"Okay, so why didn't Mary blow up?"

"She knew what was involved. That's what the drugs were for."

"Doesn't make sense. She was using agents to shunt the energy around thirty years ago. Why not repeat that process in Paris?"

"Because, in Paris, she had Tanner's surveillance to contend with. LaRue was pretty sure he was being paid off."

"Hold on, I just said he was a snake. First we got Fantello, now Tanner. All of a sudden, everyone's being paid off?"

"It looks like it. Bribes come in many forms. Money is the least of it."

"Lemme guess who's doing the bribing."

"He's here, Finney. I know it. We'll uncover the last rock, and he'll be there, like always."

"All right. So, Avery was on to the transfer business. God knows how. So Johanson found a link between Paul and Mary and he came running to Frisco. It means he's using this Lupu kid."

"It also means that making us focus on Mary was his diversion. It kept our eyes off what was happening here."

"And the file on Luna," he said to himself. "It probably never existed."

"I hadn't thought of that."

"When we're playing with Johanson, anything's possible."

"I want him, Finney."

"We all want him. We're here to finish it, once and for all."

"I want him," I repeated, staring out the window. "Johanson's mine."

Finney sighed. "Sure, Mollitor. You've got seniority. Just kick his ass once for me, too."

Vox slowed the hover as we moved out over the bay. He angled us down, cut the booster and glided onto a wide strip of concrete next to a series of short chimneys.

"The third one leads directly in," he said, unbuckling himself and swinging open the hatch. "Iorg will stay with the hover."

I looked at him. "You feel all right, Val?"

He shrugged.

"Can you hear?"

"The right side's coming back. I'll be fine. You just be careful of that leg."

"What is this?" said Finney. "I'm the only healthy one here? I should get paid more."

We headed down the shaft single file. My leg hurt like

hell, but it wasn't having any trouble holding me up so far. Finney and I scanned. At the bottom was an empty room with passages leading away in opposite directions. I was picking up vibes from the west.

"Smother the alarms," I told Finney. "I'll take care of any guards."

The corridor took us in a wide curve. Most of the rooms we passed were empty. Some had monitor screens, others bunks and tables. There was a huge amphitheater in the center of a wide circular corridor with lots of arches leading in, but the room itself was demolished. It looked like a recent battle. I kept scanning for Dawson's impress, but was getting only isolated guards. No alarms as yet.

Picking up anything? Finney flashed.

I don't like it. I should be able to spot Dawson.

Maybe everything's autoblanked.

Maybe she's not even here. I had enough of this wandering around in the dark in Paris.

We've still got to find the big J.

Damn it.

She's down here, Mollitor. Stop worrying.

I sensed movement ahead. Voices. They were all blanked, so I estimated with a spatial probe.

Seven or eight, forty feet up the curve.

Check. Get their weapons.

I hand-signaled Vox; he moved across the hallway to the inside of the curve, and flattened against the stone. The voices got closer. Finney was hanging back a few feet. I glanced at Vox and nodded.

The first four guys came into view. I fused the mechanisms on their guns and ripped away their shields. Vox swept three of them to the ground, bounced some heads and stayed low. Finney leaped into the center of the hallway and blew two backward with two shots, while I needlethrusted two more and fused the remaining guns. The last guy, disarmed and scared, decided to charge Vox barehanded. The Baron jumped to his feet and simply blocked the way. They slammed into each other and Vox wrapped his arms tight, squeezed the breath right out of the guy. He let him drop, looked back at me and smiled.

Finney put the gun back into his belt. Then all hell broke loose.

The corridor behind us exploded into flames. I crashed into the wall. Flat on my back, I watched Finney sail over me, twisting in midair, to crumple farther down the hall. The Baron's coat was on fire. He shook himself, slapped his shoulders and neck, struggled to free himself of the cloth. He pulled it over his head, as a trapdoor opened above us and a huge guy, nearly Vox's size, landed in the hall. He swung from the knees, and Vox never had a chance to block. He went right over, crashed to the floor. I got up and tried to lock the guy's nerve center, but he was well-shielded. It was weird, though; not a natural block, and no helmet. I scanned again. I knew it—it was an oscillator. Then something hit me in the forehead. Down I went again. Another blast. This time I knew it was psi. I blocked and flashed a needle back along the frequency. I stood up.

Vox was fighting from his knees, blocking a whirlwind of kicks and jabs with his arms, protecting his head as best he could. The big guy was trying to finish Vox off quickly. I refocused on the wave attacking me. I had to pinpoint the source. I stared back down the hall we'd come, parrying another two thrusts, and then it occurred to me: *trapdoor*.

I covered my head and cracked the concrete roof in a forty-foot line. Lots of dust, but it held. Damn it. I wished I had Dawson's attack power. I blasted it again and my shield took a tremendous shot. I staggered under the blow, and hit it a third time, and the stone came crashing into the hallway. There he was. Johanson levitated down toward me and I covered my eyes, exploding the oxygen between us. It blew him backward and sent me skidding the other way.

Finney had his gun out, firing at a line of thugs farther down the hall. He must've been using needlethrusts as well as the blaster because, somehow, he was forcing their retreat. It was a reckless assault, the gun in both hands, no cover at all; he was just walking into them, firing and psi-flashing. Same old Finney.

Vox was on his feet now. One side of his face was bloody. Neither he nor his opponent were connecting with many blows, but the ones he'd already taken had done their damage; the other guy wore steel knuckles on his fists.

You need help? I flashed to Finney.

He took one hand off the pistol grip, waved me away without looking back. I spun around and locked shields with Johanson, coming around the corner, charged him. He tried exploding the concrete at my feet, but I'd figured he'd try that. I neutralized the vibration. I punched him in the stomach and grabbed for his neck, but he jerked his head into my chin. He kicked, and my legs went out from under me. I blocked his psi-thrust.

Johanson leaped straight up, grabbed the opening in the ceiling and vanished. No way, I thought, not this time. I glanced down the hall at Vox, listened to another volley of blasts from Finney's pistol. Hold down the fort, guys. I braced a force shield around my leg and took off after Johanson.

XXIII

Dawson made a point of not opening her eyes. There was no way to scan—she could feel the oscillation collar around her neck—but she could hear someone breathing in the room. It felt like a small room. Her hands were manacled to the wall, and her unchained feet just barely reached the floor, by tiptoe. Definitely bare tiptoe against stone. She was naked. Her shoulder sockets ached like hell and both hands were numb, but aside from that, she didn't feel injured. She gauged the time; it must've been over twelve hours since the explosion, maybe more. Where was Darby?

With that thought, she opened her eyes. The room was a ten-by-twenty stone cell. The door was on the long wall to her right. She was the only thing on this wall. The body in the far corner was collapsed in a lump, but it obviously wasn't Darby. The hair was too dark, the body too scrawny. It moaned and rolled over a little. The hands were chained together, as were the feet. He had a collar around his neck and his clothes were ragged. She smiled grimly. The Rat had certainly come down in the world.

Dawson locked onto the oscillation vibe in her own collar as Lupu opened his eyes. The code felt slightly different. It became apparent; the two collars were inter-coded. Neutralize one, and she'd free them both.

Lupu pulled himself against the wall and stared at her. He was trying to scan. He put both hands on the collar, but he couldn't break the reinforced leather. He tugged a few more times, then gave up. Dawson dug her heels into the wall and lifted her body up a little, taking the weight off her wrists. She wriggled her fingers, forced the blood back up to her hands. Lupu smiled, watching her.

"Well," he said, "that's one consolation. I couldn't have picked a better-looking cellmate."

"Look all you want, Lupu. You'll notice my legs are free. Come within range, and I'll break your neck."

He shifted to a more comfortable position. "No need to get nasty. I didn't arrange this. I don't even know how we got here."

"You've got a lot to learn about trusting Johanson."

"Ah, yes. My former partner. It is odd. Do you suppose the explosion left him completely unharmed?"

"Johanson is very resilient."

"Mmm, I suppose you would know." He reflected a moment. "I can't believe Bruno would join him, though."

"Johanson can also be very persuasive. Anyway, Bruno is probably dead, or incapacitated."

"Why?"

"Don't be stupid, Lupu. His loyalties make no difference. If that big bastard were up and around, he would've torn me to pieces hours ago."

"I would've loved to watch that," he said, leering.

"That figures. Voyeurs can never get it up themselves."

Lupu jumped to his feet; Dawson braced one foot against the wall.

"You fucking bitch."

"Three more steps, Lupu. I guarantee you won't wake up this time."

He relaxed and retreated back to the corner, looked around the room. She watched his eyes finally rest on the door. The handle was within range of her foot. It figured. Lupu couldn't get to the door and Dawson didn't dare neutralize the collars. It was a standoff, with Johanson the victor. What could he be planning? He could take over the Rat's setup, but that wasn't his style. Johanson already had one international gang; the last thing he needed was a bigger turf to run. No, he wanted the secret of the psi-assaults. That had to be why he left both of them alive. Cover all the bases. Johanson had no way of knowing which specific clue would lead him to the prize.

She could feel her hands again. She dropped the weight back onto her wrists and tested the chain. It was heavy steel; the last ring was imbedded in stone. Maybe Vox could bust it loose with a quick jerk, but Dawson just didn't have the muscle.

She looked back at Lupu. He was sitting down again, not looking too happy. Hmm, twelve hours. Johanson would've spent the time checking the Rat's files against the Frisco Pool's, looking for clues, probably setting an ambush for Mollitor as well. Damn it, was Darby alive or not?

The Rat had stopped glancing around. He seemed content to just leer at her.

"You look delicious hanging there," he said, licking his lips. "Come on, bitch. Spread your legs. Get me hot."

Dawson ignored him.

"Mmm, boy. Just thinking about all the things I'm gonna do to you when you fall asleep . . ."

"Sleep?"

"You'll fall asleep eventually."

"I wouldn't base your plans on outlasting me at anything, Lupu. You deliver a good shock wave, but that's it."

"Yeah?"

"Yeah, punk. You're playing with the pros now. Just sit there and keep your mouth shut."

"Nobody talks to me like that!" He jumped up.

"Like I said before, big shot, come on over here and do something about it. Fucking wimp."

Lupu controlled himself. He turned to the wall and smacked it with his fist. Dawson knew this was going to be tricky. At some point—and she hadn't yet decided on the moment—she was going to deactivate the collars. Lupu obviously had no idea she could do it. She'd have about five seconds before he caught on, but those seconds would have to be used to get out of her chains. Even with perfect timing, the Rat could overwhelm her shield faster than she could land a punch.

The door opened suddenly and a guard poked his head and shoulders in. He was a small guy, laser in hand, wearing the gray uniform of Lupu's soldiers. The first thing he saw was Dawson hanging there.

"Murry!" shouted Lupu. "Get me out of here."

The guard looked over at him. Dawson's heart began to pound.

"Murry," she said softly, "I can offer you a lot more than he can." He looked back. Dawson writhed sensually against the stone. Murry's eyes went very wide, his attention riveted to the naked body. He took a step in, the laser still ready.

"Don't listen to her."

"It's yours, Murry, all yours," purred Dawson. "Do what you want with me." He took another step, the gun hand lowered, his free hand reaching out for her skin.

Dawson kicked off the wall, got her legs around his neck and slammed the body against the wall. She reversed and slammed him the other way. The gun clattered to the floor. She let go and kicked him full in the chest with both heels, cracking his sternum, driving him into the far wall, next to Lupu. His shoulder blades hit and his head snapped hard against stone. He crumpled. The gun was right below Dawson's toe. Lupu stared at the unconscious form.

"I can't believe that idiot!"

She gave him an icy look. "You let your guards in on too many rapes. They've developed one-track minds. They're easy to beat."

The door was still ajar. From somewhere far off came the sound of an explosion, then a second. Lupu listened closely for direction.

"Johanson seems to have a rebellion to put down," he said.

"Don't count on it. You're not such a beloved leader."

"Then what was that?"

"Could be my reinforcements. Could be the police. Could be Johanson falling into one of your traps."

His face brightened. "It could, couldn't it?"

Good, thought Dawson, he *does* have traps set. Nice to know. She glanced at the door; someone was in the hallway. Now what? The same trick wasn't going to work twice, not with a body on the floor. She calculated quickly. One step in, and her toe would just barely reach his head. Would he be leaning? In order to turn toward Lupu, he'd have to get another inch closer. Time and space enough to land one lousy toe, and that had to knock him out *and* keep his weapons outside Lupu's range. Just great. The odds couldn't be much worse. Sure they could; it could be Bruno out there. She took a deep breath; the Rat noticed.

"It's a trap. Look out!" he shouted. Dawson just smiled at him. She hooked her toe around the trigger of the fallen laser, aimed it roughly at the doorway. She'd take off a foot at best. They'd shoot her dead where she hung. Or worse. She felt remarkably calm.

A small, hooded figure peeked in, one hand on the door, a bundle under the other arm. No gun.

"You proper, lady?" said a tough but tiny voice.

"Feena! Thank God. Grab the gun."

The girl stooped and picked up the laser, then spotted Lupu. She shrank against the wall with a whimper.

"It's all right, he can't hurt you. He's chained."

"Come here, little Feena," said the Rat softy. "Come here and I won't rip your—"

"Shut your fucking mouth, Lupu!" Dawson snarled. "He's trapped, Feena; he can't send any waves. Just stay where you are."

The girl tossed back her hood and looked up at Dawson. "What's the glim, lady?"

"Can you shoot that thing?"

"Target."

"Get my chains. The left one."

Dawson leaned her weight onto the right wrist, braced her leg against the wall. She kept both eyes on Lupu, daring him to advance. Feena aimed with two hands and severed the chain with a short, sweeping beam. Dawson's arm dropped free, trailing chain.

"Give me the gun."

She took it and shot herself loose. Then she carefully severed the manacles around both wrists.

"What's the package?"

"Extra cover. I glimmed you'd been through a session. Here. Get suited."

Dawson took the bundle and handed her the gun.

"Watch him," she said. She put on the trousers and pulled the hooded tunic over her head. Very tight fit; these were obviously the girl's. Dawson walked over to Lupu. "Now then," she said, "what was it you were going to do to me?" Lupu just glared. "Come on, punk, open your mouth now. Maybe you'd like it if I hung *you* on the wall, naked. I could let Feena do what she'd like. You think you'd enjoy that?"

"Lemme twist him, lady," said Feena, from behind. "I'll sparkle him proper."

"Shall I remove your chains, Lupu? You want to swing at me?"

The Rat seemed to know that silence was called for. His thin face twisted, flushed red, but he didn't say a word. Dawson unclenched her fists and walked away. She'd leave him here. When Mollitor arrived, they could overwhelm his psi-impulse and interrogate him at will.

"Come on, Feena," she said. "Let's go."

Dawson started out the door, but the girl was still facing Lupu, the gun in her hands, eyes blazing. This wasn't just another mission to her, Lupu wasn't just another thug.

This was The Rat, a creature whose whims had dominated much of her life, someone she'd grown up in terror of. The sheer incongruity of having total power over him now was proving too much for her to handle. Her teeth clenched.

"Feena," said Dawson, "don't do it . . ." but Feena did. She fired a sustained blast at the Rat's head. He dodged and slid into the corner, but the light exploded all over the wall, and blood flew everywhere.

Another series of explosions sounded in response, from down the hall. The oscillation collar around Dawson's neck deactivated itself. She grabbed the girl's arm and dashed out of the room, slammed the door, keyed a triple impact lock. She took the gun from Feena, fused the firing mechanism and dropped it, then touched the metal plate directly across from the door, priming an impress.

"Come on," she said, not letting go of the girl.

"Lady, I had to," said Feena in a shaky voice. "He owed me the twist. You didn't let me slice him total. Lady, why didn't—?"

"That's enough. We're getting out of here. Just stay close to me."

They started up the hall, toward the commotion. From behind, the cell door exploded. Then again. Still intact.

"Good thing it's a triple," muttered Dawson. She looked at the girl. "Can you get away?"

Feena pointed to a tiny archway high up one wall. "Sneakhole straights to the tunnels. Book to the bay."

"Okay, go." Dawson levitated the girl up the wall.

"Lady," she called, once in the opening, "come on. We—"

"Go on, Feena, get moving. I'll handle Lupu. Thank you for everything. For God's sake, just run."

The girl's face screwed up, her eyes got glassy. She bit her lip and swallowed. Then she turned and vanished.

Dawson blanked, floated to the top of the corridor and hovered backward toward the big battle. The cell door exploded a third time and crashed out into the hall. She popped the yellow bulbs a hundred feet in each direction and stayed high, in the shadows.

The Rat stumbled into the hallway. The left side of his head and neck was a bloody, blackened mess. The ear was just about gone. Feena's shot had severed the collar. He was a wounded and furious beast. Dawson kept moving away. She bounced a needlethrust off the primed plate next to him and he screamed, wheeled around and blew a hole in the metal. She split the concrete at his feet and he tumbled to the floor, screaming again as his head bounced.

The explosions from down the hall were receding. Dawson crawled quickly along the wall and ceiling, while Lupu got to his feet. With a savage yell, he filled the corridor with an overwhelming force wave. It blew Dawson's levitation vibe away. She grabbed the edge of a doorway and flipped herself in. Flame filled the corridor behind her.

Two of Lupu's guards were at the far door, their backs to her, shooting handblasters through the opening and dodging away from the return fire. She tried scanning them. Shielded. She caved in their doorway and handsprang/bounced across the room. One of the thugs was on her side of the dust. Dawson landed five feet away and pushed off with her hands as he turned. Both legs wrapped around his head, and she did another somersault into the next room, snapping him high into the air. The body sailed forty feet and crashed into the wall. The other guy was sitting on the floor, blaster in hand, the fingers useless. He blinked at his very broken arm; no pain, still in shock. Dawson walked over and pinched a nerve in his neck.

She looked around. The walls of this room were scored and chipped from dozens of missed shots. Two arches were cut into the wall thirty feet up. Four more bodies were lying on the floor, dead. She levitated to the arches, heard a fireball go off back in the first room.

"You can't escape me," Lupu called.

She stayed blanked. The main thing was to keep her vibe smothered. What the Rat couldn't sense or see, he couldn't attack. She'd have to drop the blank-out to do any scanning herself, though.

The archway opened onto a tunnel. Dawson ran along it, crouching, moving steadily upward. God knew where, in this installation, she was. She ran a few hundred feet and it widened out. She heard sounds of fighting ahead. The hell with it, she thought, and scanned. There was a sort of room up there, really just a huge clearing. As she scanned, she felt Lupu's wave lock on from behind. She fell against the wall and countered, flashing a charge back along his wave. There was a dull grunt and he came stumbling into view. Dawson slipped a thrust around his shield and felt a concussion hit her own. She staggered back another step. Lupu winced, his shoulders spasming, and fired again. He was walking toward her, chopping up her shield, lancing white needles across her brain, ignoring whatever damage was being done to him.

Dawson followed suit. She stood where she was, her body shaking with each successive blast, amazed that he was walking right in to her. The Rat's teeth were clenched, his eyes wild, shreds of burnt skin hanging from the whole left side of his face. He blasted her again. Dawson's right eye closed, involuntarily. She caught her breath, took two steps and smacked him in the mouth. He stumbled back and caved her shield in. Dawson hit him again, cracking his jaw. He flashed a nervethrust and her right arm went numb. They had circled one another; the sounds of the battle were now in back of Lupu. Dawson shifted frequencies, locked waves. She spun and kicked him forward ten feet. He got up, tightened the wave; the pressure in her head was becoming unbearable. She caved in two of his ribs with another kick, and straight-armed him ten more feet. The Rat caromed off the walls, one side to the other, and the wave eased. Then they were around the bend; Dawson could see figures fighting. Lupu let go of the double wave suddenly, taking her thrust in order to score one himself. They both went down, temporarily blinded with the pain. Dawson groped past him, yanked his arm back, dislocating the shoulder. He screamed and chopped down on her neck with the other hand. Dawson rolled away, her head spinning. A laser blast took out a chunk of wall right next to her.

"Would you please finish him off and give me some help," she heard a desperate voice call.

Her eyes cleared. Finney was ten feet in front of her, flush to the wall, firing both around a corner and at the open passage ahead. The return fire seemed to indicate at least six gunmen. Finney was in his usual ripped trench coat, his face smeared with dirt and sweat. The fingers of his gun hand were all bloody.

On the other side of the room, Vox and Bruno circled each other, feinting, kicking, grappling and jumping away for another attempt. They both looked tired. The Baron was in his vest, his shirt torn down one side, his white hair splotched with red. The shuriken belt was at his waist, empty but for one star directly in back. Bruno looked like a cornered gorilla, terrified and snarling. He shot a kick at Vox's head, the Baron dodged and swept across for the leg, and Bruno regained his balance in time to block the counter-punch.

"I'm doing what I can," said Vox.

A volley of blasts powdered the wall at Finney's head and he ducked down, firing blindly in a spray. Dawson scanned Bruno; he was shielded. She didn't get a chance to rip the shield away.

Lupu shambled out of the passage in back and fired a needlethrust. She blocked. Her shield was barely at half-strength; it wasn't going to hold up much longer. Her only advantage was that Lupu wasn't pacing himself at all. His legs shook so, he could hardly stand. With a dislocated shoulder, a couple broken fingers, a shattered jaw, half a dozen cracked ribs and a badly charred head and neck, he was still firing thrusts for all he was worth. He was overriding his nervous system to block the pain and, consequently, was unaware of what the internal bleeding was doing to him. He was beyond caring. He fired a crackling sheet of force and Dawson doubled up, hit the middle of the floor in pain. Her right arm was still out. A stray laser blast seared across her hip and she cried out.

"Dawson," shouted Finney, glancing at her. "I told him you were down here." Blasts hit the wall. "Excuse me." He turned back, firing.

Lupu locked Dawson's wave, bore down. He pulled himself forward, holding onto the wall. She struggled to her feet, then dropped back to one knee, the room reeling before her eyes.

Hold on, was all that went through her mind— *He can't last. Hold on.*

Vox slipped a punch, came in hard against Bruno, hip to

hip. He got his hand under Bruno's chin and jerked it up. The muscles held. Bruno shot two fingers into the Baron's throat and Vox choked, pivoted, spinning Bruno around. He grabbed an arm, twisted it way up Bruno's back. Bone snapped. Bruno groaned and kicked at Vox's knee, lashed out with his good arm. Fingernails raked across the Baron's eyes as he stumbled back. He went into a crouch again, blood streaming down his face. Bruno looked down, twitched his shoulder; the arm hung limp.

"Come on, big man," said Vox, spitting the blood away.

"You can't even see me," growled Bruno.

"You're right in front of me. You've only one arm to swing with. What do I need to see, fool?"

Finney fired, and two bodies fell forward out of the passageway.

Bruno peered at Vox, one way, then the other.

"What's the matter?" said the Baron. "You think I've never fought blind? You mean you've never fought with just one arm? Hah!"

Bruno feinted with a kick, but Vox didn't react. The next kick was real, and he moved lightly out of the way. He waited for the punch. When Bruno threw it, Vox jumped back a step and caught the fist in both hands, twirled and brought it down hard against his knee. The elbow cracked. Now Bruno couldn't use either arm. The Baron hit him openhanded in the nose, knocking him back.

"Fighting is not physical," he said, advancing. Bruno spun off the wall, rolling away, his nose smashed. Vox turned his sightless eyes, following every move. He hit Bruno in the stomach. "It's mental." He hit him in the head. "Your mind fights illusion. Your force of will unmasks the shadows." Bruno threw a kick in desperation, and the Baron sidestepped it, chopped down, breaking the kneecap. Bruno screamed, staggered back against the wall.

"Enough," he said. "Please . . ."

"All space around you is an extension," said Vox, kicking the other leg out from under him. Bruno hit the floor and tried to get away. "Even your opponent is an extension of yourself." He lifted Bruno off the ground by the shirt, held him pinned to the wall. "There is no sight," he said, very close to Bruno's face, "—And no motion. You are already part of all space. *You*, however, are a brute. You have nothing to say." He snapped a fist across the jaw, splitting the bone. "I leave you to consider, with one leg on which to stand. Use it."

The Baron let go and turned away. With a whimper, Bruno slithered to the ground.

Finney fired, and another two bodies fell into the room. Then a hail of shots cracked all around him, and three holes smoked his left side. Another hit his foot.

"God damn it!" he grunted, and dropped to his knees, still shooting.

Vox sensed Dawson on the floor, her fists clenched, trembling under Lupu's psi-attack. He turned unerringly toward the Rat and threw his last shuriken, then fell as a laser blast grazed his side. He couldn't see the star bounce off the wall of force surrounding Lupu. The Rat stood against the wall, his face twisted into a howl, firing everything he had, but, suddenly, Dawson was off the receiving end. She lay pressed to the floor, too dazed to move, and watched him. He was enveloped in something, fighting for his life, a wild soundless battle taking place within a cone of force. She could feel energy fields crashing off the walls, a huge psychic scream building from all directions at once. The passage holding the remaining gunmen collapsed with a dull *boom*. Finney groped for her arm, and Dawson looked up, trying to focus.

"We've got to get out of here," he said. Blood covered one side of his coat, and his eyes were glassy.

"Finney, what is it?"

"He's being assaulted. Come on." He helped her to her feet, then collapsed against her, coughing. Neither of them could stand without help. "Baron, come on!" he shouted. "This guy's gonna blow the room, fighting it."

Vox dashed over, scooped Finney under one arm and put the other arm around Dawson's back. They hobbled out, Dawson directing, Vox supplying the strength. Her head was still spinning. The last she saw of the Rat Lupu, he was frozen to the wall, engulfed in energy fields, fighting an invisible enemy with all his mutant power.

Then she was in a long corridor, heading upward, leaning heavily on the Baron's shoulder. She could make out daylight above, the damp salt smell of the ocean. Dawson strained her ears. She wanted to hear a gull, so badly wanted to hear the sound of a big white bird gliding over the waves.

The tunnels behind her exploded in a fury of psychic energy.

XXIV

My leg was killing me. The last thing I needed was a half mile of running and climbing. There wasn't much choice though; Johanson had a slight lead to begin with. As long as we remained belowground, he'd keep adding to it. I kept moving.

Up a series of rungs, then a long ramp, then more rungs. I couldn't get a fix on his shield but, blanked or not, he wasn't going to lose me. This was more than a chase through some old tunnels; we'd been evading each other's traps for three decades. This was the latest round in a long, long game, and I was determined to make it our last.

I felt much safer knowing this wasn't Johanson's turf. His ambush below had obviously been spur-of-the-moment. The spider was far from his own web; it put us on equal footing.

We were in a duct, suddenly; steel walls. I sprang off the rungs, levitated, and electrified the metal. I heard a yell from high up the shaft; I locked onto his shield. There was nothing we could do now but maintain pressure; levitation took too much specific concentration. No time for tricks.

Daylight above. Johanson had to have already made it out. I released his wave, blanked for a second, then threw a shield around the opening above me. I came out into the air covering my eyes, ready to dodge, but there was no ambush. The long, double-decker Bay Bridge was to the right, looming high above me, more of those short chimneys all around and the water spread out on three sides below.

We were still on Treasure Island. Johanson was thirty feet away, at the bottom of a long stairway running up the side of the bridge. He looked as exhausted as I felt.

"Mollitor," he said, holding out a hand. "Listen to me."

I crashed through his shield, knocked him back against the steel steps.

"Listen to me, dammit! I found the secret. Energy transfer."

"Big fucking deal," I said and flashed a nervethrust. He deflected. I shifted frequencies and he winced and deflected again, locked shields.

"Mollitor . . ."

"You're wasting your time, Johanson. Either fight or surrender. Just don't give me your speeches." I dissolved the shieldlock and fired a thrust. He blocked a piece of it and retreated.

The thing about fighting Johanson was that we knew all each other's moves; every attack mode, every frequency modulation was an open book. He was better with weapons, and I could take him apart hand-to-hand, but unarmed and thirty feet apart, there was no advantage available for either of us. For the millionth time, I wished I could focus energy like Dawson.

"What do we gain by killing each other?" he said. "Look at it logically. We both want the same thing."

"Do we?"

Johanson kept retreating up the steps as I advanced.

"Of course. We want order. We want the culmination

of psionics. Look at this world. ENCOM and the Mafia keep making money and everything else goes to hell. How long can it last?'' I shifted the vibration; he winced and modulated in return. ''Mollitor, would you cut that out? Listen to me. We were colleagues for thirty years and enemies for thirty more. What did we accomplish? Not one damn thing. We're old men. We're at the end of our lives.''

''Speak for yourself.''

''We can help each other.''

''*You owe me*, Johanson. You owe more than you can pay. If I trade information with you, it'll be in Chicago, with you bound, gagged and mindlocked.''

The concrete of the bridge was alongside him now. The wind whistled in our ears and the bright sun had us both squinting.

''Don't be a fool. Between us, we've solved the transfer problem.''

''I don't care,'' I said, and exploded the concrete next to his head.

He almost fell. The blast blew him off the stairway, but he held onto the rail. Johanson was still agile. As he flipped himself back on, I electrified the entire staircase. One of the dumber moves I've made in my life. He was farther up the stairs. My whole body shook with the sudden voltage as he leaped to the cement bridge. My ears were ringing. I jumped and grabbed the bridge as Johanson doubled the current and the steps began crackling.

I swung myself over. Traffic all around. I blasted Johanson's shield as hard as I could and knocked him into the first lane. He threw up a force field in self-defense, bounced the first car high into the air. I held onto the bridge support and redirected all my energy toward my own force shield. Hovers careened all over; two exploded. The drivers with fast reflexes veered off the main line, out into the open space above the bay.

Johanson ignited the air in front of my face and blew the support I was holding in half. I somersaulted, came down right next to him. Half-blind, I swung and connected. He gave a grunt, stumbling away, flashed an explosive thrust, but I got my shield up in time, and the deflection cracked the top of the bridge. I leaped at him, landed a solid kick. He rolled ten feet and ignited another patch of air. I slid under it and flattened against the ground as a hover skipped twice, out of control, and hit the wall between us. The explosion blew me to the other side of the bridge and caved in a section of concrete. I couldn't see Johanson through the flames. I got up and scanned, hit his wave as it was coming for me. The recoil must've hurt him too. A white flash seared across my mind, knocked me back over. The whole bridge shook from the concussion. We locked waves and pushed. The vibrations started to build; the bridge was shaking.

"Is this the way it has to end?" he said, stepping around the burning car. "There's no deal we can make?"

"Compromise is nothing more than a tactic to you, Johanson," I said, standing. "Don't play games with me."

"No games."

"Bullshit. I don't scare you and you don't fool me. What's the stall for? You really expect me to be your partner?"

"Not partners."

"What, then?"

"We can solve the puzzle. I know what causes the energy static to congeal. You know how to tap energy into the reservoir. It fits."

"Sure it does."

"Damn it, think about it. You found Weatherly's papers before I did and I got to Lupu first. We both know what's involved here, Mollitor; there's nothing to hide. A deal is to our mutual benefit."

"That's what you say. Where's Dawson?"

"She's in a cell below. She's unhurt. You can have her."

"That's real good of you. Liar."

"It's true!"

"Where's Darby?"

"He's dead. He and I did what you and I are doing now. It demolished the room. It's going to destroy this bridge as well."

"Nowhere to run, Johanson," I said, bearing down. "No way to escape."

"I don't want to escape. Don't you understand?"

Sure I did. It was all painfully simple. The man had no reason to lie at this point. He probably did have the source of the assaults figured out. I could do it. Compare notes with Johanson. Trade our two pieces and make it whole. One unified theory. Insight would have the answer it needed to evolve. Yeah, and Johanson would become an invincible opponent. Some deal.

"I understand," I said. "Surrender, and we'll deal."

"Never," he snarled.

"That's more like it. That's the bastard I remember."

The stone at our feet was breaking up. Johanson leaped and grabbed a support, began climbing to the upper level. I exploded the top of the support, and the bar pulled loose; he swayed lazily out over the water, holding tight with one hand.

"You complete ass. Very well."

Another fireball went off in my face, singeing my hair. The bridge kept shaking; a big chunk broke off and fell. Johanson ripped my shield away with a double thrust and locked my nerves. It was too fast; I couldn't stand all of a sudden. Both legs were dead. I broke the fall with my hands and another fireball exploded. My strength was giving out; he could sense it. My shield wouldn't hold against another blast.

"I don't need you, Mollitor," he gloated. "It would've made things easier, but I've got enough information of my own."

"Time is what you don't have, Johanson," I shouted back. "Look at you. Gray, wrinkled. The clock has run out. You'll be dead within a year."

"Not with transfer. I'll go beyond you or Mary or even your precious Weatherly. I'll go—"

"The only place you're going is to hell."

I closed my eyes and focused my remaining power, concentrated on everything Dawson had ever said about neural beams. Somewhere in my mind, the energy swarmed and narrowed to one searing point. It was all split-second.

I snapped open my eyes and blew Johanson's hand off his wrist.

The look on his face was one of utter shock. He tried to catch himself, but there was nothing to grab the support with. His head turned to his bloody wrist, his legs tried to wrap around, everything seemed to move in slow motion. I lanced two needles into his astonished brain as his head turned back toward me, the mouth twisted into a scream, falling away, out of sight, two hundred feet into the gleaming waves. The bridge kept shaking.

I dragged myself to the edge and looked over. A thousand ripples in the endlessly swirling waves, but not one looked like anything special. Nothing but water. Gulls wheeled across the bay, screaming. I kept staring.

Was that it? For thirty years we'd been fighting, building to a culmination. Was this really the way it ended? This wasn't revenge; it didn't seem real. The sun still shone, the wind still blew, the world hadn't changed at all. How could Johanson just *be gone?*

I got back to the stairway as some more of the bridge busted loose. I still couldn't use my legs. Hand over hand, I lowered myself along the railings, while the sky rained concrete dust.

XXV

Finney had four holes blown right through him. One lung was collapsed, and he was coughing up blood with the other. No telling what additional damage there was; Dawson was no doctor. It looked bad, though. She scanned, set a neural block to stop the one lung from spasming, kept scanning. There was little else she could do.

The sky was full of dust, and the bridge, off to her right, was rumbling; it took no telepathic sense to realize that. Vox was standing at the entrance to the duct they'd escaped through, dabbing at his forehead with a handkerchief.

"Baron," called Dawson, "can you see?"

"It's still blurry. Don't worry. No one is coming out of that duct in one piece."

After an explosion like that, she thought, it's pretty much guaranteed. Still, it was always a relief to have Vox guarding your back.

"Iorg is coming with the hover," he said, looking up.

"God, I hope so. Finney is in bad shape."

"Where's—? Ah, hah. Dawson!" he pointed. "Over by the bridge."

Dawson fought the impulse to look. She knew who it was. She removed the edge of her focus to flash, *HURRY*, and kept both hands on Finney's bloody chest.

* * *

Mollitor stumbled, levitated, stumbled again, started hopping on the one leg that was working, finally did a huge levitation/leap and landed on his hands and knees next to them. Dawson moved away and refocused her scan onto Mollitor, relaxing the muscles locked tight across his back and legs, easing his neural rhythms. It took only a quick probe for him to realize he couldn't do much for the little Irishman. There were just too many internal organs damaged.

Finney, you there? Hold on.

The return wave was very weak. The eyes stayed closed. Mollitor blocked Finney's cough reflex, stopped the muscular spasming as best he could.

Don't try to talk.

Don't be silly, Mollitor. I'm a telepathic agent. You think I'm gonna bother talking?

Redirect the structural waves to your left lung. I'll try and plug the holes.

Never mind that shit. Did you get him?

Finney, please. Just—

God damn it. Did you get him or not?

I got him.

Dead?

I think so.

Mollitor, you son of a bitch, don't lie to me. If he escaped again . . .

He didn't escape. He fell from the bridge.

Finney's body relaxed.

God bless the undertow.

Finney, hold on. We'll get you to a hospital. Listen to me, will you? You've got to redirect—

No time, old buddy. Just loose ends. He killed Darby, didn't he?

Finney . . .

Tell me.

Yeah.

Mollitor, that kid— He started coughing again. *Lupu, the power. He—he's not it. Mollitor, he's—it killed him. Assault.*

Would you please concentrate? The lung, Finney—redirect—

No use. I feel it. I'm done. Johanson. He's really finished?

He's finished.

Good. You got your licks in. Now I'll get to kick his ass in hell. We'll show him no peace, Mollitor.

Finney.

We'll show . . .

Mollitor held on for a few moments, then released the wave and looked up. The dust from the bridge had pretty much dissipated. The wind blew the salt spray into his face, and the gulls continued their piercing song.

"He's gone," said Dawson, rubbing his shoulders.

He nodded and reached for her hand.

Iorg landed the hover. Vox opened the hatch and helped Dawson in, then Mollitor. The Baron knelt over Finney, gently lifted him and laid him across the rear seat. He sat next to the body, signaled Mollitor to close the door.

"Iorg will pilot. Tell him where to go."

Mollitor turned, looked at Dawson.

"San Francisco HQ, I guess," he said. "We should contact the Old Man." The hover flew. "You all right, kiddo?"

"Just a burn on my hip." She was quiet for a few minutes. Then, "Darby's dead?"

"That's what Johanson said. I'm sorry."

"He saved my life. Again."

"He was in love with you."

"A lot of good it did him."

"Dawson . . ."

"And we still don't know anything! Lupu overloaded, just like Paul and Mary. Now Jack's dead. And Finney. Damn it, how many more people have to—"

Mollitor froze in his seat. "Dawson!"

"What?"

"Elena. I just remembered."

"Oh, my God. No."

"No, she's not dead. The Mafia blew the cafe, or someone did. She left me a clue. Dawson, what does *Jeux sans frontière* mean?"

"It means, 'games without frontiers.' "

"I know *that*. Why is it so familiar? What is she trying to tell us?"

Dawson put a hand to her chin, frowning, her eyes in a faraway stare. "It's, uh—wait, wait a minute . . ." She hummed something to herself. "It's a song, I think."

"A song?"

"Yes, it's an old song. Something about the cafe—it's—um, oh I know! It *is* the name of a song. Very old, 1970s or '80s. Tanya used to play it on her cassette."

"Do you remember the words?"

"Oh, come on. I'm not *that* good. It was about games. Kids playing practical jokes. The chorus was 'games without frontiers.' They'd sing it in English and French. I can't really remember the tune."

"Kids. Like McIntyre's last impress."

"Like your children's program here," said Vox from the back seat.

"That's right," said Dawson, meeting Mollitor's eye. "Like Lupu."

Mollitor nodded to himself. "Lupu was abnormally powerful, right?"

She snorted. "You don't know the half of it."

"It begins to make sense then. Lupu, these kids trained from birth to focus psionics—it inflates the total static. This is the spot. San Francisco is psychically loaded to the hilt."

"What static?"

"Increased use of psi energy throughout the world creates a background field that makes it more and more difficult to channel the flow. Take my word for it. That was the jewel in Weatherly's papers; equations and all."

She still didn't look convinced. "All right, but why not Chicago? Why do everyone's clues point here?"

"This is the center. Mary was doing transfer experiments here in the '50s, using agents as storage areas. That got the ball rolling. It pumped up the psi static tremendously."

Dawson frowned. "Static is one thing," she said quietly. "That's passive resistance. The congealing fields of energy are an active assault. Did Weatherly hint at anything of that nature?"

"No."

"And he never warned us directly about this static. I wonder why not?"

"Who the hell knows? He didn't like Insight anyway. We were sullying his pure and noble psionics. If we were doomed to inflate ourselves out of business eventually, why bother warning us?"

"On the contrary," put in Vox, "he wrote papers on transfers, presented ways to actually increase the static."

Mollitor turned in his seat. "Finney had a feeling someone put the idea into Mary's head."

"He found something?"

"No, just a guess. Still, Finney had a reputation for shrewd guesses."

"It's possible," said Dawson. "She was here in San Fran. So were the kids. Maybe it was a subtle way of undermining the Pool."

Mollitor shrugged and turned back to a comfortable position, started massaging his legs. Dawson helped Vox clean up the cuts he couldn't quite reach, then leaned back and tried to relax her nervous system.

She needed time to think, had to forget about Darby and Finney for the time being. They were beyond her help; figuring out the source of the psi-assaults was how she could best mourn their passing, avenge their deaths.

Lupu had teased Johanson about the suicides; he'd hinted that he knew nothing about it. It seemed, from his actions, that he'd had no real interest in energy transfer anyway. If this was indeed the case, it meant he'd had nothing to do with Avery's death. Why in the world had he accepted Johanson as a partner? It had served only to attract attention; Tanner had to be paid off, the ENCOM file had to be rigged, dozens of minor details had to be arranged. Why take all that on? Perhaps he needed Johanson's know-how to suppress the report Avery had logged on his activity; Johanson would, at least, be better prepared to bribe Fantello. It was also likely that Johanson had fed the young man's ego with all his talk of Empire. Who knew? Maybe Lupu had told the truth in that momentary flash of anger, maybe the old man had simply been an interesting toy to have around. Still, it meant that the partnership had been a whim to Lupu, whereas Johanson had purposefully sought it as a means of figuring out transfer. Who had been using whom?

Hey? she flashed.

Yeah?

Fill me in. What did Johanson say at the end?

He claimed to know how the static congealed into the assault fields.

So they are connected.

Said Johanson.

But he didn't know about it in Paris. He learned it here. In fact, he only figured it out since the big fight yesterday. That's when he sold out Lupu.

Looks like it. He wanted to trade that information for what I knew about the transfer reservoir.

You didn't believe him?

What's the difference? Can you see us trading info with Johanson?

He double-crossed him, Mollitor. It means Lupu was expendable. He wasn't the source.

Something down there was. Maybe J. figured there were others just like Lupu.

No. There's no one else. Apart from transfer and energy fields and all, he actually was *a superpsychic. People that strong can't remain hidden. We'd know.*

You don't know that. Maybe they'd just develop their power slowly, eliminating high-level opposition before they made their move.

Can't be. In the first place, they can't be both smart enough to congeal the static into an assault and too dumb to know where the attack would best serve their purpose.

Chicago?

Of course. Why hit random agents all over the globe, when a dozen hits on HQ, starting with you, me and the Old Man, would create mass confusion?

Point.

Secondly, if there were *a group of superpsychics, Lupu's high-profile operation would've scared the hell out of them. Way too much attention drawn. They would've dealt with him when he set up shop two years ago. Anyway, I saw him, I fought him. He didn't strike me as a renegade, or as any part of a group at all. He was proud, in fact, of being a mutant. He offered to join forces with me.*

That must've been cute.

Johanson was there at the time. I didn't feel much like laughing.

All right, so there are no more superpunks. Then what did Elena mean?

I don't think it was anything more than a way to tell you to go to San Francisco. If anyone else found the message, it would mean nothing to them.

I was coming to Frisco anyway.

Elena didn't know that. She had to point you in this direction herself.

Dammit, why?

We'll find out. We're here.

The hover touched down on the roof of a three-story converted warehouse. Actually, the outside of it didn't appear at all converted. Two fire doors jutted out of the flat, graveled roof, the windows all around were smoky gray with wide iron gratings, the big bay doors of the garage in front showed off gleaming steel padlocks against the rusty brown metal. Unobtrusive, slightly dilapidated, exactly the front you want for Pool Regional Headquarters.

Mollitor scanned the fire doors.

"Which way in?" he asked Dawson.

"Usually, the front door. In this case . . ." She peered along the edges of the metal. "I'd rather not deal with Fantello and the receptionists and agents and all. Too much fanfare if you and I go waltzing in. We're blanked, for the moment."

Mollitor smiled.

"You did it too, huh?"

"You're not the only one who's overcautious," she said, smiling with him.

"Okay, how do we get in quietly?"

"I can decode these locks, smother the initial alarms. I mean, I primed them, way back when. But the sensor system in there is pretty sophisticated. Paul and I made sure no one would override it."

"Okay, so we don't use any psi energy. We happen to have some brute strength with us."

The Baron looked at him. "I beg your pardon, Mollitor. I deal in finesse."

"Excuse me, Val. Please. Finesse the door open."

Dawson carefully disengaged the vibelock and both the inner and outer impact trips. Vox planted himself before the door, narrowed his eyes, concentrated the focus.

"That door's awfully strong metal," whispered Dawson.

"Don't worry, kiddo. The framework isn't."

Vox let out a short, piercing shout and threw a heavy sidekick. The metal door bowed in and snapped back; the frame cracked at the top. He hit it with another kick and the frame split down one side. He backed off a few feet and threw a crossover, putting his full weight into it. The top hinge sheared away and the upper half of the door caved into the opening. The Baron brushed his leg off and turned to them, bowing slightly. His formality contrasted with the torn vest and shirt, the blood-flecked silver hair.

"Some finesse," said Mollitor, laughing.

"After you, my friends."

"A stoic to the end."

Dawson led; she best knew the layout of the place. They moved quickly through the upper floor, checking rooms at a glance, carefully shutting the doors behind them. All the rooms were empty.

"I don't like it," she said, half turning her head while continuing to peer forward. "There's no one here. I don't even sense any vibes. Mollitor?"

"Yeah. It's not muffled; the waves are blanked, or they're not even there. It does feel weird."

"Like the building is holding its breath," whispered Vox.

"You feel it too?"

He nodded, rolled his eyes to and fro, trying to pick some meaning out of the silent shadows.

"The stairway's right around this corner," said Dawson. "Maybe downstairs, we'll—oh!" She stepped back in surprise.

Vox leaped past Mollitor, landed beside Dawson on the balls of his feet, eyes focused, hands up ready to strike.

The man at the top of the stairs posed no threat to anyone. He lay on his stomach, head on the first step going down, arms spread before him. He wore a brown tweed suit. Dark hair. Vox turned the body over with his foot. The face was drained of color, eyes open, teeth clenched, the muscles across the face drawn tight. His fists were knotted, with blood running from where his fingernails had cut into the palm. There was no sign of any injury.

"Recognize him?"

"Sure," said Dawson. "It's Fantello."

Mollitor knelt and scanned him.

"Dead maybe two hours. Same as the others; no imprint frame."

"But we're talking about the boss. Somehow I figured he was mixed up in this."

He stood up.

"Face it, Dawson," he said, "—it's not planned. Like I told Val back in London, we're up against the inner nature of psionics, the details we never understood."

"But which Gil did."

He looked at her. The implications were becoming undeniable and it made him ill. Weatherly had seen the train coming and simply hadn't told them to get out of the way.

Mollitor gripped the scarred wooden railing and started down the stairway, feeling old again. There was no caution in his step, no tensed readiness in his bearing. He flashed a widebeam scan throughout the building.

"Mollitor," shouted Dawson, sensing it, "what are you—?"

"It doesn't matter," he said. "There's . . . two—no, three—people alive in this whole damn building. Main office. Come on."

Dawson and Vox hurried down after him. The whole next floor was a mess. The hallways were strewn with bodies, office doors ajar with the occupants dead, reaching for the handle, phones off the hook. All power in the building was out, the computer boards silent, the satellite relays blown. It had been one hell of an overload.

"Mollitor," said Dawson, scanning a few bodies, "it all happened a couple hours ago."

He stopped at the stairway leading to the ground floor, turned.

"Yeah? So?"

"About the same time Lupu overloaded."

"So he was a biggie. Unleashing all that force triggered a series of assaults at the spot of greatest concentration. HQ. So what? I'm tired of—"

"Would you stop being so damn resigned?! Whoever's left alive in the main office may very well have control of it."

"Look," he snapped, pointing his finger, "they're either our friends or our enemies. I don't really care which anymore. If they're friends, we'll corroborate our guesses."

"And if not?" said the Baron.

"They tried to kill me once and failed. They try again and it'll be the last mistake of their lives." He took Dawson's arm. "We're it, kiddo; we're all that's left. For all we know, the same blasts have already leveled Chicago. Let's just finish this while we can."

They stared at each other. It was all the same, their hopes, their fears, their history; all the conclusions meshed. It was balanced. Every thought came out equivalent, both flashing as one,

He knew it was coming.

He didn't warn us.

The office was down the stairs and to the left. The door was ajar. More bodies. Mollitor pushed past two and got the door open all the way. There was no danger in here; the three vibes he'd sensed were unconscious agents, two men and a woman slumped across their desks. He scanned them. Comatose, but stable. They'd blanked in time. He gently moved their bodies to facilitate easier breathing, made sure nothing was bleeding internally.

"Signal the hospital, will you, kiddo?" he said. "I'm going to find the hotline."

Dawson walked over to the window, concentrating. Mollitor scanned the vidscreens on the desks. Nothing. The main monitor board was dead. He scanned the remainder of the furniture until he found it.

"That big bureau, Val. I'll smother any impact trips. It's probably only primed for psi-tampering, anyway."

Vox splintered one side of the cabinet with a kick, then reached in and ripped the door from its hinges. The hotlines weren't red; they were black, just ordinary-looking antique telephones. They couldn't go dead in a power outage since they were operated by the individual user's psi energy. They linked, by satellite relay, every Pool station on the planet with the Old Man in Chicago. Mollitor keyed the emergency code.

"They're on the way," said Dawson. "You get anything?"

"Not yet. You know, we've still got one unanswered question."

"What's that?" she said, sitting on the edge of a desk.

"Why the energy fields? Why did the static congeal? Without that one effect, Gil would've gotten exactly what he wanted. Psychic power would've just ground to a halt, with no one able to generate enough force to punch through."

"Oh, I don't know. We would've figured a way around it. Who knows? Maybe he blew the equations. Maybe this really is in the natural scheme of things."

"No," said Mollitor, looking down. "Gil knew exactly what he was doing. That's what scares me." He glanced up. "It's coming through. Tap in."

Dawson linked her awareness to an edge of Mollitor's vibration, listened as the connection flashed.

San Francisco acknowledged. Please key agent code.

ML-1. Request direct to OM.

A pause.

I'm sorry, no such code originating from SF Pool. Please—

This is Mollitor, dammit. Get me the Old Man. Now! Aloud, he said, "They're alive, Dawson. Maybe the chain reaction went no further than the city."

Then a familiar vibration came on. Mollitor flashed a basic rundown to the Old Man. Chicago had noted a surge of energy coinciding with Lupu's implosion, a surge staggered all along the western seaboard.

There's a lot more, Mollitor. We've got Tanner under guard in Paris and a crew on the way to Frisco right now. How bad's HQ?

Bad. All dead but three.

There was silence for a moment, then, *We received the*

Greenland transmission a few hours ago. It fits with our other information.

Other information?

Concerning Weatherly.

Mollitor looked at Dawson.

Details?

You'll have a report by tonight. I want both of you to coordinate the cleanup out there.

What about—

Hold on, Mollitor. I'm keying in someone else.

The vibration shifted, the output dropped way down, then jumped back up full. It was a low-level psi flash, artificially amplified. A smile broke across Dawson's face.

Hello, Doctor.

Elena! You're all right?

I'm fine. Physically, anyway. I'm just relieved to know you two are alive. You got the message, eh?

Why San Francisco, Elena?

I couldn't be sure. It was either there or Chicago. But I was coming here anyway, so I thought you should check the other.

What *was either here or there?*

The strongest concentrations of psi energy output. I thought Chicago at first. But then I realized I was forgetting where Mary came from. And all those children in training. Oh dear, Mollitor, I'm afraid it was too much for him. The disappointment.

What? Who? You've got me completely—

I'm sorry. Gil. Gil Weatherly. He did it.

He didn't warn us.

If that were his only crime, we could forgive him. Mollitor, he set it up in San Francisco—a device to amplify and focus the energy. Feedback. He planned it. He knew this would happen once the levels grew strong enough.

You can't be. . . . Planned?

I'm sorry. I'm sick about it, but it's true. It was his game. Games without frontiers. A deadly game waiting to detonate at some point in the future. We didn't know how serious he was when he railed against your Pool. We never suspected how bitter he was. . . . Mollitor?

I'm here. I'm just stunned.

I know. So was I. I only half believed myself, until your chief here identified it positively. Some sort of tunnels in San Francisco.

I know about the tunnels.

You sound tired, Mollitor.

I am, Elena. I'm older than you, remember? You're always pointing that out to me.

Bah! It's an illusion. You've got plenty of strength. Go on now. A lot of work for you to do. I'll see you later.

Of course.

Give my love to Dawson.

Of course. Take care of yourself, Elena.

As always, Doctor. Ciao.

Mollitor let the receiver go, and it hit the carpet with a thud. He shook his head slowly, blinking as he glanced at the bodies in the room.

"That son of a bitch," he said through his teeth. "I can't believe it." He turned to Dawson. "Why would he do this to us? It makes no sense."

Dawson sighed.

"It makes complete sense. What Insight was doing horrified him. He couldn't act against us directly, so he kept quiet about the trap we were running toward and beefed up the magnitude of that trap for when we actually hit it." She shook her head and slid off the desk. "It's sick, but it's logical."

"My God," said Vox. "You mean LaRue was killed by the man whose papers he was looking for? A dead man?"

"A dead man," intoned Mollitor. "Fifty years dead. No one to take revenge on." He snorted. "As if I could kill Weatherly anyway."

Dawson stared at him, then at the bodies. The muffled wail of ambulance sirens sounded from up the street. She walked over, took his hand.

Come on, love. It's over. Let's help these three.

Is it really?

Sure. The assault on Lupu destroyed the device, triggered this whole mess in here. Not even Gil could foresee a T-path of his power. The tunnels are all collapsed.

And we're alive.

That's right, Mollitor. We're alive because Gil planted the device here and not in Chicago.

What?

Think about it. There was no less chance of the Pool discovering it in San Francisco. He chose to keep the main thrust away from Chicago for only one reason.

What?—to spare you and me? Oh, give me a break.

His old buddies.

Look, it's bad enough as it is. You don't have to make it worse by telling me shit like that.

It's true.

That doesn't make it any less disgusting. His old buddies. Yeah. Like hell.

Mollitor disengaged and walked out of the room. He stripped away the impact trips on the front door, fused the sensor alarms and threw the big metal doors open. The wind blew mist into the front hall, spattered his face with moisture. Not quite dusk. He went out onto the sidewalk and leaned against the stone pillar, arms folded. The world felt ugly.

A goddamn waste, he thought. From every direction, nothing but a waste of bodies and minds.

The ambulances hovered up, doors opening and slamming.

"First door down the hall to the right," he said to the medics rushing by him.

The wind kept blowing, a warm breeze. The ocean was still out there, the city still stood. Mollitor was still a top agent of Insight, still kicking, still breathing. He could have what he wanted in this world, everything except vengeance. How do you take revenge on history? Answer: You keep on living in spite of it.

He turned and stared back at the front doors. Vox was leaning on the porch railing, watching the clouds roll in from the ocean, breathing slowly, lost in his thoughts. Dawson followed one of the stretchers out, patted the Baron on the shoulder as she passed him, frowned up at the sky, then trotted down the steps toward Mollitor.

"What are you smiling about?" she asked him softly.

"You," he said. "That's the most ridiculous outfit I've seen in a while." He flicked the hood on the tunic. "About nine sizes too small, would you say?"

She looked down. Feena's clothes came to just past her elbows and knees, torn in a dozen places.

"You think this one is ridiculous? You should've seen what I traded in for it."

He put his arms around her, hugged.

"Hey?"

"Yeah, kiddo?" He let go, watched her shake the blond hair away from her face.

"It's been a day and a half since I ate anything. I am absolutely starving."

He scowled. "Food?"

"Food."

"At a time like this?"

"Well, generally, it works best when you're hungry."

"You're cute, kiddo." He scratched his head, sighed. "Well, I guess we're about eighty years late for Smokey Joe's. What do you say to a pizza?"

She thought about it.

"Keep the anchovies on your half."